LEGACY

THE CRONIN CHRONICLES
BOOK ONE

PAUL EBERZ

A
JUST
SUGAR
PRODUCTION

DEDICATION

To those who helped me survive my most desperate hours.

Acknowledgments

Carrie Murgittroyd – Editor extraordinaire, Diane Dean.
Fellow authors, advisors, critics and motivators.

A
JUST
SUGAR
PRODUCTION

Cover design and formatting by Paradox Book Cover Designs & Formatting

ISBN:

978-0-578-71010-5 paperback

978-1-7352566-4-1 hardback

Printed in USA

Editor: Carrie Murgittroyd

CHAPTER I
FEATHER RIVER VALLEY, CALIFORNIA
JANUARY 1866

Rufus, like the Old Man, was asleep. He lay on his stomach, his head resting on his paws, eyes closed, perched atop a neat pile of split firewood stacked against the north wall of the cabin. Actually, Rufus was just resting, unlike the Old Man who was sleeping like the dead.

The pair, alone in their mountain cabin, shared guard duties. During the day, Rufus might find a warm place in the sun to drift off, or nap after dinner when Amos was cleaning his rifle. But at night, when his friend was vulnerable, the dog was alert even with eyes closed.

Except for the winter storm that earlier had been raging outside, this night was like every other night of their partnership. After the end-of-day chores and a chapter or two from a book, the Old Man fueled the fireplace with an evening supply of wood. He would then fling a thick blanket on the crest of the woodpile like he was saddling Puddle, the horse. Rufus would leap to his perch, knead the blanket into place, then settle down on his watchtower

1

position. A place where he could keep lookout on the cabin's door and the bed where Amos Cronin slept.

The fire, warming the cabin against the icy winter, made for a comfortable and well-deserved sleep for Amos Cronin. Especially this day when the Old Man's daily chores were made much harder by the drifting snow and biting cold. Rufus, on the other hand, spent the day patrolling the property for unwelcome guests like coyotes, bears, or killer rabbits.

Their cabin in the mountains was a fortress, built over the years to withstand the mountain's worst weather. The four-room cabin's walls were made from long, carefully trimmed logs, laid high and mortared tight with mud and horsehair. Thick roof beams and wide cut planks held hand-cut cedar shingles which sealed their home tight against the hardest weather the mountain could render. It stood solid, in a clearing near a river, miles and miles from the nearest neighbor but it was exactly where they both wanted to be.

This place was their mountain keep, their castle, their home. And the years of sometimes back-breaking work made wilderness life almost comfortable— certainly tolerable. However, a few issues that other humans might find difficult remained. The two were accustomed to each other's habits and quirks, even bad ones, even strange ones. However, this time of year, one serious problem was true for both occupants.

Rufus, being a dog, did dog things, like wallowing in different combinations of disgusting things he found on the forest floor. Predators like wolves, mountain lions, even bears, found prey scarce in the cold of winter and a lone dog wandering though the mountain forest would make a tasty morsel. But the scent Rufus gave off must have been unidentifiable to any predator. He toured his domain free of the beasts of the forest. They must have focused their hunts on something more familiar, like deer or rabbits or raccoons. Or perhaps even something that had died, because even an old decaying carcass smelled better than the big dog during the winter.

Amos Cronin, on the other hand, was a bit more sanitary. He washed his hands because he washed dishes. He occasionally even washed his face when forced to by a messy pot of stew. He did perform one task of hygiene with daily regularity: he brushed his teeth.

The two battled for stink supremacy, a battle made possible by the winter, since neither one had seen hot water or soap since the first snowflake fell.

The night wind had calmed. The crackle of the fire, now dimmed to a red glow, was the only sound in the cabin.

Suddenly, Rufus's head popped up, tilted, eyes focused on the door. His ears slowly twisted, straining to hear. The cabin had many sounds; the wind blowing over the roof, the fireplace popping, the creaking of the fortress-like walls occasionally making sounds wood makes. But what woke Rufus was none of those. It was something odd. It was a sound that didn't belong.

A minute went by, then another.

He heard it again and jumped to the floor. Slowly, noiselessly, he stepped one foot at a time toward the door. He froze halfway there, his head turning side-to-side, staring, listening.

Small puffs of snow were blowing through the gap at the bottom of the door.

Again, he stepped forward, stopping a few feet away. No sound.

He closed the distance to the door. The stream of cold air from under the door breezed across his paws. He bent his head low, almost touching the floor, then pressed his nose tight against the gap.

He heard the sound again, but it had no smell.

The silence of the cabin suddenly broke when Rufus snorted two gray streams of hot air under the weather-beaten door planks that stood between the log cabin and the desolate cold. He drew the night air back into his nose and continued to sniff and snort, sucking in, then blowing out, torrents of air.

The door was made of seven wide planks of thick ponderosa pine, strapped together and fitted tight against a solid oak frame. Rufus's ears bent forward, twisted, and with one more nose gulp of air, he finally put a smell to the strange sound.

Rufus spun around and trotted quickly into the room where a polished but sagging brass bed held the white-bearded man. Rufus slowed as he neared the bed. He stopped, his nose several inches short of the man's face. Rufus stood still, staring at his friend. The dog hesitated a second more, then leaned forward and nudged the Old Man's blanket-covered shoulder.

The Old Man continued to snore.

Rufus nudged his arm again, this time harder.

There was a grunt followed by a grumble, "Uhhh," but the man's eyes remained closed.

Rufus, undaunted, put his nose an inch from the Old Man's weathered face, then snorted loudly. "FRUMMMP."

"What the—?" The Old Man sat up in the bed with a start, rubbing blurry eyes and grumbling unrecognizable words. He looked down and saw Rufus staring at him.

As suddenly as he awoke, the Old Man's defenses took over. He lowered his voice. "What's wrong?"

Rufus fixed his gaze on his friend, lowered his head, and let out a long, low, deep, growl from way down inside. The sound resonated, filling the quiet room.

For an instant, only an instant, cold fear came over the Old Man. It ran up his spine and sent a shiver through his whole body. He shook his head, then wiped his eyes with his big leathery hands, dismissing the strange feeling. He shot a glance through the open doorway of his room and could see the front door was still closed. He pushed the blanket off, swung his legs over, and put his bare feet on the floor. In the same motion, he reached for his rifle which was leaning against the foot of the bed. He quickly levered a 30/30 caliber shell into the chamber of his Winchester rifle.

Rufus stepped back, ears still twitching.

The Old Man stood up and walked slowly out of his bedroom. He surveyed the far wall—windows still shuttered, nothing out of place. He looked past the kitchen fireplace, its embers still glowing ruby red, to where pots and pans hung from the steel rack above the sink and where a table was set neatly for one. It was all as it was when he went to bed. The fog of sleep had disappeared. The survey was mandatory and now he knew for certain no one was in the house for two reasons. First, nothing was out of place and, second, if someone had gotten inside, he would have not been awakened by a bark but by screaming because Rufus would have been chewing on somebody's leg.

Holding the rifle in one hand, he walked to the front door. There was a small panel in its middle that opened, allowing a quick view of who might be on the porch. The Old Man took hold of the handle but didn't pull it open.

Again, the chill ran up Amos Cronin's back. Fear swelled up within him. He shivered but he shook his shoulders, willing it away. Rufus pushed up next to his friend's leg and barked once.

The Old Man decided to minimize the situation. He chose to

deny that his friend was hardly ever wrong, choosing instead to think what was lurking outside was probably just a wandering bear looking for a meal.

"Okay, okay." He waved his gun hand and walked back to his room. "I know you're just looking to irritate me." He plopped down in a chair and pulled on his pants and a heavy flannel shirt, then shoved his big feet into the knee-high, fur-lined moccasins.

Rufus barked once again.

"I'm coming, I'm coming." The Old Man stood up and stretched, his joints cracking as he rubbed his slow-to-respond muscles. When he got back to the door, he reached for a buffalo skin coat hanging from a deer horn hook on the wall, but stopped short. He looked down at Rufus. The dog didn't have an 'it's just a bear look.' Amos left the coat on the hook thinking it was too heavy and would keep him from moving quickly. Instead, he buttoned his long flannel shirt all the way up, wrapped a scarf around his neck, and pulled a fur hat tight over his head.

Rufus pawed at the floor.

"Okay, okay. I'm ready," but as the Old Man reached for the handle, he hesitated again. He saw a shadow on the door in front of him. He turned around and saw the source of the light— the fireplace. If he opened the door with a light on his back, he would be highly visible and very vulnerable. He didn't want to get shot coming out the door. The fireplace was still glowing and fresh air pouring in from an open door would cause it to flame up. If that happened, his big frame would be outlined in the door opening, making for a perfect target. If it wasn't a hungry bear and somebody was out there, the light would make him an easy shot the instant he walked through the door.

Rufus pawed the floor again.

The Old Man now growled at Rufus. "Wait." He hurried across the room and dragged two chairs from the kitchen to a position between the fireplace and the door. He took the buffalo coat from the hook and draped it over the chairbacks which blocked the firelight. When he opened the door, he would be just a shadow.

Satisfied, Amos put his hand back on the handle.

Rufus stood motionless, muscles tensed, poised to bolt the instant the door opened.

Amos took a breath, depressed the lever, and pulled.

Like a flash, Rufus bolted through the opening and disappeared into the darkness.

The Old Man stepped out quickly, pulling the door closed behind him. He moved sideways, putting his back flat against the wall. He stood motionless in the night shadow of the porch waiting for his eyes to adjust.

There was a bright three-quarter moon surrounded by winter stars on the westerly horizon. The clouds which had brought snow earlier had moved across the sky but still covered half of the eastern horizon. The moonlight from the clear sky was following behind the clouds and creeping across the open pasture like a sunrise.

The barn stood a hundred feet away, and directly in front of him. It housed two horse stalls and a pen for six cows. A small one-story structure with a hayloft above, it had a big double door in front and a fenced-in paddock off to the side. From where he stood, he could see that the door was still secured tight, exactly as he had left it hours before, when he put Puddle in his stall with some fresh oats. The shuttered window on the hayloft was also closed tight. No footprints in the snow meant no intruder near or around the building.

He couldn't see behind the barn but there was a steep bank that led down to the river which, covered by a very thin layer of ice, was impassable. If someone tried to cross, they would fall into swift moving water which would claim the victim, man or beast, without remorse.

Satisfied that the area was secure, he scanned to his left, across the pasture. The blowing wind occasionally tossed fresh snow into the air like the spray off an ocean wave. The meadow he'd cleared of timber many years ago was where the cows and his fifteen-hand horse Puddle grazed. It was wide, stretching to the rocky edge of the mountain forest. Like the snow around the barn, the snow that fell during the night was unspoiled in the meadow.

His gaze moved to his right and the field where he planted winter wheat in the fall and corn in the spring. It, like the pasture, stretched out several hundred yards to the foot of the forest on the edge of the mountain beyond. It was also pristine.

Rufus had disappeared and remained hidden, somewhere beyond his sight. The dog would travel in the deep fluffy snow, poking his head up occasionally but would be for the most part undetectable.

The Old Man cleared the areas he could see but was still standing on the porch. The longer he remained, the more vulnerable he felt. He had to move. He took a small breath and eased his grip on the rifle. Cold air filled his lungs, but suddenly fear filled his mind again, forcing him back against the wall.

Again, he shook off the unfamiliar feeling then started to move. Stepping side-to-side, back still close to the wall, he slowly moved to the edge of the porch. Staying in the moon shadow of the porch roof, he slipped down to the ground. He stepped quickly through the knee-high snow to the woodpile near the barn where he could hide and wait. The snow made his movement completely silent.

A thought occurred suddenly, how did that fool dog hear anything in a new snow?

He made it across the moonlit terrain and sat down hard behind his new vantage point. He rose up, peeked over the top of the pile, and selected a place to rest the Winchester. It was a perfect view of the back of the cabin and from this vantage point he could easily shift to cover the east and west perimeters. With the icy river behind him, he now had the advantage and felt secure. He could defend this position against one or two or ten, it didn't matter. He had a fifteen shot Henry and rarely missed his aim.

He shook the snow from his bear-like hands but didn't blow on them even though the cold metal made his fingers feel like icicles. At this temperature, the moisture in his breath would freeze on his hands, making them colder not warmer. Instead, as painful as it was, he shoved his icy fingers under his shirt to his bare skin. In a few minutes, he had the feeling back.

More time went by. His eyes, now accustomed to the light, found it easier to examine the distant clearings. The snow clouds had retreated farther east, and he could see into the forest at the edge of the pasture. He never let the undergrowth gain ground on the pastures by clearing the ground in front of the trees of the forest every spring with controlled ground fires. It was a trick he learned from the Indians so no enemy could hide in the brush on the edge of the forest.

The wind was pushing cold air through his shirt.

He scanned the edge of the hardwood forest again just beyond the shadows of the wheat field. About two hundred yards away, coming out of the shadow of the rock fence, he saw a movement. It was low to the ground. Suddenly, a form rose up, moved, then fell over.

It was a man.

The Stranger struggled to his feet and began to walk. He took one high step, lifting a leg up and out of the snow, then perched like a bird before putting his foot back on the ground. His wobbly step made him stumble and twist awkwardly, and he fell forward, face first. Amos watched as the Stranger pushed himself to his feet again and feebly shook the caked white crust from his body. He stumbled along for about ten steps before swaying sideways and falling again. This time the Stranger didn't get up.

A part of the Old Man told himself to go back to bed and float what would be a frozen carcass downriver in the morning.

He stood up shaking his head, and said out loud, "This is a big mistake."

Amos left his safe observatory and crossed the field like he was walking up to a rattlesnake ready to strike. He took a long way around, coming up behind the fallen man and studying the tracks of the Stranger's path. The footprint trail led down from the mountain to the wood's edge behind the stone wall and then to where he lay face down in the snow.

He must have come down from the logging road.

The footstep trail wandered erratically from the forest to the rock wall.

He could have been watching the cabin for a while. Was this a delirious man frozen beyond sense or reason, or was this a fox stalking a prey?

Amos continued his slow approach. As he got closer, he lifted his nose high up into the night and sniffed the air, a habit he had learned from the dog. From ten feet away, he could smell beer and whisky mixed with tobacco. The Stranger wore a thin coat over city britches and fancy boots. He wore no hat, and his head resembled a porcupine, hair frozen stiff in black spikes.

Amos came up to the body and stood over it with the Henry ready.

Fear returned to his stomach.

Balancing his weight on his back foot, he pushed the toe of his front boot into the middle of the Stranger's back.

The Stranger didn't move.

The Old Man shifted the Winchester to his left hand, safety off, finger on the trigger, but had the barrel pointing up. He leaned over and with his right hand, reached for the fabric on the Stranger's coat.

Suddenly, the Stranger rolled over and kicked his right foot up, aiming at the rifle. His other arm swung a thin blade towards the Old Man's chest.

Amos saw the glint of the blade and pulled back just enough to let it flail harmlessly past his body. The kick hit its mark but failed to part the Old Man's iron grip on the rifle.

The next thing the Stranger saw was the face of a dog from the darkest depths of Hell. From what seemed out of nowhere, Rufus pounced on the Stranger after bolting full speed from behind the rock wall. Rufus leapt from ten feet away and landed with an impact that knocked both the wind from the stranger's lungs and the knife from his hand. The dog's bared teeth were dripping saliva. His deep, black eyes held no mercy.

A full minute went by without a sound or movement from the intruder.

Finally, the Stranger whispered, "Help me."

Rufus instantly growled from somewhere so low and so deep it caused even Amos to pause.

Amos scratched his beard, contemplating the situation. He wondered what would happen next. Rufus listened to him—most of the time—but sometimes the dog had a mind of his own and, if that man moved the wrong way, there would be nothing that would stop the dog from protecting his domain, or his friend.

The Stranger, desperate, tried another approach. Slowly, very slowly, he turned his head away from the dog's paralyzing eyes and said softly, "I didn't know if you wanted to kill me. I was lost out here and...I must have passed out or somethin.' When I woke up you were standing there...and...I thought...oh, please, mister, don't kill me. I was just protecting myself."

Amos ended his long silence. "Maybe that explains the knife, and maybe it don't." He studied the skinny, long-nosed, pale-faced man, then said, "I should just walk away."

"Please, please, don't leave me here mister. I'm freezing to death."

His voice came out too loud and Rufus growled again.

The Old Man poked the Stranger with the barrel of his gun. "Why are you here? And meanwhile don't be movin' around 'cause I don't really know what the dog will do next."

Softly and slowly, the Stranger said, "I was traveling on a stage from Tucson to San Francisco and one of the passengers said I stole money from her while she was sleeping. The wagon master believed her instead of me." He started to get firm again, "Believe that? A woman instead of me? I shoulda know'd he had it in for me from the beginning. I could tell." He squinted his eyes, looking to the Old Man for an understanding that didn't come. "So, he stopped the wagon when she started yelling and me and the wagon master had words." His face changed expression, trying to muster shock. "Then...he pulled a gun on me."

"How much did you steal?"

"Nothing," he stammered. "The bitch told him I stole her money but that wasn't true. I had money...but it was mine. I done won it playin' poker. It were mine."

Rufus growled—then bit The Stranger's arm.

The man screamed and Rufus bit him again.

"I told you not to move," said the Old Man softly.

The Stranger, wincing in pain, continued, "He said he was going to turn me over to the sheriff at the next stop and wouldn't let me back inside the stagecoach. Well, I told him that wasn't fair, and I wasn't going to take that from the likes of him."

"And?"

The Stranger's voice softened a little. "I pulled that knife out." He stuck both hands in the air. "But just to protect myself."

"Like just now."

The Stranger gulped. "I guess so..." He paused, judging Rufus's next move. "Then he just drove off. He up and left me up there on the trail. He said it was a couple of miles to town."

"Eight. Eight miles to town."

"Eight! That lying son of a—"

Rufus pushed him down in the snow again.

He gulped but continued. "The snowstorm came up real sudden like with the wind howling and blowing and all. I started walking but I wandered off the trail in the snow and wound up lost right up till you found me."

"I didn't find you...he did."

Rufus growled again.

The Old Man stood for a long time just looking and thinking. He thought about the story he had just heard. He knew it wasn't true. He knew this man was a liar.

Amos shook his head but lowered the Winchester to his side. Somewhere inside he knew he could handle this one, but he also knew there would be another just like him, sooner or later.

Amos began to feel the cold beneath his shirt, and his toes were numbing up. He flipped the rifle to his left hand, stared at the Stranger for a minute, and then without a word turned and started walking towards the cabin.

"Hey," the Stranger whispered as loud as he dared, "what about me?"

Rufus growled again and shifted his weight on the Stranger's shoulders, pushing him deeper into the snow.

The Old Man continued walking away, silent.

The pressure of Rufus's big feet was almost as painful as the cold.

With his back to the dog, Amos commanded, "Rufus."

Instantly, the dog bounded off the Stranger and a half second later was two steps in front of the Old Man.

The Stranger rolled over to his side, watching the two walk away. Struggling to his feet, he groped around in the snow, found his knife, and stuck it back into the hidden compartment inside his boot.

He thinks he's pretty tough. He wiped the snow from his hands. *He was lucky this time. Nobody beats Sid Stull. Not that high and mighty wagon master or this old man.* He sneered, revealing pointed yellow teeth. *Why if it wasn't for that dog, I'd—.*

Rufus stopped and turned, staring at the Stranger.

The look the dog had on his face made the man stop thinking.

Rufus then spun around and with two quick bounds caught up to his friend.

The Stranger struggled to his feet and tried to hurry along behind the retreating figures, attempting to follow by placing his feet in the Old Man's footprints.

He could not.

CHAPTER 2
FEATHER RIVER VALLEY, CALIFORNIA
JANUARY 1866

Sid Stull, seated on a flagstone hearth, cradled his knees to his chest. The fireplace was huge— biggest he'd ever seen. His arms outstretched wouldn't touch the sides, and the thick wood mantel framed a nearly head high stone firebox. He'd been sitting quietly, rubbing his feet with one hand and gripping a steel cup filled with coffee in the other. The ice that had clumped in his beard and hair melted away, staining his red flannel underwear. He sat still and silent, but his eyes were darting back and forth like a perched hawk searching for its next meal.

The Old Man was seated at a table across the room, head down, busy cleaning the Winchester. He was broad in the shoulder, thick through the body and, now exposed by rolled-up sleeves, had arms like a blacksmith.

Stull took a breath, discontinued rubbing his feet, and stroked his wet, stringy black hair. Turning to the Old Man, he opened his mouth, his voice cracking a little when he spoke. "Guess I'm...," he cleared his throat, "pretty lucky there's no frostbite."

The Old Man didn't turn around or respond.

Stull heard a rustling sound up high.

Rufus, perched atop the woodpile and watching the Stranger's every move, slid forward an inch or two.

Stull peeked at the dog who was staring at him with unblinking black eyes. It took a minute, but he shrugged off the dog's attention and used the Old Man's lack of interest to continue to inventory the contents of the cabin.

Suddenly, a log burning right next to him broke in half and fell to the hearth, causing hot sparks to fly into the air. Most landed back in the fire but several flew out and fell on his outstretched legs.

"Yeeow." Stull lurched forward, spilling his hot coffee and further injuring his leg.

Rufus immediately rose to all fours, ears peaked, neck lowered, teeth bared. He growled, then barked what seemed like an order in Sid's direction.

Stull saw the dog poised, looking like it was daring him to move again. He brushed his legs slowly, trying to ignore the spilled coffee. Very slowly, he leaned back, fixing himself to the stone wall.

The big dog growled once more but dropped back to his 'resting-but-ready' position.

The Old Man stood and walked up to Stull, holding a towel. He held it out then shook it when Stull hesitated to take it.

Stull took it. "Thank you."

The Old Man walked back to the table.

Stull smiled a little as he rubbed the fabric between his boney fingers. *Miles from anywhere and this Old Man has fine towels.*

Sid set the cup on the hearth and wiped the rest of the melting ice water from his head and neck. When done, he hung the towel over a straight metal post that was sticking out of the stone wall inside the fireplace, close to the heat of the fire.

The fireplace, built of round fieldstone, was deep, and he could walk straight in under the mantel. In addition to the hook with the towel there were a lot of black iron gadgets mounted into the sidewalls that Stull assumed were for cooking. He didn't really know anything about cooking more than sticking a rabbit on a stick over a campfire or someone handing him a steak on a restaurant plate. But even to him it was obvious the long iron shafts and hooks were hinged to swing out over the fire at different levels. On the wall nearby, a few copper pots were hung and a few more made of black iron were stacked neatly on a shelf. One big round steel pot whose purpose mystified him was built into one side of the fireplace. It looked like an upside-down water barrel with iron doors top and bottom. He examined it for a while. Finally, without thinking it through, he stretched out a bony finger and said, "What's that?"

The Old Man looked over, paused, then stood up. He picked up the now-clean rifle, faced Stull, and reloaded the magazine, levering the action that placed a round in the chamber. He held the rifle across his chest and broke his silence, "It's an oven."

Stull grinned slyly then winked. "No kidden...you a regular old biscuit boy then, huh?"

The Old Man gave the Stranger a cold stare. It was kinda like the dog's but without the fangs or drooling spit.

When Sid saw the deep, dark, scary eyes, he realized his mistake and pulled his knees back to his chest, pretending, unsuccessfully, to be unaffected.

The Old Man disassembled the gun cleaning rod and put it, the can of gun oil, and a neatly folded rag into a wooden box. After wiping off the table, he walked past Stull, across the room, and through an open door.

Stull could see a brass bed and a dresser with a picture in a frame on its top.

The Old Man rested the rifle at the foot of the bed then walked back across the cabin and into the kitchen. A sink fashioned from mortared flat stones held an iron pump handle. He washed the gun oil from his hands, then rinsed the coffee pot.

Sid watched the Old Man complete his chores while continuing his thief's inventory. The cabin was centered on the fireplace dividing the kitchen on one side and a great room on the other. There were rooms on both ends. The one with the open door was the Old Man's bedroom but the other had a closed door and remained a mystery. The wind was still blowing against the long thick logs, set carefully with horsehair and mud mortar. The roof wasn't the usual mountain-built shanty with sagging beams and black water stains from a leak. It had a high A-framed ceiling with thick beams and wide purlins covered with hand-split cedar shingles. It was built like a fort—a stronghold against the weather, and against those who would do the occupants harm.

In the kitchen there was a table and chairs, shelves stocked with tin cans of all shapes and sizes, and jars filled with preserved food, enough to last the coldest winter. On the other side of the cabin there was a large desk, and two long floor-to-ceiling shelves filled with books, papers, and stacks of boxes that Sid knew held special treasures.

Stull shifted again, his neck straining to see into the bedroom and his head filled with curiosity of what was in the room behind the closed door. The gun lay against the bed, which the only thing he could see. It had two big pillows and a thick woven blanket. Sid hadn't seen anything like this outside of a hotel room in a town with at least two saloons.

A lot of gold built this.

Stull stretched and yawned, his fatigue growing as his body warmed. He repositioned his spindly legs and, when he bent over, he saw the foundry mark stamped onto a steel plate on the black oven in the fireplace.

Tibbets Metal Works
Philadelphia, Pennsylvania

He had this shipped all the way from a city in the East. Yes indeed, this old fool's got a lot of money, that's for sure.

Everything the Old Man owned was of interest, but it was the firearms that really whetted his appetite. Eight guns hung on a wooden rack bolted to the wall near the door. There was a long-barreled shotgun for ducks and a small-bore bolt action rifle. Under them were two perfectly preserved muzzle loaders. One he didn't recognize but the other was the coveted Kentucky long rifle. Next there was a heavy barrel, large caliber, buffalo rifle which had a wide sling adorned with colored beads and what looked like an eagle feather hanging from the stock. The gun Stull's eyes fixed on was hanging in a leather holster. It was a Colt 45 Peacemaker, the best and most reliable pistol in the West. He had seen several lawmen use that model when they were pointing at him.

The prize of the collection, however, the one Stull desired the most was leaning against the wall near the Old Man's bed. It was a Winchester lever action repeater. He heard about it but had actually seen a Calvary Captain at Fort Scott carrying this new rifle a couple of months ago. He saw it again in Arizona on his way north. Fortunately, the lawman chasing him was a bad shot and the horse Sid had stolen was a little faster than the sheriff's.

Sid had an old beat-up, unreliable six shooter, or at least he used to have one. All of his stuff was on the stagecoach. Pistols were okay, but pistols were hard to conceal, bulky, heavy, and misfired a lot. Not to mention you always had to be faster than the other guy. The little derringers were not accurate, and most times couldn't stop anybody. He preferred a knife. It could be hidden and used when not expected. It was noiseless and the way he used it, deadly. He was good with knives but over the years he'd had too many close calls. If he had his druthers, he would now much rather shoot from a distance. He could hide, shoot and kill, then escape without being seen. If only he had a good reliable rifle —like the Old Man. That Winchester lever-action rifle could pick off a whole posse before they could return a shot. Sid swore he would have one just like it one day and then there would be hell to pay.

"Like that gun?" asked the Old Man, observing the Stranger's interest.

Sid startled, caught staring. "Ah...nah..." He paused awkwardly then added, "well... yes.... I do. I saw one like it a while back. I like it just fine."

"Which end of the gun were you on?" It was more a statement than a question.

Sid said nothing. He was afraid of the Old Man up close and not just because of his size. He was a big fella all right, but he had tangled and bested big men before. It was something else that scared him.

The buttons on the Old Man's flannel shirt were pulled tight. If he hadn't had long gray hair that was pulled back like the Indians, Sid would have guessed him younger. The one thing that defied his guess was the Old Man's hands. They really told the story. They were large, leathery, and marked with crooked scars each of which could have told a story. His fingers appeared to be made from long strands of steel.

Those hands did a lot of hard work.

He looked down at his own hands which were thin, delicate even, like a fancy woman's hand. Embarrassed, he stuck his free hand under his leg.

He continued his inventory. There were tables and chairs around the room that were store-bought. There were even pillows, which were on the chairs and had been covered with brightly colored fabric.

Where did this old fool get all the money for these store-bought things?

Without paying the Stranger any mind, the Old Man stoked the fire with the poker, put an additional log in the right location and then crossed the room, went into his bedroom, and lay down on his bed.

Sid sat still on the slate hearth, now finally dry.

The Old Man rolled over and turned his back to Sid.

Sid looked at the long black poker that was not two feet away. He looked at it, then judged the time it would take to cross the room and bash the Old Man over the head. Then he looked at Rufus.

The dog was perched on his woodpile, eyes closed, head laying down on his two front paws.

Sid looked at the poker again, then the Old Man, then the copper pots. He moved just a bit.

Rufus didn't even open his eyes. He just growled a low guttural sound.

Sid stopped.

Without rolling over to look at him the Old Man said, "I'd sit real still, if I were you."

Sid sat real still for the rest of the night and slept leaning against the wall.

CHAPTER 3
FEATHER RIVER VALLEY, CALIFORNIA
JANUARY 1866

Sleep came to Sid Stull in spurts. He slipped into fitful darkness only to be awakened by shooting pains from sleeping while sitting up against the stone fireplace. The hearth where he sat was narrow and left no room to stretch out. Laying on the floor was not an option. Every time he attempted to move the damn dog would snarl at him. So, he stayed put, drifting off despite muscle cramps and stabbing pains.

Morning found him with his head back against the wall, mouth open and a small amount of drool on his chin. The dog woke him growling fiercely from about an inch from his face. His heart barely had time to recover from the panic of the wolf-dog's threat when the Old Man announced, "It's time for you to go."

Sid grumbled but complied. He was being forced out into the cold again without sympathy or coffee.

The Old Man left the cabin, leaving the dog to assist in Sid's exit. Stull pulled on his now dry clothes and stretched painfully as he walked to the door.

Rufus followed him out then sat on the porch.

Stull turned to pull the door closed and gave one more look around the cabin, cementing images of its contents in his brain.

Amos sat on a single horse-drawn wagon, staring straight ahead, with the reins in his hands. He had on a buffalo skin coat and there was snow on his boots.

Rufus almost knocked Sid down as he bolted off the porch, jumped down into the snow, then leapt into the hay trough at the back of the wagon.

Blinded by the sun's reflection off the snow, Sid raised his hands to his eyes. He stumbled down the steps, then walked around the front of the horse—judging this tethered animal less dangerous than the blood thirsty monster perched in the back. Amos's form blocked the sun and Sid's effort to see the man with the reins yielded only the shadowed outline of a man twice his size. Sid gripped the seat and pulled himself up.

"Come on git, Puddle." The Old Man gave a gentle snap with the leather strap which made more noise than impact.

The wagon bounced along the seldom driven path bordering the pasture. It was flat until they reached the tall pine soldiers lining the beginnings of the mountain greenery. The trees leaned on each other, slim at the top, but wide in their foundation. The forest song was playing. Branches kept the beat while birds sang, and the wind conducted the melody.

But Sid heard nothing. He wasn't listening.

The wagon meandered up through the forest at a decent pace until the path started up a steeper slope. The wagon slowed and the horse pulled harder, the path switching back and forth as it climbed up the mountain. It was slow going and more difficult because the road had large ruts and washouts that needed navigation. Twice the travelers had to dismount to remove fallen branches impeding their journey.

Sid thought the road would never end, but eventually the trail crested, and the Old Man pulled back the reins when the trail widened and flattened out. They had arrived at the logging road on which Sid's sudden debarkation from the stagecoach was supposed to have occurred the night before.

Amos pointed to the fresh wagon wheel tracks in the snow which indicated there had been other wagons on the road that day. "The road is open."

"So?" Sid was genuinely puzzled.

Puddle began pawing at the ground.

Amos looked at Sid then pointed down to the ground. "Get out."

Stull went into shock. "What...out? You're not leaving me here? There's no town...no people." He raised his voice and made no effort to dismount. He shook his head. "I'm not getting off the wagon."

Amos ignored him and stretched his arm out, pointing down the road. "Walk that way. Keep the sun at your back until you come to a fork in the road. Take the road that puts the sun on your right shoulder. If you do that and stay on the trail...and walk steady...you'll see Carversville by mid-afternoon."

"But it's still cold," wined Sid.

"Then...walk fast."

Sid grimaced, still not moving. He was sitting with arms crossed. "I'll not go...and you can't make me." He was trying out defiance.

It didn't work.

The Old Man was also sitting still, both reins in his hands, and looking straight ahead. A few seconds went by.

Sid still didn't move.

The Old Man shook his head back and forth a little.

Sid remained firm, crossing his arms tighter.

Amos gave Rufus permission. "Rufus."

The dog instantly leaped to the front seat and, using his big body, pushed Sid down to the ground.

Stull landed on his side, but his face still caught a lot of the impact. He rolled over and sat up, snow and small sticks on his face. "You haven't heard the last of me," he yelled, pointing his boney finger. "I'll see you again." He brushed some debris away. "Bet on that. I'll see you again."

The Old Man softly murmured, "I know you will."

Amos maneuvered Puddle to turn the wagon around to head back down the mountain.

Rufus sat perched on the seat, head turning as the wagon did, never taking his eyes from the Stranger.

After a minute or two, Amos had the wagon pointed the right way. He paused a second, then gave Puddle another gentle tap with the reins. "Git up."

The wagon, with Amos Cronin looking down the trail, and Rufus's gaze still fixed, started moving away from Sid Stull.

Sid, standing and brushing the snow from his clothes, took a few hesitant steps down the road where Amos had pointed. He looked forward then back over his shoulder towards the retreating wagon.

Rufus jumped from the front seat to the hay trough.

Sid, his face red with anger, pointed at the dog, then made an exaggerated gesture and spit in disgust in the direction of the disappearing wagon. "I'll get you for this." He added a dramatic fist shake.

Rufus leapt so high it looked like he was almost flying, hitting the ground at full speed.

Sid, at first, saw only a cloud of snow suddenly rise from the ground. The next thing Sid saw was Rufus appearing out of the white cloud, with his mouth open, tongue flapping, and teeth bared.

Sid's eyes got as big as saucers. He stumbled backwards, then turned and broke into a full run. Stull got only a few feet before a toe of his boot caught on a root and he pitched forward to the ground. He landed sliding forward on his hands and knees, ending up crouched over, head down, and butt in the air.

The teeth penetrating Sid's pants instantly made him forget the pain of falling on the frozen road. He screamed in pain.

Rufus held on for only one good head shake then let him go.

Sid rolled around, grabbing his bleeding behind.

Rufus sat down and calmly watched.

With a face scratched, bruised and full of snow, Sid looked at the dog and snarled, "I'll make a rug out of you."

The big dog rose and crouched like a lion about to strike. His eyes went black. Snarling, he took a slow step forward, his head low and teeth bared.

Sid instantly put his hands up to fend off an imminent attack, while deeply regretting his remark.

"Rufus." The Old Man yelled from the wagon, which was now only partially visible.

Rufus turned and bounded away, casting snow on Sid's face.

Sid struggled to his feet, brushed off the snow, pulled up his torn pants, and started limping away with the sun at his back as the Old Man advised.

Rufus stopped once and looked back, then quickly caught up to the wagon, and jumped up to the seat.

"Happy now?" Amos looked at his friend with half a grin.

Rufus barked once.

Amos scratched the dog's ear. "You better keep those eyes and ears sharp, my friend. He'll be back...with friends, sooner or later," the Old Man said with sad conviction.

The trip going back to the cabin was downhill and a bit faster. Certainly, easier on Puddle. The wagon came out of the evergreen forest and drove around the pasture, arriving on the south side of the cabin in front of the barn. Amos pulled the wagon up to the doors, unhitched Puddle, and walked him to his stall. He grabbed a brush, groomed the big black horse, and thanked him for the ride. The trip earned Puddle an extra bucket of oats for his effort.

The Old Man stood in the doorway of the barn. He was proud of what he, or rather the three, had built. It had been hard work. Of course, the gold made it much easier, but the effort resulted in a pretty good life. The cattle in the pasture, seeing the activity, meandered back to the barn hoping for an early lunch. He put feed in the trough for the late arrivals then shut the door and sadly thought, *It could have been a lot different.*

He slapped the barn door with his hand. "Stop. It's too late now."

He was talking to no one because no one was there.

Rufus sat waiting on the porch.

Amos walked slow toward the cabin. The thought wouldn't go away. What was only coming in his sleep was now haunting his days. He walked up then sat on a step. Rufus sat beside him.

They would have loved it too, but they never saw it.

The danger had past, for now, but deep inside he knew that it was almost time. He interlaced his fingers and ducked his head down. The moment of pride disappeared. His mind drifted back to the chill that had run up his back.

Maybe the feeling that overtook him last night wasn't brought on by someone threatening harm. It certainly wasn't that skinny runt, or even the threat of him returning with a gang of his friends. He wasn't afraid of that stranger, or any stranger. Maybe it was something else.

Years of surviving in these mountains had taught him many lessons. One of which was there were no excuses and no recourse. Mountain life was as sure as nightfall and sunrise. Every tree, every blade of grass, every soul that lived...eventually died. But now, somehow, he knew the cold that ran up his spine wasn't death.

It came to him in a flash, he knew what it was. He slapped his hands to his knees and stood. He took a deep breath of cool air, feeling invigorated. He had much to do before he closed an eye.

It was time!

A plan had been there for a while but in pieces, but now, suddenly, it came together. Steps would have to be taken. It would take time, and he had to be careful. There were a lot of strangers hiding in the dark.

He wouldn't be around to protect him. It wouldn't make up for what happened but maybe—if he was smart enough—his son would know what to do with his legacy.

Amos looked out across the pasture at the tops of the trees gently swaying against the new breeze.

Maybe, I'll see the boy one time.

CHAPTER 4

PHILADELPHIA, PENNSYLVANIA

APRIL 1866

Patience wasn't a virtue Henry Cronin possessed in any great quantity. His fingers drummed the desktop, ears perked listening for a bell that just had to ring soon.

It must be three o'clock any minute.

The headmaster was a diligent man whose fastidious nature meant punctuality. He made a ritual of ringing the dismissal bell every day exactly on time.

Minutes seemed to eke by like the slow drip of tree sap.

At the front of the classroom, Mr. Ellis was droning on and on about the war finally ending. With only minutes before the end of the school day, he stood in the front of the classroom conducting a battle to keep the attention of eleven boys and two girls with a lecture about the political implications of the Union's victory. He was losing this skirmish.

The pudgy, grey-haired, teacher wore a black waistcoat buttoned to the throat that had a bit of chalk dust on the tail. Under it was a starched white shirt complete with a stiff celluloid collar. A silver watch chain dangled from the pocket of his perfectly creased vest.

Henry, and the rest of his classmates, knew when Mr. Ellis's inner actor was about to take over his lecture. They knew the chain appeared when he was about to recite a famous quote or dramatize a battlefield hero's story. It was his prop, rolling it gently between his fingers, his chin raised to the sky, eyes gazing to the distance, poised to deliver a stage actor's soliloquy.

The chain and watch appeared, and the seven boys and two girls collectively groaned.

Henry gazed out the window, fingers still marking time with a slow beat. He saw a wagon loaded with soldiers, pulled by a team of army mules, pass by on its way to Fort Mifflin. Mr. Ellis's lecture that day was about General Lee's recent surrender marking the end of the Civil War. Henry speculated that these boys were either coming back from the war or had won a game of chance in being new recruits who were no longer needed for battle. The soldiers' uniforms seemed new, so Henry assumed the latter.

The war's end meant good news as his service in uniform was no longer a discussion. The first university in the country was now his destiny. It was all arranged. He would graduate from Penn Charter in June and attend Ben Franklin's University of Pennsylvania in the fall. His marks weren't impressive, but several teachers' recommendations accompanied his application, all concurring in the opinion that while not a great student Henry had enormous potential. A fact, in the headmaster's opinion, that would be proven true—someday. However, his acceptance to university did not necessarily need glowing references. It was never in question, as his tuition for all four years was pre-paid in full.

Mr. Ellis's speech was coming to an end, his audience restless and profoundly unappreciative. A low murmur arose from the audience. He shot a stern look in all directions that elicited obedient silence and obtained their undivided attention again. All the students regained focus, save one.

Mr. Ellis leaned forward, pointed his nose in Henry's direction, and tapped his foot. "Mr. Cronin."

His name being called aloud snapped Henry's attention back from the travelers outside the window. However, he realized his complete and total disinterest in Mr. Ellis's performance was written all over his face.

"Have you someplace better to be?" The teacher said the words slowly, dragging out the 'to be.'

There was a pause. Every face in the class turned to look at Henry. Their faces had looks of anticipation.

"Well?" Mr. Ellis's face was also anticipatory and for good reason. Henry Cronin wasn't always respectful toward authority.

There was another pause as Henry stood, took a pencil from his pocket, and began to twirl it like a watch chain. "Mr. Ellis—."

The headmaster saved the day. The dismissal bell suddenly rang loud, echoing freedom down the hall.

The children jumped from their seats and started running to the exit.

"Wait." Mr. Ellis stuck a hand into the air to stop the onslaught.

The children obeyed, almost. They were still slowly shuffling their feet toward the door.

Ellis grumbled, "Mr. Cronin, you show little interest in this class." He lowered his voice. "Yet somehow you get decent grades." His voice raised again. "Your disinterest in my lectures about the future of our country and overall complacency to your education indicate to me that you're headed down the road to...

nowhere." He grinned a little, seemingly pleased with his impromptu dissertation.

Henry grinning mischievously, looked at his classmates, then back to Mr. Ellis. "Well sir, if I've been going nowhere, then from what I have heard in here, nowhere is a better place...to be."

The second bell rang, and the floodgates opened. It was hard to tell if the cheers that erupted were for Henry or the bell.

There was no stopping the exodus now, and Henry escaped with the crowd.

Mr. Ellis stammered, pointed aimlessly, stammered again, then replaced his watch chain as he had run out of script.

About sixty or seventy kids ranging from twelve to sixteen ran out of the arched double doors of Penn Charter School. They came out in groups, girls laughing and boys pushing and shoving. Their enthusiasm had been accelerated because all the windows had been open becoming an irresistible lure, teasing the students with fresh spring air and a bright, warming sun. It had been a typical northeastern winter featuring numerous snowstorms and days and days of bitter cold. However, those days had been replaced with blooming trees and spring flowers. The need to cover up against the freezing wind became a desire to embrace the breeze.

The weather didn't make it a hard winter all by itself. For years the war had been raging on and on and the lists of those killed in battle were published in the newspapers almost every day. But, finally, just as the winter started its retreat, the newspaper announced the fall of the Confederacy's capital, Richmond, and, a few days later, the headlines were of General

Lee's surrender at Appomattox and the end of the war. It was joyous, and celebrations were everywhere. There were bands playing and fireworks lit the night sky. People were happy and relieved that it was finally over. The fact that it meant the Union was preserved was important to those who stood for principle and won. It was important to Mr. Ellis and his lecture and to the boys in the wagon who wouldn't face death tomorrow. It also lessened, for a while, the sorrow dwelling in the houses of the ones who wouldn't return. Henry didn't know one person who hadn't lost someone in the battles, and who didn't have pain that would never retreat.

On this day the war, like the winter, was in the past and the warm sun lifted spirts and reminded everyone that hope was still possible.

There was a long sidewalk leading out to the avenue where, every day, students traveled to and from school. Almost all the students, and most of the faculty, headed home traveling east to the Germantown section of Philadelphia. A few, the headmaster, the dean of faculty, and a few children of politicians and bankers, went south into center city where they had well-to-do residences around Rittenhouse Square.

Every day Henry walked west to Laurel Hill. He lived in a house just on the border of Fairmount Park, a beautiful, pristine stretch of land with huge trees, great stretches of open space, and carefully manicured city gardens. He lived with his Aunt Betty in a big brick house with a lookout on the third floor where one could enjoy long views of the Schuylkill River. There weren't a lot of houses in the Hill, only a few, and they were coveted by the well-to-do of Rittenhouse Square.

He preferred to walk the distance to and from school by himself. When he first began at Penn Charter, Aunt Betty arranged for Gerald, the groom who cared for the horses, to take the carriage and drive Henry. That didn't work out. Henry convinced his aunt that showing up in a horse-drawn carriage every day would make him stand out among his classmates. He told her he didn't want to be different. He just wanted to fit in. So, he walked, starting when he was twelve. Rain, or snow didn't matter, he stuck to his guns. Aunt Betty, undeterred, had Gerald follow him from a distance anyway. A practice that continued until the beginning of this term when she decided that Henry could take care of himself.

His daily journey, not including the weather, wasn't without its perils.

Over the past six months, Henry had become a target for a group of three boys. At first, they just harassed and threatened him. On the watch for trouble, he managed to get past them, but they eventually cornered him, took his money, and beat him up. Henry knew his aunt would be horrified at his torn clothes and blackened eye, but still wanting to maintain his independence, he told his aunt that he fell cutting through the park.

He avoided the gang's next attempts by taking different routes and being more alert, but they trapped him again and gave him another beating. Henry no longer carried more than a few pennies and was fortunate, this time, that he was only punched in the stomach and arms. So, he was able to conceal this attack from his aunt.

It took a while to plan out. Henry spent hours sitting in his room, thinking, spending so much time that Aunt Betty became concerned.

"Henry." Her voice was as soft as the knock on the door. "Are you alright?"

He jumped up from the bed and quickly swung it open. "I'm fine. I'm sorry, I didn't hear you calling me. Do you need me to do something?"

"No, no." She smiled. Her concern was diminished by the sound of his voice. "I'm just worried." A grimace took her smile away. "You've not been yourself lately."

"I'm fine, really." He stepped into the hall, put his arm around her waist, and headed her toward the stairs.

She slowed, stopped, and looked up at him. "What's wrong, dear? You know you can tell me anything, don't you?"

Henry wasn't going to lie to her. Never had before and never would, but there were some things he thought better to keep private.

She gave him a hard stare with no indication of giving up.

Henry smiled a toothy grin, patted her shoulder, and gently continued to guide her toward the stairs. "I am just working on something, Aunt Betty. It's kind of a surprise."

Her concern seemed to fade a bit. "Really, that's nice...but not for me, I hope." She tightened her shoulders and pointed at him. "I don't need anything, so—"

"No, no. Not for you," then he added quickly, "not that you don't deserve a surprise once in a while."

"Henry." Her smile returned.

"It's for some kids I met at school."

"New friends?"

"Not exactly friends but then who knows what the future holds."

She patted his hand.

Henry changed the subject. "Am I correct in thinking you were baking a cake?"

She nodded happily. "Indeed, I was. Your favorite."

Henry started down the stairs with her at his side. For the first time, he realized he was a full head taller than her.

CHAPTER 5
PHILADELPHIA, PENNSYLVANIA

MAY 1866

Henry worked the problem as well as he could, but the more he thought about it the more variables became evident. He certainly did not want another beating and yet the only way to end this threat was to put himself at risk.

Why they had singled him out was a mystery to him. There were other boys walking about, but Henry knew he was different. His clothes were better, without wear. His school was the best, most elite in the city and he lived in a house that not even the wealthiest shop owners or businessmen in the neighborhood could possibly afford. But the fact remained he'd become a target, and their persistence increased with every encounter. He knew the best result of this plan would be that he remains unscathed, and helping his tormentors to decide to look elsewhere for entertainment. It was the goal of his strategy. However, he foresaw obstacles that might lead to something sustainably short of a happy ending.

He lay on his bed, staring at the ceiling, one leg crossed over the other, making notes on a pad of paper. The early morning light coming through his window and streaking the floor was gaining on his bed. It was almost time to go.

Ten pages had been marked with hand-drawn maps of different routes he'd explored. He had noted the time of day he'd seen the boys on the streets, their favorite hangouts, and their names and where they lived. It had taken days of hiding in alleys and ducking around corners to accumulate the information, but eventually the data helped him calculate the odds of success. It helped determine the when and where. There was risk, but he couldn't go through an entire summer hiding from his persecutors.

He closed the book of notes and began dressing for school. He'd made the decision knowing the success of his plan was decidedly uncertain, but no matter, today was the day.

He wasn't really a friend— Henry didn't have any real friends— but Georgie Pickney was someone whom Henry liked enough to talk to occasionally. The boy was Henry's age but was far less worldly. Henry suspected Georgie, like many of his other privileged classmates, was sheltered from regular city life. The family was well off – enough. They had a semi-privileged life, and the boy seemed to want for little. Georgie was not a handsome physical specimen. He was average height with blond hair, a round face, and pink skin. He was smart, but only from the books he read, not the lessons they taught.

"Georgie, are you headed home right after school?"

"I am indeed, Henry." His father was British, his mother French, so Georgie was born pretentious. "Why do you ask?"

"Just curious. I was wondering if you were still avoiding McMichael Park."

George went from slightly pink to slightly red. "I...I. Yes, I told my mother that she needs to do business with another apothecary, one closer to our home. I shan't be going near that part of the city to pick up packages for her any time soon." Georgie was struggling to act manly.

Henry leaned over in his seat and lowered his voice. "Those boys who beat you up—"

"What..." Georgie stammered. "Yes, those boys were ruffians, bullies..." His eyes welled up then his voice changed. "Henry, they hurt me." His eyes went to the floor. "They really hurt me."

Henry patted him on the shoulder. "You're not the only one who has had trouble in that neighborhood."

Georgie looked up. "You too?"

Henry nodded.

"Really?"

"Yep. I have to walk home that way every day and they've gotten me three times."

Georgie looked surprised and relieved, possibly because now he knew he wasn't the only one.

"I have it on good authority," Henry paused and looked back and forth like someone might be listening. "Those boys might be running into some trouble of their own."

Georgie perked up and so did his voice. "That would be magnifique."

Henry winced at the French Brit offspring.

"Mr. Cronin," Professor Ellis's voice boomed. "Are we having another problem?"

"No sir," Henry said obediently. "Sorry, sir."

Georgie grinned broadly and nodded at Henry.

Henry nodded back but then turned his attention to the window and the street scene beyond.

The school bell rang precisely at the appointed hour and Henry began walking, taking his usual route. He knew he would be safe until he entered the four-block realm of the bullies which was halfway between school and home.

The path from Penn Charter led to McMichael Park. On this bright and sunny spring day, the road surrounding the park had a constant stream of wagons and carriages moving in the concert of daily commerce. He navigated the crowded street, thinking and rethinking his plan. He slowed as he approached Queen Street where houses and stores were built close together and marked the beginning of the four blocks where all the attacks occurred.

They had caught him three times, each fight more violent. He could have traveled around the area, but the small square of the city was where they lived. He knew, sooner or later, they would expand their territory the additional five blocks toward his house. He also wasn't about to allow his life to be ruled by fear. He was outnumbered and outsized, so he just needed to be smarter.

He slowed his gait as he approached the first block of their territory. His objective was half-way in, an alley behind the stores on Midvale Avenue. To get there he needed to cross, unseen by the boys, three well-traveled roads. The wagons and carriages were abundant, so he could duck behind one going his way and maintain a low profile. He could do that until he wanted to be seen.

He almost made it.

One of the variables he couldn't anticipate was early detection.

The short, fat boy with black greasy hair and a very high voice was standing on the corner at the end of the block Henry was navigating. Henry saw him first and tried to hide, but the wagon being pulled down the street that was providing cover suddenly turned, leaving him exposed.

The fat boy turned, cupped both hands to his mouth, and yelled. "Hey...over here."

Henry froze for a second, quickly calculating speed and distance. The fat boy was half a block away. The entrance to the alley was still two blocks west. He knew he could easily outdistance the fat boy, the second lad in the group also wouldn't be a problem, he was skinny and awkward.

The third boy was the problem. Henry found out that his name was Tommy Gunderson. He was the ringleader and much bigger than his buddies.

He was also bigger than Henry.

Gunderson was the one who hurt Henry the most, causing the black eye and what was possibly a broken rib. He would be faster than the other two, and the one Henry had to beat to the alley.

"Over here, over here." The fat boy was now frantically waving at his friends. He was jumping too, but not very high.

The other two boys came around the corner.

The fat boy pointed.

Henry waited a couple of seconds more, then ran.

Gunderson had come around the corner running and didn't hesitate a step. "Let's get 'em."

Henry had a good block head start. Far enough not to get caught but close enough to keep them chasing.

He ran along in front of the stores until a door opened. Henry spun around it and the lady coming out. "Sorry ma'am."

To catch up, the boys were running in the street which was muddy from the horses tromping and wagon wheels rolling. The fat boy slipped and fell sliding forward on his chest. The second boy stopped and laughed a goofy laugh, but both recovered quickly and continued running behind Gunderson.

Henry peeked over his shoulder and realized he was too far ahead and slowed up a little. He took in a breath and was surprised that he wasn't scared. He smiled a little, realizing that he was a lot faster than he thought.

Tommy Gunderson was twenty feet behind and his comrades, who'd almost caught up were ten feet behind Gunderson. The three were now running next to the storefronts and looking serious.

The alley was only five steps away. It was long and narrow and ran behind all the stores on Midvale Avenue. Two-story red brick walls lined both sides of the alley. The only interruptions in the brick were single, windowless doors every thirty or forty feet, each a backdoor to a store facing the Avenue. It was dark, the only light coming from the space between the roofs of the buildings.

Henry counted. *One.* He ran thirty feet, passing a door. *Two.* He passed the second. Thirty more feet. *Three.*

Gunderson was right behind. "I got you now." He raised his hands, arms stretched out straight.

Henry stopped abruptly, turned and faced the threat, his feet spread, anticipating the blow.

Gunderson grabbed Henry by the shirt and threw him against the third door.

Henry pulled his hands up like a boxer protecting his face.

Gunderson yanked Henry off the door, then slammed him back into the door again.

The other two boys caught up. They started shouting. "Hit him, hit him. Knock him down. Get his money."

Gunderson made a fist, pulled it back, and held it a half a second.

Henry ducked his head just as the punch was thrown, and Gunderson's fist hit the door full on. Henry heard a bone crack.

"Yow." Gunderson, still holding on to Henry's shirt with one hand, shook his punching hand while grimacing with pain.

"Let us at him." The other boys were pushing in close, but the alley was narrow and didn't give them much room to maneuver.

The skinny kid threw a punch over Gunderson's shoulder, but it only glanced off the side of Henry's head. It too hit the door.

Gunderson regripped Henry's shirt with one hand and used his forearm to bang Henry into the door again. The back of his head banged hard off the door. He saw a white flash and his body went limp for a second or two.

"I think you broke my hand." Gunderson spit. "You son of a bitch."

As the word "bitch" came out of his mouth, the door opened.

A big man wearing a white butcher's apron smeared with blood appeared in the opening. He had both hands on his hips and a growl on his face.

Gunderson let go of Henry and looked up, suddenly scared.

The other two stood like statues, frozen and silent.

Henry was working hard to maintain his victim status while suppressing a smile.

"Tommy?" The man had focused on Gunderson.

"Dad."

It was almost too good. Henry plopped to the ground and leaned back against the wall about to enjoy the fruits of his plan.

"What's going on?" The man's growling face turned meaner.

Gunderson started to speak but it was apparent he hadn't

gotten a good lie together yet so what he had to say came out as a stutter. "I'm...I'm ... I mean we just."

Henry joined in, immediately drawing the man's attention. "These boys were chasing me, trying to steal my money, and beat me up."

The man's gaze went to his son, then back to Henry. "What's your name, son?"

"Henry Cronin, sir."

"Henry..." He instantly recognized the name. "Cronin...Henry Cronin?"

"Sir, yes sir."

The man leaned over, getting close to his son's face. "Do you know who this is?" He reached out and grabbed his son's shirt, lifting him up into the air with one hand.

The other two boys became unfrozen and bolted.

"This is the nephew of Elisabeth Nichols, who happens to be one of my best customers. Not to mention she is one of the nicest people your mother and I know."

He looked down at Henry. "You alright, son?"

"Yes sir. It wasn't that bad..." he waited a second then added, "this time."

"This time?" The man went red in the face. "This time?" He grabbed Gunderson's arm and threw him through the open door.

Henry's smile was trying hard to bust through. He was doing everything to hold it back.

The man put a hand on Henry's shoulder. "Don't you worry. Tommy will never bother you again." He paused a second, stared harder, and added, "Ever."

"Thank you, sir." Henry nodded. "And...could they not beat up the other kids at school too?"

Henry could see the man's teeth grinding. "Give my best to

your aunt, please." He turned and walked slowly through the door and gently closed it.

Henry turned to walk down the alley, and home.

The smile finally broke through.

CHAPTER 6
CARVERSVILLE, CALIFORNIA
MAY 1866

Spring was trying hard to break winter's icy grip, the grey sky and biting cold refusing to leave. It ruled well into April, but on this sunny afternoon the struggle against the coming season seemed futile. Nowhere was the battle more apparent, and more inconvenient, than the main road through Carversille.

During winter, the wide dirt road bisecting the town's businesses was frozen but remained passable even after a big snowfall. The horses and wagons would pack down new- fallen snow, rendering the surface icy but manageable. Today, the rising temperatures turned the hard-packed snow and ice into a sloppy, muddy bog.

Carversville was built between two foothills of the western Rocky Mountains on a fairly flat plateau. It grew exponentially over the years and now had a bustling business district at its heart. A hotel and a few eateries serviced the settlers passing through, the workers at the bank, the livery stable, and a variety of smaller shops and stores. On most days, buggies, stagecoaches, delivery carts, and a stream of Conestoga wagons came and went with ease, but not today. Drivers had to carefully guide their wagons in straight lines, one behind the other, following in each other's muddy tracks. However, as the sun got higher in the sky, another layer of ice melted and the mud got deeper, causing the wagons to skid and slide, sometimes getting stuck and blocking traffic. When the horses couldn't pull them free, additional traction was needed. Travelers were forced to jump down from their wagons into the boot-high, sloppy mess. Long planks were stored near the road's edge for this very situation, and the travelers jammed the boards under the wheels for traction. It was nasty, arduous work, but necessary to extricate the mud-stuck wagons.

This warm day was a serious inconvenience to some, but it was also the source of endless entertainment to others. In an alley between the hotel and the barber shop, a group of children had spontaneously invented a game. They were busy sliding back and forth down the length of the alley on a wooden barrel top competing against each other in the categories of speed, distance, and the amount of mud accumulated per slide. All participants were covered from head-to-toe in thick oozing mud and were breaking into fits of hysterical laughter after each participant completed a run.

While the children were making the best of the situation, adults were hurrying along covered wooden walkways in front of the stores. When they came to an alley between the rows of buildings, or had to cross to the other side, they slowed and stepped carefully down to the street onto a plank resting atop the mud. They crossed the distance between the buildings with heads down and arms outstretched, balancing like tight rope walkers desperately trying not to lose their footing. However, when they heard the children's voices, chattering and laughing, they would stop and look. Poised and still, their concentration interrupted, the adults tried to peer into the dark alley. These adults, who paused their hurried schedules, couldn't help but smile at the sound even while shaking their heads knowing that somewhere mothers would be waiting with a much different view of this children's game.

The mud was affecting another Carversille's man in a much different way. Howard Goodman was dressed in his usual uniform. He wore dark overalls fastened with brass buttons, a blue flannel shirt buttoned to the neck, and two black sleeve garters. He also wore a canvas bib apron that covered his growing middle-aged belly and was almost as clean as his store. He was cursing, just under his breath, while shaking his head in dismay as he swept the porch of his General Store.

"Mud, Mud, Mud," he fussed while waging a losing effort to sweep clumps of mud from his otherwise spotless storefront walkway.

Through the sparkling clean display window, his wife, Martha Goodman, was staring at her husband with a concerned look on her plain but pretty young face. The door was open welcoming a fresh breeze. As she brushed a hair from her face, she heard the sudden eruption of laughter. She walked to the storefront where she glanced past her obsessive husband and glimpsed the children playing in the alley. She smiled briefly, then, with a deep sadness, she quickly looked down, her expression changing.

Business in their general store had been very good. The town was growing because of the loggers, ranchers, and farmers as well as settlers passing through almost every day. The couple spent endless days working, arranging for the purchase of more inventory, stocking shelves, as well as selling their wares to their new customers. Goodman's General Store was the only place for miles and miles where one could buy the implements and hard-goods necessary to begin a new life in the promised land.

The settlers who had come great distances arrived full of expectations, usually with a substantial grubstake, vastly different than those from just a few years ago. In the past, the wagons were filled with prospectors desperately looking for gold in the mountains and rivers of Northern California. Their dreams vanished as quickly as did their presence.

Martha turned and walked back to the counter and her duties. Two of the town's women were feeling the fabric that had just arrived from back East and two men were debating which tools they needed to repair a roof. The rough and often lawless past had changed dramatically in just the few years since the Goodman's arrival in Carversville. Settlers who were looking to homestead meant the years of Martha and Howard's hard work would finally pay off.

She heard the children again. She walked back to the front of the store and closed the door.

Amos Cronin sat tall on the wagon's wooden bench seat. Next to him, also sitting tall and smelling a might better than usual, was Rufus. The dog was half the old man's size but looked twice as fierce. It was quite a sight to see. They were infamous, actually, because those from Carversville, who had witnessed their comings and goings, were quick to gossip. The onlookers were prone to embellishing even the slightest detail and relaying the information with the same enthusiasm as the infrequent sightings of buffalo. The six foot two, two-hundred-and-twenty-pound man was big, no doubt, but not without equal. There were plenty of big loggers, farmers, and muleskinners, however for some reason, this man-made children stare and men stop talking. They couldn't take their eyes off Amos Cronin and Rufus. They were quite a pair.

Gossip went around fast in Carversville, and each storyteller had a different account of the duo's activities, telling and retelling, embellishing to the point that facts became unimportant to the tale. There were stories of close calls with the Indians, and one about an incident with a grizzly bear. There were stories of a couple of run-ins with ranch hands, retold by "eyewitnesses." One had Amos besting three men in short order, with Rufus handling two more. But mostly the stories were about him and gold. Some said he struck it rich and squirreled it away somewhere on the mountain, but nobody knew for sure. The truth was he gave little sign of wealth. He paid some bills in town with gold dust, but no more than others. He just didn't brag, show off, or give any sign that he'd made a strike. He hadn't even filed a claim. However, he had purchased a good deal of the land around his cabin. Nobody really knew how much land but there were rumors. The stories were legends, some parts true, some not, but because of the larger-than-life appearance of the big man and his wolf dog, it seemed that all of them were believable.

Rufus turned his head from side to side, lifting his nose in the air. The Old Man found this trait remarkable. Most dogs he had come across ground scented, but Rufus, unlike hounds, worked with his nose in the air just like the wolves.

Amos had bathed and was dressed in clean clothes. This trip to town was unavoidable but purposeful. He needed supplies, a haircut, bags of feed from the Goodman's, and to pay a visit to his lawyer.

While Amos was frowning and single focused on his destination, Rufus's head was moving around like he was watching a field full of rabbits. There was movement everywhere, and it seemed he couldn't decide who to chase first. Amos was grunting disapproval under his breath at everything he saw but Rufus's tail was wagging with anticipation.

Amos needed to come to town because he'd gotten used to comfort. He could afford it, and he liked it more when he got back to the cabin, but he hated himself for the weakness, as he knew it was a fault which someday would cost him.

The wagon rolled slowly on, passing businesses and storefronts, Amos staring straight ahead. He winced passing the laundry and the stable which smelled terrible.

The laundry reeked because the soapy water ran from the big tubs inside the building to a drainage trench that was used all year regardless of weather. During the winter, the water would freeze, so it just lay there turning into a pile of dirty brown ice. Today, the sun was melting a winters worth of filth.

Every stable had its own aroma. Everybody knows horse stalls can be unpleasant but when they are neglected it is awful. This business belonged to the mayor's brother-in-law, Tom Hopkins, who was a lay-about. When the stalls were occasionally cleaned, the leavings were dumped into a pile to rot just behind the big wooden building. Today, the sun was cooking the horse hay stew, and the stink filled the street. There was a point on the road where the two smells met. Eyes watered and occasionally someone lost a meal to the sickening odor.

Amos disliked the town and almost everybody in it, almost. He loathed people who didn't care, and those who cared too much. He detested them and showed it, not being one to hide disapproval. Rufus on the other hand was liked by adults once they got over the initial shock of turning around and staring at a huge wolf-like dog. Children on the other hand, loved him immediately.

Amos's wagon pulled up and stopped at the two-story building that was his first destination. Rufus spied the kids laughing in the alley and bounded down from the seat. Their laughter was taken to a much higher level as Rufus immediately joined the fun.

Amos shook his head, climbed down from the wagon, and walked up the wide wooden steps to his lawyer's office.

For most residents of Carversville, the comings and goings of the population of this little mountain town was almost a full-time occupation. It seemed like anyone who had an eye open was watching what someone else was doing. Perhaps it was a survival instinct acquired from the dangers of living in a society during a time before it tried to establish its social limits. Or perhaps it was just they had nothing better to do. Neither of those two justifications, however, applied to Sid Stull. His curiosity was more base, more dark, more evil. His interest was plain and simple greed.

The front window of Wingers Café offered a fair view of the town's goings on, and the diners could keep an eye out while eating a ranch-size breakfast, lunch, or an obscene-size dinner. Sid was consuming a stack of buttermilk pancakes and a slab of bacon when his appetite quelled at the site of the Old Man coming down the street. With syrup dripping from his chin, he stared as his grey-bearded foe climbed down from the wagon.

Sid wiped off the sticky drizzle as his mind went back to that night at the Old Man's cabin. He remembered the cold, and the snow, but mostly he remembered the cabin.

That Old Man has gold.

The guns, the furniture— that steel oven. He had it alright, lots of it. He was certain of that, but where did he hide it? Now, that was the question.

"What are you looking at?" Soapy Smith, a man about Sid's age whose nickname was far from accurate, poked Stull with his fork.

"A gold mine," Sid remarked without diverting his gaze.

"What...where? What's that?" A second man, also unfamiliar with hygiene, grunted. The man called Bite was broad through the chest, had a bald head, a long jet-black beard, and two front teeth made of yellow gold.

The Old Man walked up the stairs and opened the door to an office that had a sign hanging. *Bogart Simpson Clark – Attorney at Law.*

After the Old Man walked through the door, Sid turned to his partners. "I'll tell you when I'm ready and," he leered at the two men, "I'm not ready yet."

He stuck a forkful of pancakes in his mouth. In the months he had been in Carversville he'd survived by teaming up with these two drifters. At first, they were rivals he ran into at the saloon, who he fought with over who was going to rob which drunk. But eventually Sid took control of the trio, and they widened their range of crimes to raiding and robbing wagons that were passing through Carversville.

A wagon would stop in town for supplies. The three would then assess their wealth and strength. They were careful, picking only wagons with older husbands and wives, and were without children —most of the time. Once a victim was chosen, the three waited on the road about a day's ride out of town behind a boulder or hidden in the trees. The victims would just disappear and, being unknown settlers traveling a dangerous path, no one went looking for them.

The three men left no witnesses and little evidence.

Stull finished his pancakes, more syrup dripped into his beard. He glanced to the Lawyer's office again.

He should be making out a will.

CHAPTER 7

CARVERSVILLE, CALIFORNIA

MAY 1866

A tall Grandfather clock sounded a rhythmic heartbeat from deep inside its dark oak, hand-carved, cabinet. Amos always sat in the same chair next to the wooden masterpiece whenever he visited his lawyer's office. He found it worthy of close inspection. A craftsman with God-given talent had spent countless hours carving the intricate piece. Today, Amos studied the eagle, the focal point of the carving, focusing on the feathers of the majestic bird's back and wings. They had perfect symmetry, every groove flawless, every ridge sanded as smooth as river stone. The artist had captured a moment of motion, and the depth of expression in the eagle's eyes gave the illusion it might fly off to freedom.

Amos eased his big frame over for a closer look, but his weight-shifting movement caused a loud sucking noise to emanate from the leather chair.

Bogart Simpson Clark's secretary, Miss Margaret Dewitt, a matronly woman with her hair pulled back as tight as her expression, looked up from her work, startled by the rude noise.

Amos noticed her reaction and stammered, "God damn chair."

"Mr. Cronin," DeWitt scolded, "I am a Christian woman and I'm offended by the use of that type of language in my presence."

He held back a grin. "Well...Miss Dewitt, I'm sorry about that." He paused for a half a second, then added, "But I'm not the one with the farting chair."

"Umph." Her face reddened immediately. She crossed her arms and raised her chin to the ceiling, showing her righteous contempt for the salty attitude. "This type of foul behavior might be acceptable in the backwoods—"

"Amos." Bogart Simpson Clark, Esquire, entered in the nick of time. He extended his right hand in greeting, "Good to see you." The lawyer had been standing inside the open door of his office, allowing for his best client's mandatory clock-inspection-time to expire. However, he intervened before the confrontation between Amos and his secretary, the self-appointed spokeswoman of God, elevated. Simpson raised his left hand to the old man's shoulder and guided him to his office and away from Miss Dewitt's formidable wrath.

"She's a bit prudish, and I apologize Amos," he said, closing the door. "I hope you understand how hard it is to find someone with legal office skills in this part of the world. I'm afraid she's equal measures of a blessing and a curse." The attorney's hand was still gripping Amos's bear paw.

A high-backed chair across from Simpson's long, wide desk was where Amos had sat in the past. This time, however, he looked at it, paused, then silently walked to the window where he parted the curtain.

"What can I do for you today, Amos?" Simpson crossed behind his client and sat, noiselessly, on the leather chair behind his desk.

"I want to write a will." The Old Man's voice was slow and low.

"Okay...a will. Hmm. Of course...no problem." The lawyer

pushed the chair forward, pulled a stack of white paper from his desk drawer, then fumbled for a pen. He seemed unnerved as the paper arranging went on for a minute or two.

Amos was still looking out the window.

Simpson abruptly stood up. "Amos, would you excuse me for a moment, please. In order to honor your request, I'll need to prepare a few things." He came around the desk quickly and headed for the door. "Can I get you anything, water, tea, coffee, maybe something stronger?"

Amos didn't look at him or reply.

"I'll be just a minute or two."

Bogart's mind was racing.

This is it. I'll be the only person who knows.

As the door closed, he turned to Miss DeWitt. "I won't need you anymore today. Take the rest of the day." He motioned to the door.

She looked confused. "I haven't finished transcribing—"

Maybe for the first time since she began working in his office, he raised his voice. "Miss DeWitt, you're not needed for the rest of the day. I need you to please leave the office as quickly as possible."

Confused and indignant at the same time, she pushed papers into a pile and began putting her things in a drawer.

"Miss DeWitt." He gestured to the door, again.

She rose and walked with her hands clutched at her waist, leaving without another word.

The second the door closed, Simpson bolted for the stairs leading to the second floor where he and his wife lived. He climbed the steps and pushed open the door at the top. "Amelia. Amelia."

"In here."

He moved quickly to the bedroom, finding his wife sitting at the dressing table fixing her hair. She saw him in the mirror but didn't turn around.

He took a breath. "Amos Cronin is here."

Blandly she replied, "I'm aware."

"He wants to write a will."

Her face elongated as her mouth opened but no words came out.

He nodded at the image in the mirror.

"He's writing a will?" She turned. "We're going to know."

Amos had found something else besides sculptured wood to entertain himself while waiting. There was a bookshelf lining the interior wall of the office. Most of the shelves held groups of books that were similarly covered and numbered in a fashion to help identify their legal purpose. There were a few large thick volumes bound with metal rings that Amos thought must contain maps and deeds. There were a few that were leather-bound and appeared significantly older than the rest. He took one down. It was entitled *The Letters and Journals of Lord Byron*. He put it back. Another, its cover fresher and stiffer, was by Mark Twain, titled *Letters from Carson*.

The door creaked as it opened. "Twain. You have a book by a Mr. Mark Twain there." Simpson pointed. "He's a new author, American, from the south I believe. I bought his book after reading some of his newspaper articles."

"Ah huh," Amos grunted and returned it to the shelf.

"*The Iliad*." Amelia Simpson stood in the doorway holding a tray of cups and a pot of hot water for tea. She waited till both men turned to her then added, "Or *The Odyssey*. Right side bottom shelf. Those are the only books he has worth reading."

Amos didn't like the way she dragged the word he.

The attorney, usually not at a loss for words, was silent.

She didn't ask but started to distribute the cups. "They, of course, are not my cup of tea." She tittered at her clever irony. "I'm a fan of the works of Emily Bronte or Elizabeth Browning, myself." She finished pouring. Amos didn't reach for the cup, so she placed it on a small table near a chair opposite her husband's desk.

"When I told Amelia you were here, she insisted on greeting you, personally." Simpson nervously rattled his cup.

She remained standing, hands clutched at her waist like the departed Miss DeWitt. "I must insist you stay for dinner, Amos."

There was silence.

"My wife is a fine cook—best fried chicken in the county."

More silence.

"Well then, I'll let you get on with...whatever matter needs his...consultation." She hesitated a second then walked past her husband on the way out. She leaned close to his ear and whispered, "You, find out."

Simpson fingered his vest, coughed, then uttered, "Now, about that will."

Amos stretched his arms when he exited the office, a yawn followed. It was late afternoon, but there was still time to return to the cabin well before dark. A few wagons were still navigating the road. The volume of traffic had diminished, giving the mud a chance to dry out a bit.

Amos started across the street to Goodman's General Store. The last chore for the day was buying and loading his list of needed supplies. He walked on the plank laid earlier that day. However, it now was almost as muddy as the road beneath it. He saw Martha and Howard standing side by side on the porch awaiting his arrival.

"Good afternoon, Amos," Howard wore a salesman's smile which was almost as disturbing as his wife's curtsy.

"Howard. Martha." Amos walked past them into the store.

Following behind quickly, Howard stammered out, "What can we do for you on this fine day?"

Amos stopped a few steps inside and looked around the store without responding. He surveyed the inventory and decided he needed only the necessities on a list he handed to the storekeeper. "I'll pull the wagon up to the front. Okay?"

Martha tried to mimic Howard's smile. "Mr. Cronin...Amos... Howard and I would love to invite you to stay and have dinner tonight."

Howard jumped in on the period of her sentence. "Martha makes the best fried chicken in the state."

"There should be a contest." Amos muttered.

"Pardon?" Martha looked puzzled.

Amos became less intimidating and more friendly. He'd helped them out over the years. They were good people and always treated everyone fairly. He'd witnessed them do kind deeds for those not as fortunate as well. "Thank you, but no thank you. The road back gets a might tricky after dark."

Howard's smile was earnest. "Of course, of course, Maybe next time you come in you'll keep us in mind. It's an open invitation."

Martha reached out and touched his arm. "Please Amos, next time."

Amos nodded, almost smiled, then grunted a bit. "I'll pull the wagon up."

Puddle, still hitched to the wagon, was content in the shade of the alley near the lawyer's office. Amos mounted the wagon then guided it to the General Store. He stood up but before dismounting surveyed the area, looking for Rufus. He yelled out, "Rufus."

He heard kids in the alley but couldn't make out what they were saying. Suddenly, Rufus burst from the alley running at full tilt. At least Amos thought it was his friend. The thing charging at him bore a resemblance, but barely. It had four legs and two ears, but the form was just brown mud with eyes.

The children, who followed him out of the alley, weren't much better, also things that sort of resembled children.

Amos climbed down to the ground and put up two hands. "Stop."

Rufus continued on, as did the kids.

"Stop, you filthy beast."

Rufus pulled up, coming to a sliding stop just in front of the porch.

"You're not riding with me like this."

Howard Goodman was loading the back of the wagon with bags of oats while Martha stood on the porch with a mixture of horror and disgust on her face.

Amos walked over to the dog, grabbed fur with two hands, one behind the neck, and one near his tail. He picked Rufus up off the ground, which was no easy feat, and walked him to the nearest horse trough where he proceeded to dunk his friend over and over again until he resembled something close to a dog.

While Mrs. Goodman was horrified, the children were in hysterics.

Amos turned to them. "Go on, git. All of ya, and you'd better get dunking yourselves before your mamas see you."

They ran back to the alley, still laughing.

Rufus shook hard several times, spraying water in every direction, then jumped up to the seat.

The loading completed; Amos climbed on board. "Howard, give your bill to George at the bank. He'll take care of it as usual." He snapped the reins lightly and Puddle pulled forward. Amos tipped his hat to Mrs. Goodman. "Martha."

The wagon moved slowly up the street. Rufus occasionally provided a shake, which sprayed Amos with muddy residue. On his right, Amos nodded to Howard and Martha Goodman who were still watching from their store porch. Across the street, Lawyer Simpson was at a window also watching Amos leave. His wife, however, was not looking. She was there, beside him, but turned sideways, her face a few inches away from Simpson's ear, her mouth moving fast. Amos could see the red in her face even from this distance.

A pair of mud-coated children, held up on their tiptoes by their ears, were being led by a distraught mother down the wooden walkway to her own version of a horse trough bath. Rufus barked once at the children. One of them managed a wave.

Puddle pulled the wagon at a steady pace. His work would be easier once they got away from the mud, the smell of civilization, and back to the sweetgrass and the spring breeze coming down from the mountain.

Passing the saloon, Amos saw Sid Stull out of the corner of his eye lurking on the porch. Two other sub-humans were beside him, and all three had eyes fixed on his departure.

They would come sooner or later.

Amos giddyupped Puddle with a roll of the reins.

The pace became a little quicker as Amos guided the wagon past the last house of the town. It sat up on a rise, off the main road, surrounded by a white fence. There was an arched gate with a sign posted on top. Long script letters spelled out the name Cudworth. A stone path wound up to a large, two-story house that overlooked the rest of the town like a judge's bench in a courtroom. The other buildings in town paled in comparison. Manicured bushes bordered a path to a wide country porch with swings. Tall black shutters protected sparkling clean glass windows that were mounted in walls of painted white clapboard.

It was the home and office of Reginald Cudworth, the self-appointed future of Carversville. He had the influence and the power. He held all the keys, except one.

Amos did not peek out the corner of his eye. He looked straight up to a window on the second floor where he knew Cudworth would be watching.

A window curtain was pulled back. No light shone inside. No image could be seen in the darkness behind the glass.

Amos let the rein slack.

Puddle slowed then stopped.

Amos continued to stare at the window.

Puddle pawed at the ground.

Finally, Amos turned his head back to the trail ahead.

Rufus shook the last of the water from his coat.

Amos snapped the reins. "Gitup."

They would come. Sooner or later.

CHAPTER 8
PHILADELPHIA, PENNSYLVANIA
JUNE 1866

"Henry."

He grumbled but didn't respond.

"Henry Cronin."

The voice came from a distance. He recognized it and wanted it to stop.

"You need to get up."

One eye opened. The other was still buried in a pillow.

"It's 6:15. If you don't get up now, we'll be late."

Even in a state of near unconsciousness he knew not to curse. He knew how but now was definitely not the right time.

"I'm getting up, Aunt Betty."

Knowing she was waiting at the bottom of the stairs to hear him rustling around, he stomped his feet on the floor.

"Your suit and a fresh shirt are hanging in the closet. I'm making breakfast. Shake a leg."

"Okay." He scratched himself awake, brushed his teeth, ran a comb through his hair, made his bed, then took the suit out of the closet.

A damn suit.

He tossed it on the bed and wondered if it still fit. It had been several months since he needed a jacket and tie. Aunt Betty had dragged him to dinner at the home of Claude LaGrande, the president of First Bank. It wasn't till he arrived that he discovered his aunt arranged a matchmaking between him and the First Bank's first daughter. She was a fair maiden who giggled incessantly the entire night.

The suit fit. She hadn't.

"Well, don't you look handsome." Aunt Betty wore a proud smile and a red and white checked apron over her Sunday go-to-church outfit.

"Sit, boy. We have pancakes and bacon. Do you want eggs instead?" She pointed toward the stove. "It will only take a minute."

"No, no, really this is great. Thank you."

She smiled. "Sister Joseph Mary said we needed to be at church a half an hour before the service." She looked at the clock on the counter. "Time for you to eat. You know how you get if you don't eat. So, eat up."

"You want me to eat, then?"

She chuckled, then scuffed the back of his head. "Come on now. It's the students' mass. I know you don't like these things, but it's a tradition, and besides, it's only once a year." She shook a wooden mixing spoon at him. "So, you be good."

He looked down so she could not see his sardonic grin.

The Basilica of Peter and Paul opened for business early in the year, after a ten-year build. It was beautiful, and its construction finished in record time. The mammoth structure took only ten years to complete even with the Civil War raging on for more than five of those years. The Catholic church was the most magnificent structure in the city and its caretakers cleaned and polished it regularly. The nuns and priests were dedicated to replicating the ceremonies and traditions of the church's long history. The newest ritual to be introduced was a children's mass that previously had been performed at local parishes but now had a grand stage—the huge, magnificent, marble-columned, stained-glassed, copper-domed cathedral.

Aunt Mary's donations to the building fund had a lot of influence on invitations to special events, preferential seating, and even occasional recognition from the pulpit. On this occasion, Aunt Mary would sit in a front pew to the right of the altar while Henry, along with the entire catechism class, sat in the front left of the church.

"Children." Sister Mary Joseph stood at the steps leading to the front doors. "Children, gather round."

About fifty schoolchildren varying in age from ten to seventeen were milling about waiting for direction. Henry reluctantly, hands in pockets, moved toward the sister.

"Form two lines." The nun, covered from head-to-toe in a black habit, raised two arms indicating where to form up. Her order's uniforms were comprised of flowing robes, secured with sashes and beads, topped off with a starched white headpiece, which Henry thought did the same job as blinkers on a horse. A nun could look straight ahead but her side views were restricted. However, Sister Mary Joseph's vision mystified Henry as she seemed to have some kind of mystical power and could spot a disrupter, such as himself, regardless of the head gear. She was tough. She never smiled, never laughed, and had zero tolerance for tomfoolery. She would root out all offenders and discipline the heathens with holy terror.

Not today, sister. I have a plan.

From the balcony high above the church floor, a choir sang an unfamiliar processional song, but it had rhythm so the children could walk in sync. All of the choir selections, as well as all of the proceedings were in Latin; everything was, except the priest's sermon, which was in fire and brimstone.

The children entered with the nun in the lead piously marching down the aisle, with hands folded, to pews reserved with white ribbons. Sister Mary Joseph directed traffic to the assigned seats, row by row, making sure each child sat three feet apart. She then moved to the front of the group to stand her post.

In addition to the procession and seating, another issue needing supervision was the sitting, kneeling, and standing during the service. These physical responses to the importance of the ceremony were a mystery to all the children. It wasn't their fault they didn't know what to do. The frequency of attendance varied, so their knowledge of the liturgy and the proper etiquette was somewhat lacking. Sister Mary Joseph decided that a prompt was needed so the children would know what to do and more importantly when.

The good Sister obtained a children's toy, which was a small strip of metal that had a flexible bubble in the middle. It made a sound like a cricket when pressed. Sister had used it several times during services previously and it had worked very well. At the proper moment, she would click once and the children knelt, twice meant stand, and three times meant take a seat.

This day the mass was fairly well attended by both children and adults. Everything was moving along as expected. The choir sang. The priests did what priests do, and the children were either paying attention or pretending to.

About halfway through the service, Sister Joseph clicked twice. The children stood. At the next proper moment, a single click rang out and the children knelt down. A few minutes later, Sister Joseph clicked twice, and the children rose again.

But then, suddenly, a single click rang out and the children knelt down in unison.

Sister Mary Joseph removed her hand from her voluminous sleeve and stared at the clicker.

She turned, looked at the children, held out the toy and clicked twice, bringing the children back to their feet.

Three clicks rang out and the children sat.

Sister extended her arm, holding the clicker out like a pistol and clicked it two times. Half the children stood, the other half remained seated, and they all were snickering.

The priest had stopped doing whatever he was doing, and he and the altar boys were staring at the good sister and the children. The adults were looking around and mumbling.

Sister Mary Joseph had turned a color of red Henry had never seen before. She was a spectrum of color, the fingers gripping the clicker were white, and her lips were blue.

He had a plan. It was a good plan.

There was, however, a flaw— Michael O'Doul.

The seventh grader had long been an admirer of Henry who, together with most of the classmates, always anticipated Henry's next show of insubordination. This stunt, which would no doubt be inflated to much greater proportions in the future, might well have caused internal injuries to his young devotee.

Henry heard a snort to his right. He looked down to Michael who was seated beside him. His face was red, his eyes bulging. Liquid began running from his nose. Two more snorts came out in rapid succession. The other classmates, whose heads were on swivels looking for answers to the clicking mystery, heard

Michael's nose blasts. They saw Henry, heard Michael, and a cacophony of sound erupted.

Sister Mary Joseph immediately focused on Henry's pew and flowed down the aisle at twice the speed of nun.

Michael was now laying down on the pew laughing uncontrollably.

Her arm stretched out, finger pointed at Michael, seemingly with the power to open the gates of hell.

Michael was laughing so hard he couldn't say, "It wasn't me."

I had a plan.

Henry, still standing, took his hand out of his pocket and held up his clicker, saving Michael from eternal damnation.

She was as mad as he had ever seen Aunt Betty get. "I'm so disappointed in you."

Henry felt shame at that moment, but there was still some residual elation.

"What possessed you to do such a thing?"

"Uh...I don't know really. I guess it's all just so...stuffy."

She took a breath. "You will apologize."

The last of the elation vanished. "Yes."

She sat down in the chair across the kitchen table from him. "Henry, why do you do these things, and don't tell me stuffy, that's not a reason."

Henry was pushing the corner of the tablecloth back and forth. He looked up at her and did what he always did, answer honestly. "I'm not...umm." He pushed the cloth around some more. "I don't know. Really, Aunt Betty, I don't know."

"Do you want attention? Is that it? Am I not paying enough attention to you?"

Henry looked straight up at her. "No...God no. You have always been there for me."

"Then why such disrespect? The teachers, now the church, really Henry, I don't understand."

His face was blank. There was no answer. He didn't know why.

"I don't know, Aunt Betty, I just don't, but I promise I will stop disappointing you. I promise."

She smiled a little and reached a hand across the table, taking his in hers. "You know, your mother was exactly like you."

Henry lit up. "Really?"

"Indeed, she would always find ways to make my mother and father laugh...me too." She raised her hand and shook a finger at him. "Not like you...no indeed. You are...I don't know what...but you definitely have her sense of humor."

"I wish I'd known her," he said softly.

She stood up, then looked down at him. Her hands were crossed in front of her. Whatever memory she was recalling of her sister vanished. A serious look came over her face.

"What's the matter?"

"I received a telegram a few days ago and I have been trying to decide whether or not to show it to you."

"I don't understand...a telegram?"

She looked up, then down, then shook her head before saying, "This might be a big mistake."

"What is it?"

"Your father is requesting that we come to California."

Henry leaped to his feet. "When, now? Right now?"

"After you finish school in June."

"Really?"

70

"Your father wants us to take a steamship from New York to New Orleans. From there travel by train to the Isthmus of Panama and the Pacific Ocean where we will then take another steamship to San Francisco. He'll have transportation there for us to get to Carversville, where he lives."

"Wow. What an adventure." Henry's mind was racing. "How long will that take?"

"Two months." She turned and walked to the kitchen window and looked out. The trees were just starting to bloom and there was a fresh scent in the air. The river was full, racing along its banks, flowing to the sea.

"Why did you wait to tell me?"

"You were to graduate then go to university."

"I'll go when we come back." Words were just flying out of his mouth.

She didn't say anything.

Henry walked up to her and put his hands on her shoulders. He again became aware he was so much taller than her. "Is that it, just me going on to college?"

She had tears in her eyes. "Everything will change now."

Henry looked over her shoulder. "Don't worry, everything will be just fine."

She didn't answer. She just patted his hand.

CHAPTER 9
FEATHER RIVER VALLEY, CALIFORNIA
JULY 1866

Trickling water and tree branches were keeping a musical beat known only to the instruments in nature's symphony. Amos lay sleeping under a large oak tree, the sun warming his face through his thick beard. The great ball of fire appeared though his eyes were closed.

Reality began calling him back.

He squeezed his eyelids tighter together refusing to leave.

He was young again. She was here.

She called out, "Amos."

He couldn't answer.

"Darling..." she called again, "Where are you?"

From the middle of the fireball, a shadow emerged. Gradually it became a face—her face.

Something moved, something that was driven deep inside.

She was standing near the riverbank, waving at him. He was standing still, not moving, frozen.

"There you are! I was worried." She smiled brightly at first.

But then, after a long moment, she frowned. Her head began moving back and forth.

He was paralyzed, unable to speak. He watched her step on the water, moving towards him. The sun sent single beams of light down to the creek which bounced up when they touched the surface of the water. Light reflected through her flowing white gown, revealing the shadow of her perfect form. Her fine dark hair flew into the air lifted by a nonexistent breeze.

"It's not time," she whispered as her feet left the water, her image rising as she got closer to him.

He couldn't speak. He tried but nothing came out. He desperately wanted to tell her what was in his heart.

He reached for her and she extended her hand to him. He could almost touch her.

She went up and over his head and disappeared when his eyes could no longer stay closed.

Amos was at his table making a list. He was fussing over order and importance, but he was firm in his resolve to complete each of the tasks. He knew, one way or another, there was little time.

Things need attention.

Rufus, perched in his tower at the end of the day, was watching, head on his paws.

Amos looked up and glared at him. "Stop it." He looked down at the paper then peeked up.

Rufus hadn't moved a muscle.

He rustled the papers, looked up again, this time giving his friend his full attention. "I know what I'm doing."

Rufus just stared at him.

"I said…I know what I'm doing."

Rufus half grumbled, half growled.

Amos pointed at the door. "I'll put you out."

Rufus growled full-on.

Amos retreated back to his notes.

He checked - Send telegram.

Checked - Write will.

The fire crackled, getting his attention for a moment before he wrote – See Cholok

He scratched his beard, tapped the pencil, then wrote – Write letter – still not fully knowing what he wanted to say.

He eyed the paper, then wrote, <u>Fix Cudworth</u>. Another thing to do for which he had no answer. He dragged the pencil point under the name, making a thick black line.

He stood up, looked hard at what he wrote, then picked up the pencil, bent down, and wrote – Destroy it.

He put the pencil down and squared up the paper on the table. It wasn't that he needed a list to remember. It was just his way. He worked better when he planned things out. It was his habit to work though problems to determine the best solution.

The fire needed a log. It was spring, but only during the day— when the sun was up. Once the sun set, the mountain let one know it was still the master.

He walked to the door, grabbed his coat and the Henry from the gun rack.

"Let's take a walk. Puddle needs his evening oats."

Rufus bounded down from the log pile and was out the door in a flash.

His friend disappeared into the night as Amos murmured, "There's much to do."

CHAPTER 10

SAN FRANCISCO, CALIFORNIA

JULY 1866

Reginald Cudworth arrived at the Occidental Hotel in a carriage driven by a pair of black Percherons. The driver wore a grey uniform, and the horses sported matching black harnesses accented with brass bit rings. Cudworth wore a white suit over a black vest, and a hat trimmed with a hatband made of silk. His entourage, not including the driver, consisted of two young Chinese women who were responsible for his wardrobe and personal hygiene. They rode in the carriage with him, while his personal aide/bodyguard rode on the seat next to the driver. Eight suitcases were secured to the back of the carriage and were brought to his suite of rooms by the hotel staff.

Onlookers, of far less standing, watching the opulence unloaded, might find it difficult to fathom that while industries were handicapped by the lack of sufficient workforce and severe shortages of materials due to the devastating war, some commerce was booming beyond imagination. The Civil War had been in the East, far, far away from the Pacific coast. The war was over, and this part of the continent needed the infrastructure to accommodate a growing swarm of humanity. The white-suited man stepping down to red carpet considered himself to be such a shaper of destiny.

His business was multiplying exponentially, and obstacles preventing the growth of new enterprise were being overcome by any means necessary. The pages of the penny paperbacks sold in the East told tales of the undiscovered, undeveloped, savage Wild West. These stories romanticized the lawlessness, the gunfights, and the beating back of the godless Indians. But in fact, these stories about gunfighters and Cavalry charges, true or not, paled in comparison to the freewheeling captains of industry who were charged with the responsibility of the success of the Manifest Destiny promised by the President of the United States.

Cudworth was involved in many enterprises including being a part of a combine of industry giants who were financing and building a section of the transcontinental railroad. The project would open the West and cut the travel time from the east to the west from several months to two weeks. He'd traveled from Carversville for meetings in San Francisco many times, and one of the rewards of making the journey was the accommodations which were spectacular. It wasn't a hard trip, long, but not difficult, and the reward at journey's end was the Occidental Hotel.

The newly completed luxury hotel was built to accommodate every need of affluent travelers visiting the west coast's busiest port, politicians and dignitaries, and of course, businessmen. Moguls and magnates of industry met there to discuss strategies and formulate plans for their next fortune, in luxurious splendor.

This trip, however, was slightly different. Cudworth was nervous, a condition he found unusual and inconvenient. His position and power were always stable, arrived at by being diligent, vigilant, and most importantly ruthless. However, in this venture he allowed himself to fall victim to the same disease as the filthy beggars panning for gold in backwater creeks— greed. He knew how the obsession could destroy everything, but he couldn't resist the risk, as the reward at the end of this rainbow was enormous—almost too big to comprehend. He had already invested four hundred times what an average working man made in a year because the pot contained more riches than any gold strike, ever.

On a long, wide oak table in the center of the meeting room on the third floor of the Occidental Hotel lay a map. It wasn't a map of what is, it was a map of what was to be. Six men stood examining the drawing, three with fat cigars and glasses of Hyde No. 5 whiskey, three with far less expensive brandy in wide mouth snifters and no cigars. They were waiting for a seventh member of the association to arrive.

"I for one will vote to move forward on the alternate route despite the cost." The man thumbed his vest then blew a decisive stream of grey smoke into the air.

The other four men remained silent and looked toward the sixth man holding the largest cigar.

Reginald Cudworth hadn't been in a situation where he needed others to get what he wanted, and he had to use every ounce of energy he had not to explode.

A long minute went by, the group anticipating Cudworth's response.

Peter Donahue spoke first. "Perhaps we should refrain from discussing this item of the agenda until Mr. Ralston arrives." Donahue was the glue that kept the partnership running.

Cudworth grunted, "Yes, I agree," then pointed to the map diverting attention to positive progress. "How many miles have been laid on the western front?"

This cue from Cudworth was all Theodore Judah needed to step up to the bragging hitch. "More than a hundred miles since we last met, Reggie."

Cudworth grumbled, "Reginald or Cudworth if you will, please."

"Right." The engineer brushed off the request and gestured to the men to step closer. "Gentlemen."

They moved forward to the carefully inked map of the western United States from Colorado to San Francisco. "As you can see, I've drawn in the completed sections of rail west of the Sierra Mountains leading to the ultimate connection with the Union Pacific Line in Utah. That piece of the Central Pacific construction east of the mountains is making great progress." He puffed in then out.

Collis Huntington, the youngest of the group, stepped up. "Indeed, great progress. But—"

"There is no but." A voice from the entrance of the room gained their attention.

The six turned and saw William Ralston. He was a tall, thin man, with greying temples and a matching VanDyke beard. "Our friend Judah has put together an opportunity that comes along once in a lifetime. Lest we forget, he convinced Mr. Lincoln to sign the Pacific Railroad Act in '62 and that piece of legislation will make us rich beyond our wildest dreams." He approached the group with chin forward and eyebrows ruffled. "This is the greatest opportunity of a century and we, my friends, are right at the heart of it."

A waiter suddenly appeared from the shadows and handed Ralston a glass of the No. 5 whiskey. "You all know, since the find at Sutter's Mill, I've locked up every available surrounding acre possible which is proving to be very rewarding." He shook a finger in the air. "But gentlemen, building this railroad will realize more money than the value of every nugget ever discovered in those hills."

The others were silent and patient, having heard his dissertation before.

"Ahhh." Ralston looked around the table. "You still doubt the outcome. Okay, this isn't the first time I've gone ten rounds with you blokes."

Cudworth anted up and challenged his optimism. "So, you're the expert on all things then, Ralston? I've heard the property you bought on Sun Mountain isn't working out."

The silence was instant and deafening.

Ralston just smiled. "Well, if the mines at Sun Mountain are played out, like you're intimating, that's my problem, isn't it? Because none of you are involved, correct...Mr. Cudworth?"

"Correct, I'm not and...," looking around the room, "I assume by our colleagues' expressions they're glad as well."

More silence, accented with a few puffs of smoke.

Cudworth railed on. "And your speculation into these properties and the resulting drain on cash flow is the reason you brought me into this project, isn't it? Currently, the partners and you are fully vested, and need me to secure the last portions of the right-of-way."

Ralston didn't smile. The others remained quiet.

Judah then took advantage of the moment of silence to divert attention back to the map. "May I continue?"

"By all means." Huntington affirmed. "Please, let's move on."

"There are three sections along the route I planned that are still...ahh, outstanding. We hope they will be secured shortly. Two of them can be easily rerouted if there is an issue. However, the third section," he pointed to a spot on the map, "is the pivotal piece of the whole run to Utah. Without it we will have to change direction, reroute the path of construction, and purchase additional land. This naturally will be expensive, as the terrain is much more difficult. More importantly, it will cost time."

Ralston interjected, "I believe this is your turn to enlighten us Mr. Cudworth. This section through your mountains was the actual reason we brought you into this association, was it not?"

Cudworth slammed down his glass. "I've secured fifty-six miles of right-of-way. A damn site more than any of you."

"And yet here we sit on our hands because of you." Ralston fired back.

"Gentlemen please." Judah raised both hands. "I think I need to remind you how this works. The Act allows the government to sell bonds with the proceeds lent to the companies building the railroad to secure the property and build the lines. I need not remind you the repayment of the bond loan represents a paltry sum considering the income that will be realized when the line is completed."

Ralston proclaimed, "When completed."

Judah continued. "When we purchase ground and build the track, we get the bond funds for construction, and we also receive land grants for thousands of acres of surrounding property. That means in addition to the railroad we have lumber and mineral rights with no acquisition cost."

Ralston again loudly. "When the track is laid."

Cudworth bobbed his head toward the others. "Which means, when completed, the bonds will be paid by railroad revenue in just a few years and the lumber and mineral rights will be icing on the cake."

"If completed." Ralston walked to the map and stuck his finger down on the stretch along the Feather River Valley. "How about this ten-mile piece, Reggie? Every one of us suffer if we have to reroute because you can't close this deal."

Cudworth didn't have a good response. "I'm working on it."

Judah interrupted. "Look, you all know I've been surveying for years to establish the best route through the Sierra Mountains leading into Utah and the connection to the transcontinental. The section on Feather River is optimal, but it's not the only way. True, the other routes are much more expensive, and require a larger investment of infrastructure, but it is possible to reroute."

"And how much of Cudworth's right-of-way will be used if we have to change routes?" Huntington asked.

"Uh...I haven't calculated that—"

"We know you've borrowed almost three hundred thousand dollars, Cudworth, and if you can't secure the Feather River acres you will suffer serious consequences."

"I'm giving you my personal guarantee, I will secure this property...one way or another."

Ralston leaned in close. "You'd better...Reggie."

Cudworth sucked in his anger and held his glass straight out. The steward appeared and poured more fine, rare whiskey.

Huntington walked over and took Cudworth aside. "The projected revenues from the railroad when completed will pay off all the construction costs in less than five years. Every railroad tie, every bridge, every iron rail will be owned free and clear. The rerouting will be painful, but you'll still do fine. If you can just get a quick decision we can move on—"

Cudworth interrupted. "I don't want a portion; I want it all and I'll get it done." He went from anger to determination.

Ralston had him going, but somehow, he pulled back and calmed down. He turned to the group and held up his glass. "Gentlemen. I know there are more things on our agenda today, and this meeting got off to a rough start, but I want to make a toast."

The men looked at him with little enthusiasm.

"To success."

Huntington and Judah raised their glasses, the others did not.

CHAPTER II
CARVERSVILLE, CALIFORNIA
JULY 1866

The weather had been temperate this spring, unlike the previous two years, one of which was dry as a bone, and the other non-stop rain. This season the precipitation was tolerable, making a mess of transportation only occasionally. Whenever it rained, Main Street was a problem; however, a solution was in the works. Cobblestones were being placed on the main road through the town, and it was a very welcome public works project.

Carversville was booming. Businesses were thriving. A second church was under construction as well as another, bigger, grander hotel. These new buildings required a new road. Raising the money to facilitate the latest public improvement was much easier than expected. A municipal bond for public works allocated ten thousand dollars a month for the project with the expectation of completion in six months. Every business in town invested in the bonds, and a road that was navigable in all weather was under construction. Reginald Cudworth did not buy a bond but was benefiting. He had the construction contract.

Cudworth was supplying the labor and material to build the

road. Chinese laborers, on furlough from the inactive railroad line construction company he owned, were shipped to Carversville and were being housed in a makeshift tent city. Not only was he reaping a huge profit, but Cudworth had a contract which kept his labor from deserting to other crews in the West while the rights-of-way for the connecting rail lines in the East were still being secured.

Every day, half of the workers waded into Feather River to find pot-lid sized stones worn smooth by centuries of water flowing to the sea. The rocks were loaded into wagons and transported six miles to Carversville. The other half of the crew painstakingly prepared the road, unloaded the tons of rocks, then placed and mortared the stones in place. It was hard, back-breaking work, but it was less dangerous than laboring on the train track, bridge, and tunnel construction. No one had died building the road, yet.

The stone pavement began where the road coming down from the mountain passed the Welcome to Carversville sign and continued to the big white house at the end of Main Street. It stopped where Cudworth sat on the front porch of his big white mansion looking down at his stream of worker bees busy making him money. He was enjoying this king-like view of his power and wealth at work.

There was a time when his favorite pastime was weighing the sacks of gold that his schemes reaped. However, that joyful distraction had been diminished since the war. Paper money had become, not only popular, but the way big business was being conducted. At his feet, next to his chair, was a canvas bag with brown leather straps he'd received from City Hall. It contained ten thousand U.S. greenbacks for the month's work.

A man opened the front gate and began walking up the path. He was short, had a round belly, a straggly beard, and a shock of red hair sticking out from an otherwise shining bald head.

"O'Dyer." Cudworth begrudgingly acknowledged when the man got close. "You're here to collect the month."

"Indeed, I am."

"How much, this time?"

O'Dyer shook his head. "You ask me the same thing every month and every time I say the same thing. It's twenty-five dollars a month, per man, plus three hundred dollars to me."

"How many?"

"Dollars or men?"

"Men, and don't get smart with me, there are plenty of other scoundrels like you willing to take my money."

"One hundred and twelve men." O'Dyer laughed out loud then added. "If you could find someone two bits cheaper, I'd be down the half-finished road."

Cudworth shook his head. "It's too much. Twenty-five dollars a month. It's robbery."

O'Dyer, apparently now tired of the act, got angry. "Give me the fecking money now, and if'n you give me a hard time again, I'll be gone— me and the bleedin' chinks. There is plenty of work on the western rail."

Cudworth put up his hand and signaled a stop. "All right. All right. No need to get hostile."

The Irishman spit a stream of black on Cudworth's plants. "You're a real piece of work, you are. I just happened to find out you're gettin' seventy-five a month per man. So, I don't want to hear any bitchin'."

"Who told you that?"

O'Dyer spit more tobacco juice and stuck out his hand. "I'd appreciate it if you hand over the money you owe me, and I'll be on my way."

Cudworth picked up the bag and, while keeping the inside hidden from O'Dyer's view, took three bound stacks containing one thousand dollars each, and counted out one hundred dollars from a fourth. He finished, withdrew his hand, but held onto the stack of money. "I'm wondering if you might be interested in taking on another task for me. I have a problem that needs attention."

In one quick move, O'Dyer grabbed the cash. He counted it twice, then stuffed it into a knapsack. After putting the bag on his shoulder, he looked at Cudworth for a long minute, apparently curious, and then, as if it were against his better judgement, asked, "What task?"

Cudworth's chair squeaked as he rose. He stretched for a moment, then walked past O'Dyer down the steps to the pathway.

O'Dyer followed.

"I have a problem which needs attention."

The Irishman interrupted. "You said that."

Cudworth didn't miss a beat from his rehearsed speech. "There is a man preventing you and those chinamen of yours from working the railroad."

"Right." O'Dyer spit black tobacco juice once more. "And what would you be wantin' me to do?"

"I need you and a couple of your men to convince this man with whom I have the problem to do business with me. If you're successful, it's a month's pay."

O'Dyer stared at him for a moment then crooked his head and pointed his finger. "First of all, you don't give a good shite about me. And...despite what you might think of those yellow bastards they are not a gang of cowboys or a bunch of saloon roughnecks."

The speech had gone off the rail. "I just want—"

"Listen Cudworth, despite what you think of me, I'm not a killer, and not one of those yellow bastards are either. Don't get me wrong, I don't care if they live or die, but they are not thugs, and I'm not crazy enough to do what I know you want me to do."

"I—"

He held up his hand. "No." He didn't spit, he just turned his back and walked away.

Cudworth headed back to the porch.

I need another plan.

Sheriff Alex Long had two thumbs in his britches, a chaw in his cheek, and a toothy grin on his face. "We are making some serious progress aren't we Mr. Cudworth?"

Cudworth didn't respond, being more concerned with the dirt accumulating on his suit than anything the sheriff was saying. The crew laying the cobblestones was shoveling and compacting dirt and raising a mighty cloud of dust. Cudworth used a monogrammed handkerchief to try to brush clean his shoulders and waistcoat. Giving up, Cudworth nodded to the door of the café. "Inside."

A young woman sporting a brilliant smile rushed over to the two men. "Why Mr. Cudworth and Sherriff Long what can I get for you?"

"Privacy." Cudworth pushed past her to a table near the rear of the restaurant.

Sheriff Long followed behind then sat opposite and waited for Cudworth to speak.

Cudworth began by looking at Long and giving him an unconvincing grin. "We are making progress, I agree Sheriff. Good things are happening for the good people who elected you. However, I've heard, from some of the people who put you in office, you've been unsuccessful in removing all the bad elements from our town."

Long stammered uncomfortably. "I...ah...well yes, there are a few of them hanging around..." then with enthusiasm added, "but I'm working on that."

"Who are they? And I don't mean the lumberjacks who roll in once a month to get drunk and bust up the saloon. The bad guys, the real bad guys. Who are they?"

"Well." Long hesitated.

"Sheriff, if you want to keep your job, you'll give me names right now."

Long knuckled under to Cudworth's will as he'd done so many times before. "Stull—Sid Stull and two other guys he hangs around with. One of them is named Soapy Smith and the other one is called Bite. Those are the worst of the bunch. There are a few others, but they are the ones I can't get rid of."

Cudworth paused a second. "What did they do to make them bad guys in your eyes and so hard to prosecute?"

"That's the problem. I don't know exactly. They don't work... no job in town or on a ranch. There're certainly not loggers...but somehow, they always have money."

"What do you suspect?"

Long lowered his voice. "There is a rumor that they mark a wagon of settlers pulling through town. They trail behind them, when they move on. When the settlers get a couple of miles out of town, they ambush and rob them. I suspect they kill them and hide the wagons in a ravine or a cave. Someplace where they won't be found."

"And you know this, how?"

"Months later a couple of inquiries come through from relatives looking for people who were supposed to arrive in some town, somewhere, but didn't. Nothing official. People looking for people who disappeared. Mind you, that isn't that unusual...but those settlers definitely came through Carversville, and Stull and his boys have no jobs."

"You're certain it's this Stull character and his buddies?"

"I guess I'm as sure as I can be without any proof."

The young waitress appeared again. "Is there anything I can get you gentlemen?"

Cudworth looked up with a stare that made the sheriff seem scared. "Go away girl."

Long stammered out, "What do you need me to do Mr. Cudworth?"

Cudworth stood and brushed his lapels and started for the door. "Nothing, Sheriff. I want you to do absolutely nothing."

CHAPTER 12
OFF THE ISTHMUS OF PANAMA
IN THE PACIFIC OCEAN

August 1866

The wind was right tonight. For the past couple of days, there was hardly a breeze and the smell of burning coal coming from the smokestack kept the passengers, for the most part, below deck. Naturally, the crew, apparently used to the fumes, paid little attention, and went about doing their shipborne duties without complaint. The passengers, a dozen in all, complained constantly.

Aunt Betty had not complained and offered an optimist's outlook. "We have been most fortunate to not have had bad weather and the accompanying high seas. This trip has been smooth, and we should be thankful even though, I must admit, the smoke lingers a bit too long."

Henry was constantly amazed at the way she found positivity no matter what the situation. He almost always agreed with her assessments, at first, although as time passed, he found some of her sunshine attitude toward life misplaced. This was one of those times. The odor was something one could occasionally escape. The soot, however, was omnipresent. Henry thought he would need to purchase all new clothes, because the black grit had formed a thin coating on everything he owned and seemed ground into every thread.

Gerald Myer, the addition to the Cronin California caravan, also seemed less understanding of the coal mist but kept his opinion to himself. Gerald had been with them since Laurel Hill was purchased. He was hired to take the major role in the upkeep of the house and grounds. Over the years his realm expanded to include groom for the horses, wagon master, gardener, and security guard. It didn't surprise Henry when he was offered, and graciously accepted, the invitation for the voyage, expanding what was a pair to a trio of travelers. Henry had no issues with his aunt's decision to ask Gerald to accompany them, and welcomed the man whose company was so enjoyed by both he and his aunt.

The three travelers were sitting in a small glassed-in compartment on the deck, up in front of the boat, where the view was spectacular, and the odor somewhat more manageable. They had cracked the windows, and a non-coal infused breeze was blowing into the room. Occasionally, a spray of sea water would wash against the glass reminding them to stay inside, as venturing onto the bow deck, even in calm seas, could result in a sudden shower of ocean wave.

The SS Oregon was a flatbottom steamship with two huge wooden paddles on the port and starboard side. When the sea was rough, the bow lifted high, then slapped down with a concussion force. But the sea had been calm since they left Panama, and the captain told them they had been fortunate to choose this time of year to travel. He said in October and November, after the summer had warmed the ocean, the sea, winds, and the waves became more unpredictable and more violent.

The trio were sitting with mugs of coffee and enjoying the morning sun. Henry was quiet and reflecting on beginning the last leg of the journey, while Aunt Betty and Gerald discussed what chores would take priority when they returned to Philadelphia.

Gerald was German and looked German. He was tall, blond, had a straight nose and broad shoulders, and possessed a work ethic that was not only fastidious but appeared inexhaustible.

As Henry sat drinking his coffee, watching his aunt and Gerald chatting, it occurred to him that he'd never witnessed Gerald ever saying no to his aunt. Deep in thought, his fingers tapped the arm of his chair.

What am I looking at?

The morning coffee on the deck wasn't exactly a quiet moment where conversation was smooth and easy. There was the rhythmic beat of the paddles propelling the boat forward. There was the constant crashing of the waves resisting the boat's progress and the machine sounds echoing below deck, emanating from the boilers generating the steam that made all the gears turn. It was a bit overwhelming at first, but the travelers had become veterans of life on a steamboat after completing the Atlantic run. They'd almost gotten used to these sounds necessary to steam forward on the Pacific Ocean leg of the journey.

Henry looked over to Gerald. "I just realized in all the years I've known you I've never asked about your journey to America."

Gerald laughed. "You grew up around me, so I guess to you I appeared to have always been there. You were more concerned about growing up, than how I got to Philadelphia." He pointed to the sea. "Until now."

"Gerald," Betty chimed in, "please tell Henry some of the

stories you've told me. I'm certain he'll find your experiences as interesting as I do."

Henry looked at her, then at him.

Some of the stories? As interesting as I do?

Gerald took a sip of coffee from his mug. "I immigrated from Germany almost twenty years ago and, to tell the truth, I don't remember much about the trip because I was so seasick I barely went up on deck." He chuckled a bit.

"See," Betty offered quickly, "like I said, the weather has been a blessing. We've had calm seas, and Gerald didn't get ill. We're so lucky."

Henry stared at his aunt's face as she spoke. He could see from the way they looked at each other that there was some kind of mystical mind connection.

How could I have been so blind all this time?

The look on Henry's face must have given his thoughts away.

Both Betty's and Gerald's expressions changed. They became ridged and sat straight back in their chairs, staring straight ahead and trying too hard to not look at each other.

A moment went by.

Betty flushed and pointed to Henry. "Now, just a second young man. Don't you go inferring something you know nothing about."

Henry smiled a little, then looked at Gerald who just shrugged.

Henry jumped up, now grinning from ear to ear. He slapped his legs and howled. "How did I not know this?"

"Now, Henry." She protested again, still sitting back straight with a little panic on her face.

Gerald smiled at her. "He knows. Betty, he knows." He reached over, took her hand, and looked at Henry.

She didn't pull away.

"I came to work for Betty and you after your father bought Laurel Hill. The property and the barns, horses and carriages, all required full-time attention. The house was much bigger than where you were living on Front Street." He put his hand on Betty's shoulder. "Your aunt had no one to help take care of the beautiful property, especially while raising an infant which was a full-time job. I had done some work for the lawyer who bought the property for Betty and you. He recommended me for the caretaker's job. Betty approved of me, and I was hired."

Betty sighed, her resistance was vanishing, and she seemed committed to finally telling it all. She sighed and put her hand on top of Gerald's then looked at Henry. "We worked together every day for years, and over that time...I became very, very fond of Gerald. But," she added sternly, "I had made a solemn oath to your mother before she died, that I would raise you as a gentleman, and see to it that you received the best education possible, and help you secure a position like a doctor or lawyer."

Gerald shook his head back and forth, "You and your aunt are rich. That is a fact, and even though Betty has never forgotten her roots, she has seen to it that you've never been denied anything of importance."

"I know we are...well...wealthy...or at least my father is, but I've never really felt rich."

"That, dear Henry, was my goal, in spite of your advantages, you would never feel superior."

Gerald took over. "Ahhh...and that was the problem. The rich in society have a lot of rules, and one of them is to never accept a rich Elizabeth Nichols and this lowly stableman. If we were to openly be together, she...and you...would have been ostracized and you wouldn't have been accepted at Penn Charter or the University."

Betty smiled at Henry. "We kept apart...even though our

feelings for each other were very strong, so we could do right by your mother's wishes for your upbringing."

Henry felt himself getting angry. "So, you two have been separate...not together all these years, because of me?"

Betty smiled. "Well, we haven't been completely separate." She blushed again.

"Careful is the word I'd use." Gerald said, squeezing her hand. She nodded.

Henry grabbed his aunt and lifted her from the chair. "So now...you and Gerald are free to—"

"Henry, let's be serious please." She pushed herself back to into her chair. "This is just an adventure. A complete departure from our lives in Philadelphia. We will be in California in a couple of weeks, but soon we will have to return to Philadelphia where you will be going to university." Her voice was stern and demanding. "Nothing is going to change that."

Henry stepped back, gave a stern look to his two guardians. "You're right about being in California and going back to Philadelphia. However," He paused for dramatic impact, "My education at university is already paid. I don't think they'll give the money back, do you? Am I correct?"

"I suppose so." Betty squeaked.

I have a plan.

Henry began pacing, and his voice raised with fake outrage. "You raised me as a Catholic."

"Of course." She looked curious.

"I can tell you this, I won't be traveling with a man and woman who are not married. This is shocking, it's un-Christian... why it's un-American. I won't have it, I tell you."

Betty and Gerald were stunned into silence.

He put one hand on Betty's shoulder and the other on Gerald's. "There's a captain on this ship."

The couple's silence became smiles.

"Well?" Henry exclaimed.

Betty and Gerald embraced.

There was laughter and some tears, and a great deal of relief.

They sat talking for a bit, then moved to a window stand and watch the ocean go by. Henry took some jabs for being so blind for so long, with Aunt Betty leading the charge of ribbing.

"Wait a minute," Henry held up a hand halting the good-natured assault. "Aunt Betty, Gerald said something I didn't understand. Why did my father give the money to buy Laurel Hill to the lawyer? Why didn't he just give it to you?"

Betty answered. "The law about women owning property is not easy to navigate my dear. When your father bought the house, a woman could not hold title to a property unless she is married. Your father made a trust which put the property in the Cronin family name."

"So, you can't own your own home?"

"The law has changed, but not for all women. The law only apply to white people. Understand?"

Henry scratched his head. "Not really. Doesn't seem right but I'll work on it."

Gerald put his hand on Henry's shoulder. "It looks like you may want a career in law?"

"I vote for doctor." Betty pushed up on her toes and, for the first time, Henry saw his aunt kiss his soon to be uncle.

The night was cloudless, and stars filled the sky from horizon-to-horizon. Henry was in awe. He never envisioned anything like this night sky. No poet or author had ever captured what he was witnessing. He couldn't imagine words could ever express the overwhelming expanse of its depth or beauty.

Aunt Betty had come up behind him noiselessly, yet he was not startled by her sudden appearance.

She kissed his cheek. "Enjoying the view?"

"Indeed, I am, Mrs. Myer."

She gave him a little punch on the shoulder.

He looked out at the ocean passing by.

"Can I ask you something?"

"Anything."

"Didn't you want to have children of your own and get married like everyone does?"

She smiled and touched his face. "I have a child and the only man I ever loved was by my side and is now my husband."

Henry pondered on it for a moment then looked back at the stars.

"Can I ask you something else?"

"Of course."

"I've been thinking about how we got here, and I remembered something you said to me back in Philadelphia, the night you told me about my father's telegram."

She crooked her head, puzzled. "What was that?"

"You said, "'Everything was going to change.' I didn't understand at the time, but it certainly has."

"What's the question?"

"How did you know?"

"I always knew everything would change someday. You would go off to medical school, or law school, or get married. But," she paused. "I was taken by surprise by your father's telegram. I didn't expect it. But, somehow because of it, I knew everything would change."

She nodded then looked off to the stars, and standing side-by-side, put her head on his shoulder. "It is time."

They stood quietly for a bit then she patted his arm and stepped back. "I have a present for you."

Henry waved his hand. "Wait, that's not right. I'm supposed to give you a wedding present."

"Stop. This has nothing to do with that." She reached into a bag she'd been carrying and withdrew a small leather book. She looked at it fondly as she placed her hand on the cover.

"This is for you. It's from your mother. It's a journal she began writing on the journey across the county. She continued to write until...after she got back to Philadelphia."

Henry looked at it, then at her, his eyes wide and mouth open.

"Right before she, I mean, right after you were born, she asked me to give this to you when I thought the time was right."

"You talk about her all the time, how funny she was, how beautiful and how she lived, but not how she died." He put his arm around her shoulder. "It's okay, we can talk about it—my mother died giving birth to me."

"I don't talk about it, not because of you." Her voice cracked when she spoke. "I don't talk about it because of me." She looked up at him, her eyes filled with tears. "She's been gone almost eighteen years, and I still miss her so."

He reached out and took both her hands in his. "I know how much you loved your sister, and I know how much you love me."

She pulled a handkerchief from her sleeve and dabbed her eyes. She handed him the book. "I think the right time to give this to you is now. In a few weeks you'll meet your father, and you can ask him about her too." She leaned over and kissed him on the cheek.

"I think I'll ask him why he sent her back to Philadelphia." He blurted out quickly.

She straightened her back and said sharply almost wagging a finger, "It was absolutely the right thing to do. The mountains in the winter, no shelter, the wild beasts...no indeed. It was the right thing."

He reacted thoughtfully. "And now a telegram after eighteen years?"

She had no response but remained stiff backed. "You'll ask him when you see him."

"Indeed, I will."

She started for the stairs down to her stateroom.

Henry looked at the book he held in both hands as she walked away. "Aunt Betty."

She turned.

"Did you read it?"

"No, dear." She shook her head. "I never did. It wasn't for me. It is for you."

CHAPTER 13

CARVERSVILLE, CALIFORNIA
AUGUST 1866

Amelia Clark was poised on a chair as if she were sitting for a portrait. The occasion called for her to wear her best day dress. It had a wide pleated skirt dyed purple, cinched tight at the waist with a wide silk belt contrasting the bodice. The top was trimmed in tasteful white lace accenting a simple string of pearls. In almost every aspect it was the way a respectable, affluent, wife of a lawyer would present herself in public. Almost. She had the dress made in Sacramento from a picture she saw in a magazine of a dress worn by a Southern Bell, but she made one change. Instead of buttons in the back, she elected to add the fasteners to the front. Today for her audience of one she daringly failed to fasten the top two buttons.

Reginald Cudworth was a few feet away sitting impatiently waiting for Bogart Simpson Clark to appear. Earlier in the day, he sent his attendant to advise the lawyer of his arrival which was to be precisely two o'clock. It was now two fifteen. He was progressing from irritated to annoyed. The diversion which kept his annoyance from blossoming to anger was the possibility the third button on the bodice would pop.

"He'll be here shortly, I'm sure. And again, I apologize for the delay." She smiled, then looked at herself in the mirror hanging next to Cudworth's chair.

Cudworth was curious but not enticed.

She bent forward to brush an imaginary something from her skirt. The fabric spread.

When the fabric didn't give way, Cudworth's displeasure with the wait deepened. "I do not understand why I have to wait."

She was looking in the mirror again and adjusting herself in the seat. "I'm sorry. Bogart must have eaten something that disagreed with him. I'm certain he'll be down soon."

"Grummph."

He again, momentarily, became fascinated with her buttons but then moved on to how she was staring at herself in the mirror.

Noise from footsteps on the stairs ended his curiosity.

The door to Simpson's office flew open and the lawyer arrived looking pale and disheveled. "I apologize Mr. Cudworth for keeping you waiting. My stomach has not been right for a while."

"Whose cooking are you eating?" Cudworth asked gruffly.

"Not mine," she answered quickly, "I don't cook."

Simpson shot a look at his wife who was unphased.

Cudworth grumbled again.

"What can I do for you sir?"

Mrs. Simpson rose from her seat to leave, but in doing so bent forward, giving her button one more opportunity.

Cudworth stuck a hand out. "Don't go. I'll need your opinion as well as your husband's."

She acted momentarily surprised but recovered by looking into the mirror. "Certainly, Mr. Cudworth, whatever you require."

She paused for only a second before adding, "You may call me Amelia. May I call you Reginald?"

"No."

Her eyes went from the mirror to the floor.

The lawyer slowly moved to his desk and pulled paper and pen to him as he sat.

"You won't need paper. In fact, I don't need a lawyer or a lawyer's advice. I want information."

Now recovered from the insult, Amelia said, "My husband won't say it but I will, information costs by the hour."

Cudworth looked at her and, for once, held his tongue, accusing her of charging for her services by the hour wouldn't get what he needed.

"How can I...we help?" Simpson pushed the paper to the side.

"Amos Cronin."

"Yes, what about Amos?"

"He's a client of yours?"

"Yes."

"I need to know all about him and his dealings."

Simpson coughed then coughed again. "Why...I can't...what you're asking is not ethical. I can't betray—"

"One thousand dollars." Amelia's voice had changed, and she was no longer distracted by her own image.

"Two hundred." Cudworth countered.

"One thousand." Amelia didn't look at her husband.

"Five hundred."

"Last time," she slowed her words. "One thousand dollars, payable end of day today."

Cudworth sputtered, rumbled around in his seat, then stomped his foot but didn't speak.

"Today." She finalized her demand.

"Done."

She turned to her husband. "Tell him what he wants to know."

"But—"

"Tell him." She ordered.

Simpson had both hands flat on the desk and was sliding them around, his head shaking back and forth. "What do you want to know?"

Cudworth removed a list from his jacket pocket and unfolded the paper. "How much property does he own?"

"Actually, I don't know about that. He was in here not long ago and I wrote a will for—"

"A will?" Cudworth interrupted.

"Yes."

Cudworth shook a finger. "Good, then in that case, tell me why you don't know about property."

"I asked but he said all of the land he owned was bought through lawyers in San Francisco. He said if anything should happen to him, I was to notify them, and they would know what to do."

"Did the will designate the beneficiary?"

"Yes, his son Henry Cronin of Philadelphia."

"A son?" Cudworth was completely surprised.

"Yes, I was surprised too. Before he left that day, he instructed me to send a telegram asking his son and the woman who raised the boy, his aunt, the mother's sister, to come here to Carversville. I sent it. They confirmed and are on their way now."

Cudworth stood and began pacing. "Are there any special provisions in the will, like asset distribution or land grants. Also, what about his cabin on the Feather River?"

"Everything goes to the son."

"Not everything." Amelia had been quiet until now. She stood and walked up to Cudworth. "There was something I read in the will."

"You read his will?"

She looked at him. "Don't be stupid, I read everything."

Cudworth calmed, he knew he had an ally.

"Amos went through a list of names of people from the town. He is leaving money to the Goodman's from the General Store, old Tom Hardy the barber, those two women who own the livery. He also, left some money to the Doc, and to the Carversville school."

"Anything else?"

"He left some property to those Indians who live up in the mountains. He said they helped him build the cabin. Which frankly, I've always wondered about. Have you seen that place?"

Cudworth shook his head.

"It's really something, a big log cabin and a barn that no one man could have built alone. He never hired one person from town, yet there it is. Until he came into this office to write a will, we never knew how he managed to build that fortress. But now we know, it was the Indians."

"So, he paid them, but with land?"

She shook her head. "He said he owed them more than just labor on his ranch."

Bogart finally entered the conversation. "He told me. I mean, us...the government took ownership of land in California from Mexico after they fought the war in '48. Since then, the unclaimed land, especially acres in remote areas, sold cheap. Cronin bought the land where the tribe had been living for hundreds of years. He said it was always theirs and they deserved to have it back."

Cudworth stopped pacing. His voice got soft, almost a whisper. "Where is this land?"

"Ahh...I have to look." The lawyer went to a drawer and started removing files.

Amelia walked up close to Cudworth. "Payable today, correct?"

He nodded then used his arm to move her away.

"Here it is." Simpson read a bit, then pointed to the writing. "It's about 33,000 acres around the Feather River. I didn't pay much attention to it because it seems so worthless. It's way up in the mountain and almost inaccessible."

"He left it to the tribe?"

"No." He rustled the paper again. "One man...a Maidu Tribe elder named Cholok."

Cudworth began to chuckle.

Simpson rose from his chair, head down and looking whiter than when he came into the room. He started walking around the desk then suddenly put his hand over his mouth and ran from the office.

Amelia shook her head as she watched her husband run out of the room.

"Aren't you going to help him?"

"No." She took his arm. "Actually, I'm going to help you across the street to the bank."

Cudworth patted her hand. "Perhaps you'd like to celebrate your good fortune with a glass of fine brandy."

"Perhaps." As they began walking to the door, she checked her third button.

It was late, near midnight, and most of the people who worked for a living were asleep in bed. The saloon was the only establishment open for business, and even that had wound down. The three bandits, Sid Stull, Soapy Smith, and Bite had gone through most of their cash, and were a couple of drinks and a couple of dollars short of drunk. They sat in the back at a round table nursing what used to be cold beer but now was warm barley juice.

The bartender was cleaning glasses when a man he recognized, but did not know well enough to talk to, came through the doors. He was medium height but wide and heavy. At first glance, one might assume he would be slow or awkward, but that would be a very wrong assumption. The eyes were narrow and focused, and his mystique was amplified by a long scar starting high on his cheek and ending at his chin.

"I'll have a beer."

"Yes sir, coming up." The bartender grabbed one of the freshly cleaned glasses and filled it carefully to minimize the foam.

"Thanks." The man took a long drink, emptying about half, then placed it gently back on the bar. "Nice."

"Thanks. Keeping it cold is the problem. We built an icehouse out back, so we are able to keep winter ice frozen almost all summer. I think we are the only place for a hundred miles that has cold beer."

"Uh huh."

The man peered around the bar through the big mirror hanging behind the bar. Without turning around, he could see two men at a table near the front window and one at the far end drinking alone.

"You work for Cudworth, right?" The bartender wiped the top with a white towel.

"Yep." He finished the beer.

"I thought so." The bartender refilled the glass without asking. "So, what's he like? I've been here six years and I've seen him on the street a handful of times, but never in here."

"And you never will. When he needs something, he sends me."

The bartender looked at him curiously. "So, do you...I mean does he want something?"

"Somebody."

"Oh, who would that be?"

"A man named Sid Stull."

The bartender, anxious to be helpful, pointed. "You're in luck mister. There he sits."

The man turned and looked at the table in the back he hadn't been able to see in the mirror. He nodded to the bartender. "Take two beers to his friends and tell Mr. Stull I'd like to talk to him outside."

"Sure thing." He started away then turned and whispered, "Is he in trouble?"

The man threw a dollar coin on the bar then walked for the door.

"Thanks mister." The bartender smiled at the big tip.

All of Stull's instincts told him this was bad news. Maybe he worked for the rich guy at the end of the street and maybe he didn't. Maybe he was a relative of one of the settlers they helped to the promised land. Maybe it was the law. He moved slow, eyes darting back and forth. His right hand pulled the handle of the knife in his boot out from its sheath a little so it would be easier to throw if he had to.

He hadn't run across the bodyguard for Cudworth before, but he'd heard about him, and the description matched, including the long scar. So, he decided to see what the man wanted, but he was also ready for trouble.

The door swung closed behind him as Stull left the saloon.

"You Stull?" The big man had a black thin cigar between the fingers of one hand. The other hand was empty.

Stull approached. "Who wants to know?"

"My name is unimportant. You know who I work for?"

Stull nodded. "Cudworth."

The man grunted. He was standing in the half shadow of the porch being lit only by the light coming through the window of the saloon. "Do you know Amos Cronin?"

Stull got angry every time he heard the name. "Yeah, what of it?"

"I'm going to say something. I'm going to say it once and only once." He stepped out of the shadow. "And know this, if I ever hear one word of what I tell you come back to me from any source, from anybody at all, you will die the most painful death you can possibly imagine."

Stull tried to act as if this threat didn't scare him, but it did, to the core. "Right, and you don't scare me. I've been threatened by uglier men than you."

"Do you understand?" He said it slow, each word a full sentence.

Stull nodded; bravado gone.

"Are you a betting man?"

"What?" Stull was confused by the sudden change of direction.

"Are you a betting man?"

"I guess so."

"I am placing a bet for you and, if you accept, you are betting that something will happen to Amos Cronin before the end of the month."

"Something?"

"The bet pays a thousand dollars."

Stull was stunned into silence. He'd never seen a hundred dollars much less a thousand.

"Mr. Stull. Should I place the bet for you?"

"Ahh...sure." He grinned as greed took control.

The man started away.

"Wait."

The man turned around.

"What am I betting?"

"Your life."

CHAPTER 14
FEATHER RIVER VALLEY, CALIFORNIA
APRIL 1848

The path Feather River followed on its way to the sea was forced to change direction when its journey hit a solid wall of rock. The water became deeper and darker where it impacted the cliff at the base of a mountain. On the opposite side of the bend, a wide shallow wash sloped gradually up to the tree line. Occasionally, when storms raged, the river was filled with runoff beyond its capacity causing some of the trees growing along its edges to become vulnerable to erosion, exposing roots and making them unstable.

This bend in the river was one of Amos's favorite fishing spots. It was where several trees had fallen one on top of the other. After the river stripped the leaves, bark, and most of the branches, the sun bleached the wood so white it resembled the skeletal remains of an unknown prehistoric animal.

The fallen trees provided a platform where Amos could sit and use a handline for the whitefish hiding in the deep water near the rock face, or a net to catch trout or rock bass in the shallows.

But this day was different. He was hoping he would be lucky

and find the salmon had begun their spawning run upstream. In anticipation of good fortune, he brought a bigger net, one Rose has fashioned from twine spun from spruce roots. His plan was to wade into the roaring river and catch enough salmon to smoke and then sell in Carversville.

That was the plan, but of course it all hinged on the cooperation of the salmon which, like waiting for the buffalo to return, took patience and prayers. He had started early that morning and hiked in the dark up and over the foothills leaving Rose to fend for herself for the day. Using the wood from their wagon, long thick pine branches, and dried mud, they had built a makeshift shelter. They managed to survive the first winter in the mountains through guile, hard work, and luck. There were four horses in the team that had pulled them across the country, but two of them were pretty old and becoming a drain on their limited resources. Today, while he was off fishing, Rose told him she planned to hook up the team and try to pull some of the stumps from the south pasture so more wheat could be planted. He objected but she insisted.

The sun had been up for more than an hour, and he could hear the river just over the rise. Amos suddenly heard someone yelling. He ran forward, dodging branches and slippery rocks. He ran down the slope to where he could see the bleached white trees extending out over the bend of the river. On the farthest tree limb of the partially submerged logs, a spot where the river was rushing past at tremendous speed, a man lay flat, legs spread wide, one hand on a stump of a branch and the other holding onto a leg that was sticking out of the water. Someone had apparently fallen off the log and was now being pulled downriver by the current. The small branch and the strength of the man holding on to it were the only things keeping the victim from a certain death. Once the water passed the fallen trees, it ran through a section of rapids filled with boulders— where, once in the river's grip, no one could survive.

As Amos ran forward to help, he saw that the victim in the water was a boy maybe fourteen or fifteen years old. He could also see the man holding him and the boy were Indians. As Amos got closer, he saw the boy was stretched out and holding onto a net with both hands. In the net was a salmon. The man was yelling what Amos thought must have been 'let go of the net' but the boy just continued to hold on. Amos got to the fallen trees and ran as fast as the wet logs would allow, then threw himself down and, reaching into the current, grabbed the boy's other leg. Even with the two men pulling with all their might it seemed impossible to pull the boy back.

The Indian kept yelling, but the boy refused to let go of the fish. Together the men, eventually, re-positioned themselves, gained better footholds, and managed to make headway. Finally, they got a grip on the boy's middle and pulled. Out of the water came the boy, held by the waist, bent in the middle, but still holding the net and a salmon that may have been half as long as he was tall.

Without looking, the man took the net from the boy and handed it to Amos. He stood the boy up and hugged him. Then he gave him a good crack in the mouth with an open hand. The man then hugged the boy again.

Amos sat down on the white bleached log, trying to regain his breath and his strength. Somewhere in the aftermath, when calm was restored, Amos could see the man finally recognized him as a white man.

There was a lot of staring, the river adding the only sound.

The boy, not paying any attention to the men, was carefully examining his catch.

Amos picked up the boy's snap net, a willow sapling bent in a tight circle covered with a thin plant-root net. The objective was to hold the rig submerged in the river, while hanging over the log, so when a salmon hit the net, the willow twig bent in half capturing the fish. The key is, naturally, to hang on. Amos saw the boy's net was torn, no doubt, from catching such a big fish.

Amos walked back to the beach and retrieved a bag he dropped before he ran out on the logs. He pulled out the net Rose had made. He walked back out and handed it to the boy. "Nice catch."

The boy now, apparently also realizing the stranger was a white man, appeared more afraid of Amos then he had been bobbing for his life in the grasp of the river's current.

Amos held out the net again and shook it. "Go on."

The boy looked at the man Amos now assumed was his father, who nodded, and the boy gingerly took the new net.

Amos looked at the father, gave half a wave, then turned to leave.

"You're not even going to introduce yourself?"

Amos turned around, surprised. "Sorry, I didn't know you could understand me,

So, I—"

"You just saved my son's life. I want to know who your name."

He stood silent for a moment looking at the Indian. The man had long black hair tied back and wore leather leggings and a vest. "Amos Cronin. My wife and I have been living down by—"

"I know where your camp is. We see your progress."

"You see our progress?" He walked up closer. "You're watching us? I never saw

anyone—"

"Watched from where you can't see."

There was another pause, and neither man looked ready to break the silence.

113

The boy had retrieved the salmon from the net, and after using a knife to clean his catch, he held the fish high in the air. The tail reached down to his knees.

"The Gods have sent many fish to us today." The father picked up the new net, took the boy's arm, and spoke to him in a language Amos didn't understand.

The boy gave the net back to Amos.

"I gave that to him."

The father spoke over Amos's objection. "Help us gather what has come to help us live."

The father picked up the boy's net and, using some long strings of leather, began repairing the net. The boy took Amos's arm and together they went back to the flat spot on the fallen trees. The boy then beckoned to Amos to fish.

Amos took the net Rose had made and held it down into the water. It immediately floated to the surface and was completely ineffective in the strong current.

The boy laughed.

The father barked a command to the boy, who then ran light-footed across the fallen trees to the bank where he used his knife to cut a willow switch. Within a minute or two he was back, fed it though the loops in Amos's net, and made a mirror image of his own. Then using his hands to motion to Amos what to do, he instructed him with gestures on how to lay down and lower the net to catch a salmon.

The father observed the two and finished repairing the boy's net, then joined them on the log. The three spent the next hours netting the gifts the gods sent and occasionally laughing at the white man's ineptitude.

The sun was still high, but so were the mountains. Once it disappeared over the crest the shadows would take over, and while the sky above was still light, it would be very difficult to negotiate the trail home. Amos, tired and sore from using muscles he hadn't used before, started to collect his belongings, and a stringer of ten cleaned salmon. He hoisted it and, after checking the weight and guessing it was more than fifty pounds, knew the hike home would be arduous.

The father walked to Amos and stood staring at him as if he were making a decision.

Amos reached out a hand. "Thank you for helping me learn to fish this way. It will mean food for my wife and I for a long time."

The father held his stare and didn't return the handshake.

Amos didn't know what to do next.

"You saved my son's life, and probably mine as well. I would not have let go."

"I was just doing the right thing."

"But we are Indians."

"I don't understand."

The father smiled. "No, I don't think you do."

Amos adjusted the string of fish on his shoulder.

The father took a leather pouch from his hip. "Here."

Amos waved his hand. "No, no. What you've already done... teaching me to fish this way, is more than enough."

The father put his hand on Amos's shoulder, and Amos felt how powerful the man was.

"In our way, when a life is saved by another, a great debt is owed." He took Amos's hand and made him take the pouch.

Amos opened the tie on the top. There were five large gold nuggets inside.

"No, no." Amos protested. "This is too much. These are worth a lot."

The father shook his head. "My name is Cholok. One day I will visit you at your home, and we will talk again."

Amos thought for a moment. He knew men that would torture

and kill for half of what was in the bag, not to mention what they would do to find the source.

The boy ran over, smiled, and said, "ha-ma-ni-ya."

Amos was a little confused.

His father interpreted. "We have no word in our language to say goodbye. My son just said, 'until we meet again.'"

Amos smiled, and started walking, but after only a few steps he turned. "Cholok, where did you learn English?"

"Amos, that is a story I will tell you...when we meet again."

CHAPTER 15
FEATHER RIVER VALLEY, CALIFORNIA
MAY 1849

Puddle was grazing in the pasture, feeding on the half-grown wheat that Amos had planted before he received the telegram from Betty. Progress on the construction of the barn had stopped completely, and Amos had made only a passing attempt at stopping the leak in the roof of his shack.

He sat on the stump of a tree facing the river. Amos had been there for a few hours, and it was where he'd been sitting, every day, for the eight weeks since the cable arrived. He'd barely eaten, and sleep was almost an impossibility.

He didn't see or hear Cholok coming even though he rode out of the forest making no effort to conceal his approach. Amos didn't turn around when the Indian pulled up on the reins, dismounted, and tied his horse to a tree branch.

"My friend, you don't look well." Cholok stood near Amos, looking down, concern on his face.

Amos muttered. "She died."

The Indian put his hand on his friend's shoulder. "I can feel your great sadness." He sat down on the ground near Amos, staring out in the same direction, looking out over the river.

They sat together for a long time. The sun was behind them now. Amos looked and it occurred to him he wasn't sure how long Cholok had been by his side. He wiped his face with both hands. When he stood up, his body protested.

Cholok rose as well, brushing off his britches. He fixed his gaze on Amos and continued to stare until Amos looked at him. "I want you to come with me. You need to rest."

Amos was unresponsive but not uncooperative.

Cholok left Amos standing while he saddled Puddle who had wandered from the field and was now standing next to his horse.

"Come." Cholok guided Amos up into the saddle, then leaped onto his bareback ride. He thumped his heels into the horse's side and the two men rode away from Amos's mountain home.

Zuni had a rabbit stew made with corn and wild onions ready for them when they arrived. It was cooking in a large clay pot. Four members of the band had good fortune that day and their efforts hunting and foraging meant a full belly for everyone, including the stranger.

Her life had been disrupted because of Cholok's decision to bring the white man to the village but his wife complied and, that morning, informed the others her husband was returning with a stranger, and she needed their cooperation. Cholok advised her to save mentioning the stranger was a white man until last. She waited, then said it quickly, retreating equally as fast to avoid the questions. She had no answers for why, she had asked her husband, but he would not answer her.

There was no chief in the village, no leader, it wasn't their way. The band of twenty-eight lived without a hierarchy, surviving all disputes with conversation and compromise. The primary motivator for resolution of problems was survival, which, was an everyday group effort.

Cholok was a man of influence, and many of the tribe looked up to him both as an elder and as one who had the Sight. He also was the only member who spoke the language of the tribe that meant them all harm.

As the two men dismounted and approached the crowd of the hungry and curious, Zuni, who had finished preparations, said, "Food are ready." Zuni's English was improving.

The boy, who'd survived salmon fishing, received the first bowl. The others stood a few feet away, empty bowls in hand, staring at Amos.

Zuni filled two wooden bowls and approached her husband. Cholok nodded and gestured to hand a bowl to Amos, then waved to the others whose hunger now overcame their reluctance and moved quickly to the large clay pot hanging over the cooking fire.

All of the activity was taking place outside their lodge, which was one of several lodges built in a clearing surrounded by tall evergreens. Round cedar bark shingles covered the structures and looked as if they could withstand the summer's or the winter's worst.

Cholok waited until the others had gotten their food, finished gawking at the white- skinned visitor, and wandered away. They had all seen white people before, but only when they held weapons pointed at them.

Zuni came to sit with them. She looked at Amos and smiled.

"She doesn't like strangers." Cholok motioned with his spoon. "But Zuni seems to like you."

"Wait till she gets to know me."

Cholok choked a little then grinned. "You made a joke." He paused a second then added, "Not a good one, but a joke."

Amos almost smiled, then ate quickly.

Zuni noticed and beckoned the boy to refill his bowl.

"No. No thank you. I've eaten too much of your food already."

Cholok beckoned to the boy to fill it up anyway. "Amos, tonight there is more than enough, and we eat everything that is prepared. There is no waste."

Amos reluctantly accepted another bowl.

"I'm glad you came here."

Amos nodded. "I am too. That was more food than—"

A baby crying stopped him cold.

Zuni jumped up and quickly went inside the lodge. She returned with a bundle of baby.

Cholok made the introduction. "This is Aponi, my daughter."

Amos looked at him, then at the boy sitting in the corner and, puzzled at the age difference, and gestured to Cholok. "Yours?"

Cholok bumped his chest. "Yes, a boy and now a girl. A few years apart but..." He didn't finish. Instead, he held out his arms, and his wife gave him the baby. "Aponi," he said softly, looking down at her, "the name means butterfly."

A few minutes went by, and when the baby started fussing, Zuni took her and began breastfeeding.

Cholok motioned to Amos. "Let's walk."

They went past the lodges and walked out to a flat rock cliff with a view of the river below and the mountains in the distance. "We used to live down where the town is now. There were many more of us then. But when the white man came, we were forced out, and our band settled here in this valley."

"Why here?"

"Water, wood, hunting is good, many acorns to harvest. This valley between the mountains feeds and shelters our little band."

"Is that the only reason?"

Cholok smiled. "You are smart, Heskym. We settled here because your people don't want it."

"Wait. What did you just call me?"

"Heskym. It means...my friend."

"And what do I call you?"

"Cholok." He grinned.

Amos shrugged. "I understand but how did you come to learn English living way out here?"

Cholok sat on a rock near the edge and picked up a handful of stones. He began throwing them down toward the river. "Your people came when I was a child, about seven years old. They were Christian people and thought they were doing God's work. They took me and ten of the other children and sent us to a boarding school in Canada. We were forbidden to speak our language and taught English. We were dressed in uniforms and went to Christian churches. I learned many things there...but I never gave up my heritage."

"I had no idea." Amos said softly. "That's monstrous."

"The children didn't fit in. Even when we learned what they wanted us to learn we still looked like Indians, and no matter how they cut our hair, we still were shunned by everyone."

"What happened? I mean, how did you get to come back?"

"I escaped after many years and several different schools. One night, I put on my best shoes, stole a loaf of bread and a few apples, and left. It took me several months, but eventually I found my way back. I had some help from the Tolowa, Paiute, and the Lummi tribes. They helped me and I still have many friends there."

Amos stopped thinking about his wife for a bit.

"We've found a way to survive here. It is only a small part of what we had for many generations, but this valley is now our home."

Amos looked at Cholok, "I know there is a but coming."

"You're right, there is a but." Cholok tossed a small rock at him. "It is said by my people I have the Sight."

"I don't understand."

"They say I have visions that shows me what will happen."

"And do you?"

He didn't answer, threw another rock at the river, then stood up and started pacing. "Amos, I think you and I have a lot in common. I've been watching you since you and your wife first arrived in the lower lands. I watched what you did, and how you did it. Do I have Sight? I don't know. What I know for certain is I have instinct, and I think I need to trust you to do something very, very important for my family and this tribe."

Amos jumped up. "Wait a minute. Just wait. I'm not worthy of any trust. I can't get up in the morning. I'm not working in the field; I'm not even feeding the stock. I'm useless."

Cholok put his hand on Amos's shoulder. "You're grieving."

Amos choked up, but didn't speak.

"You know my son; the fisherman, and you just met my Aponi."

Amos nodded.

"Many years between, yes."

Amos nodded again.

"Zuni and I had three other children. Two boys and a girl. All died."

Amos didn't speak.

"We all grieve. And we all must go on."

There was quiet between them.

Cholok broke the silence. "I need you. I need your help..." he stepped back, "and you need mine."

Amos ducked his head, and walked over to the cliff.

"Don't jump." Cholok laughed. "It's not high enough."

Amos laughed.

"Come. Zuni will make tea, and I'll explain."

The shadows were getting long. Amos was feeling like he should head back down to the cabin soon, but he wanted to hear what Cholok had to say. They were sitting by themselves on benches in the lodge and drinking something hot.

"It's called Yerba. It's an herb that we use like the English use tea."

Amos didn't hate it. "Maybe Zuni will show me where it grows."

Cholok took a sip then paused before speaking. He took in a breath. "I want you to buy our valley."

The absurdity of the statement made him spill the tea on his leg. "Damn."

"I know it sounds crazy—"

"Sounds crazy?"

"Wait. Let me explain." Cholok had both hands up like he was stopping a horse from rearing up. "Our tribe lived here for hundreds of years and there were many of us. Today, we have been reduced to small bands living apart in isolated mountain passes no white man wants. This band, our band, has made a life here in this valley. My people say I have the Sight, and I say I don't, but my instinct is stronger than any vision, or dream. My instinct tells me someday your people will come and take our valley away. They will take it from us, like they have taken from every other tribe. Everything we have will be theirs."

"But Cholok, there's no way. What you're saying is impossible. I can barely afford to buy oats for the horses, much less an entire valley."

Cholok just grinned. "Amos...Heskym. Trust me."

"Trust an Indian?" Amos laughed. "You are crazy."

Cholok jumped up. "Another joke. What a great day this has been. And..." He held out his arm, pointing and beckoning Amos to follow, "it is about to get much better. Come, I need to show you something."

CHAPTER 16
FEATHER RIVER VALLEY, CALIFORNIA

MAY 1849

Amos found himself in a place where he'd never been before and doubted he could ever find again. They had walked what seemed like several miles, and they were now negotiating a narrow ledge on a sheer rock face. He didn't usually mind heights, but inching along on a ledge several hundred feet above the treetops was a little unnerving. Looking over Cholok's shoulder, the ledge appeared as if it led to a buttress of stone, and a dead end.

The Indian pointed down to the bottom of the wall of stone. There was a dark area, almost black. It looked like a shadow—but it wasn't. Cholok bent down, got on all fours, and stuck his head into the darkness. His body followed.

Amos heard an echoed voice.

"Come on, my friend. Follow me."

Amos wasn't happy about it, but he did it anyway.

The tunnel of rock was just wide enough and just high enough to crawl forward. It was dark, but for some reason Amos couldn't figure, it was not completely black.

Suddenly, Amos felt the walls of the tunnel getting wider. In a few more feet he could almost stand. A few more and they were in a great cavern. Amos judged it to be about forty feet across. At the far end there was a bend, making it difficult to estimate the cave's length. The height was its most impressive feature. It was as tall as a church steeple. A small stream of water about a foot or two wide ran along the edge. The air was moving, he could smell evergreen. Amos guessed the stream was coming from outside the cave and carrying the scent of the forest with the water. He looked around, it wasn't hard to do as there were narrow streams of light coming from somewhere up high, which lit the path, the walls, and Cholok.

"This way." Cholok disappeared around the bend in the cave.

Amos followed his voice.

Cholok had stopped and was standing with both hands outstretched. "Amos, this is the end of our journey, and our worries."

The narrow tubes of light streaming down bounced off the stone walls. Where the light hit the wall, it glowed.

Amos walked to one of the light beams and put his hand on the stone.

His heart stopped. The reflection was gold. Layers of it. Wide thick streaks of yellow that started low and arched up and around to the other side of the cave. It was everywhere. Layer after layer of bright yellow streaks were stacked between grey and deep purple granite.

Amos's heart was thumping so loud he thought Cholok could hear it beating. He breathed out, "My God."

"Something, huh?" The Indian was now grinning with all his teeth showing. "You and I are the only people in the whole world who know about this. I've told no one, not even Zuni."

"Cholok, why me...I don't understand. Why haven't you—?"

"You mean why haven't I chopped out a couple of hundred

126

pounds, and do what every other white man in America would do?"

"Yes...why not? You could own anything...everything." Amos waved at the walls of gold. "Look at it. It's a king's ransom."

"Amos," scoffed Cholok, "if I walked into town with a single nugget, the world I know, and my tribe knows, would end. Greed would be on the tribe like black flies on a carcass."

Amos wheeled around and looked at his friend suddenly understanding what Cholok had in mind. "You can't mean you—"

"Yes. I do mean. Amos Cronin, you are now the richest man in the West, and the first thing you're going to do is buy this valley."

Amos was slow to digest but eventually nodded. "Because, if I own it, the tribe can stay—"

"And nobody can take it away...ever."

Amos walked around, pondering the responsibility. "There will be problems, Cholok. I can't inquire about buying property anywhere in Carversville. I'd have to go to San Francisco, get a lawyer, figure out the boundaries and—."

Cholok waved his hands in the air. "Yes, of course there will be many problems. However, the most important thing is, you must never let anyone know about this find. Don't file any claim or take a sack of gold to an assayer. You would start a stampede that no one could stop, and any hope of this valley being ours will vanish."

Amos nodded.

Cholok looked at him almost defiantly. "There will be problems, but I know you can handle them."

"Well, I don't know that's true." Amos took a beat, then looked at Cholok. "You've been plotting this tactic for a long time, haven't you?"

"I have my friend, since the Bear Flag Revolt in '46. I was just waiting for you to appear to make it happen."

"The Bear what?"

"Amos, do you not read a newspaper? It started as a revolt by settlers against Mexico. It led to the Mexican-American War which ended last year. The US won and gained control of half of the West and California from Mexico."

Amos shrugged.

Cholok shook his head, talking to himself. "And they call us barbarians."

"Okay, okay. How does that affect what you want me to do?"

"The government has control over all the lands not claimed and documented by U.S. citizens."

Amos added. "So, I can buy whatever is not claimed from the government without anyone knowing about it."

Cholok stuck his hands out, smiled, and nodded vigorously. "And now you have the money to do it."

"Still." Amos shook his head.

Cholok stepped up and spoke quietly. "Think of your son. He will have the best of everything and have every advantage."

"My friend." Amos squatted onto the stone floor. "This is yours not mine. I can't take what is yours."

"No, you're not taking. We are partners. You are securing the homeland of every member of our tribe. We have lived for centuries without ever needing the yellow stone. We don't need to change. And like we talked about before, the wealth...this gold... they will never let us keep it. You've seen what it has done to your people, the greed, it's a disease. It will fester and kill. I don't want it to happen to my tribe."

"I understand."

"Besides...I've seen your lodge."

Amos laughed for the first time.

"I'm struggling to build a small barn by myself. Now even

with this it will be difficult. I can't hire anybody from town, everyone would know."

"My friend, you've seen our lodges. We know how to build strong against the worst of storms. We will help."

Amos looked at the gold in the wall again. He had gotten enough money to send Rose back home from three small stones, and there looked like there was enough here to buy Philadelphia.

"Come, it is getting late." Cholok started back the way they came.

Amos followed.

They walked in silence all the way back. It was peaceful, hardly a breeze. In the distance a single coyote howled.

Cholok pointed excitedly. "Hear that? A coyote. This is a good sign."

"I hear coyotes all the time. Why is this one so special?"

"Because I'm making it so." Cholok hit his chest with his fist. "There is a Maidu Tribe legend about the Coyote. It appears in many of our mythic traditions and stories. The Coyote has magical powers of transformation and resurrection. There are stories of it changing the ways of rivers, creating new landscapes, and getting sacred things for our people. The coyote was also a great hero who was summoned to fight against monsters. One of the stories is about how he was summoned by a warrior chief to fight and kill the Thunderbird, the killer of people."

Amos scoffed. "And I suppose I'm the Coyote."

"And I'm the warrior chief." The Indian stopped and turned to him. "The warrior chief couldn't kill the monster alone; he was troubled, and his power wasn't enough, so he was not able to fight by himself. He needed the help of the Coyote to defeat what would have wiped out all the people."

"It's just a story."

Cholok looked at the ground. "To you and all white men, but to us it tells us of a path that gives us hope when there is none." He paused a minute. "How different are our fables from the Bible stories I learned at Christian schools? I was taught those were stories of belief, and redemption. Stories like David defeating Goliath, or the Good Samaritan." He shook his head. "These are lessons that come to us from the past, my friend. They are the same...they are hope."

Amos spoke softly. "My friend, you've put a lot of faith in me... but I'm a broken man."

Cholok smiled and shook his head. "Not broken, damaged."

Amos had nothing to say.

Cholok looked out at the horizon. "Amos, my friend. Sometimes, you have to throw yourself on a log to try and save someone you don't know."

CHAPTER 17
FEATHER RIVER VALLEY, CALIFORNIA

SEPTEMBER 1857

He was pleased with the responsiveness of his new companion named Puddle—a name that this horse earned. Amos had been in the market for a new mount for a while but hadn't found a match. For some, buying a horse and having a working partner were the same, but out in the wilderness there were a few things that needed to be as reliable as the sunrise. On different days, different things were a necessity. Dry boots in weather, an unfailing weapon when in danger, and a horse that didn't quit—for any reason. Selection of the first two were based on one's experience, the last one was purely on a kindred personality, and Puddle had plenty of personality.

They met because of a man named Bill Jordan, a logger with a bad reputation. Amos found out later, Jordan had won the horse in a poker game. The mount was big, standing on four legs taller than most men on two. He was a horse that matched Amos's size more than any other mount he'd seen. He was black, with a long mane, muscular legs and neck, and his movement was fluid and powerful.

Amos had driven his wagon into town in time to see Jordan standing in the street outside the saloon. Amos saw him jam a bit into the horse's mouth, yank the harness strap hard, and violently pull the saddle cinch tight. Amos judged Jordan was trying to show the horse who was boss. Amos pulled the reins up and halted the wagon near the General Store. He sat watching the horse not reacting to the abuse of his owner, just occasionally turning his head, eyeing the man.

Jordan stuck his foot in the stirrups and swung his body up and onto the saddle. The man then snapped the reins hard against the horse's neck while leaning forward anticipating a sudden bolt.

The horse didn't react and stood motionless.

The man, at first, seemed surprised. He snapped again, adding a heel kick to its belly.

The horse was still motionless. In fact, the mount looked relaxed and showed almost no acknowledgment of the man beating on his body.

Jordan, obviously frustrated, began shouting a long string of curse words that got the attention of townspeople who'd begun to gather.

Amos scratched his beard.

A man appeared on the wooden porch outside the saloon. He had both thumbs under his red suspenders and a smile on his face.

Jordan yelled at him, "You bastard. This plow horse is no damn good. You owe me forty dollars. That's a lot of goddamn money and I want what I won."

The man on the porch, who apparently lost the horse in the poker game, paying no attention to the outburst, just laughed. "I wouldn't kick him again if I were you."

Jordan yelled, "Oh yeah?" then kicked the horse's belly as hard as he could.

The horse moved. It took several slow steps forward to where the laundry was dumping water into the street, then bucked its hind quarter straight up.

The man literally sailed into the air. His arms were spread out almost as wide as his legs. He traveled about ten feet, landing headfirst in the water and mud. The horse then stomped its front leg next to the man's head, splashing enough water to make him choke.

Every man, woman, and child standing nearby doubled over with laughter.

Jordan pushed himself up out of the mud, got to his knees, spit, then stood upright. His eyes were squinting, and his jaw was set with anger. "Okay, you son of a bitch...I own you and now you're dead." He reached down, unsnapped his gun from his holster, and pulled it.

The laughter stopped.

The next sound heard on the street was the familiar metal clicking of hammers on a gun cocking.

"You pull that trigger, and I'll kill you where you stand."

Jordan spun around; his gun still pointed straight out. Now instead of pointing at the horse, he was pointing it at Amos.

Amos, still seated in the wagon, had a double-barreled shotgun leveled at the man's head.

Jordan flinched. His gun lowered slightly, as did his voice. "It's my horse."

"Now it's mine."

"But—"

"Forty dollars. Now, get your harness and saddle off my horse."

The man slowly holstered his pistol.

It took a minute for him to reclaim his possessions.

As he pulled the saddle down, the horse whinnied and splashed the puddle again, causing the man to jump.

Amos got down from the wagon and handed Jordan two Liberty Head twenty-dollar gold coins and, as he did, he looked Jordan in the eye and whispered, "If I ever see you beat an animal again, I'll kill you just for fun."

Amos turned and walked over to the horse and stroked his nose. "How 'bout it? You coming with me?" He hung a loose rope around the horse's neck and leaving it slack began walking back to the wagon.

The horse followed.

The man on the porch had rejoined the others in somewhat subdued laughter. "What you gonna' name that bronco, Amos?"

Amos thought a second. "Puddle."

That sent the laughter back to double-over.

Amos and Puddle rode the rocky path which wound its way up and over the foothills and into the valley where the Maidu village was nestled. It was a sight to see. From the path above, Amos could see how well-planned the lodges were located. Tall evergreens surrounded three sides, sheltering the village from the shifting winds of harsh weather. The fourth side was leeward, downwind, and uphill from the river. It was a short walk to fresh water, but high enough to avoid flooding should the river rise. There was a smokehouse for fish and meat and a root cellar keeping hard-to-find Miner's lettuce cool, their acorn mash safe from the squirrels, and the honey they harvested away from the bears.

He could see the children playing in the common and the

tribes people attending to their daily tasks. He saw Cholok and Odina, whose name meant mountain and who resembled one, walking up from the river with a long stringer of fish. It apparently had been a good day.

Odina and several other men from the tribe helped him build the cabin because it had special requirements that he would only trust the Indians to know about.

He shifted his weight in the saddle. Reaching behind him, he adjusted the bags strapped over Puddle's back. "Almost there." He patted his new friend's neck. "Heyup." Puddle moved forward on the voice command.

A lookout he hadn't seen appeared out of nowhere and waved. He followed the path down to the village then whistled as loud as he could. The children looked up, then started running, laughing, and competing to see who would get to Amos first.

Puddle stopped when they reached the center of the common and let the children run all around him, petting him, some pulling his tail.

Cholok appeared, shooing them away, and they ran, but Amos dismounted and called them back.

He reached into his pocket and pulled out handfuls of lemon-flavored rock candy.

At that moment Amos could have run for God and been elected. He didn't smile much, but he did then. It was joyous.

Zuni walked into the commons carrying a sling filled with acorns. "Hello Amos."

Amos nodded and smiled. Her English was getting much better. He had attempted to learn their language and he could understand a bit, usually able to follow a conversation. However, every time he tried to speak in their tongue, everyone would laugh. Cholok explained that his Irish-Philadelphia accent was not helping him. He stuck to English and relied on Cholok to translate.

Amos walked over to Puddle, who by now had developed quite a few admirers. Several tribesmen were measuring and comparing, and one was brave enough to swing up onto the saddle. Puddle didn't seem to object. But to be safe, Amos shook a finger and discouraged the rider from any attempt to ride the big stallion. Amos pulled the canvas bags down.

"This one is just salt." He handed Cholok the heavy bag. "Here's the flour." It was lighter and he handed it to Zuni. He reached into the saddle bag and took out a smaller pouch that had a leather tie on top. "This is English tea. Zuni, I love what you cook," he frowned, "but I think you'll see this is much better than your Yaupon tea."

She understood but playfully hit him with her free hand. "Ya-ka-he."

Cholok whispered, "White man."

Amos smiling, said, "Yes I am, and your tea is still awful."

Cholok translated and she hit him again.

They walked back to Cholok's lodge and sat outside on a flattened log.

"You have good news, don't you?"

Amos grinned. "How do you always know?"

"Heskym, you only have two expressions...none, and good news."

Amos nodded. "Well, yes, I do have good news." He withdrew a sheaf of papers from inside his jacket. "This, Heskym, is the deed to the valley. The property goes from the windy bend upstream down to the waterfall, and both sides of the river, over the top of the ridges, and halfway down the other side."

Cholok was silent.

"My friend, no one will ever take it away from you. I've seen to it."

More silence. Cholok was frozen, just staring out at the river.

Zuni came out of the lodge with plates of fish and acorn mash. She looked at her husband then shrugged at Amos, with curiosity on her face.

"He's having a moment."

She shrugged again apparently not understanding.

Suddenly, Cholok leaped from the log, sending the plates into the air. He started yelling at the top of his lungs. Amos had heard a war cry before, and this was close to the volume, but not the same emotion.

Every hut emptied. Men came out from the forest and up from the river, all running.

Cholok ran to a boulder and leaped to the top. Amos wasn't sure he would make the jump, given his age, but he did. He wobbled for a second, then announced to everyone the valley of the Maidu Tribe would be theirs forever. He pointed to Amos and the crowd mobbed him and started slapping him on the back to a point where he winced from their enthusiasm.

It took about an hour for the jubilation to die down, but it did, and new plates of food appeared.

Cholok, now apparently famished, tore through a plate of food and signaled for more.

A bonfire was started in the center common, and children were dancing and playing games. The adults were gathered in small groups and all of them were peeking at the white man who'd become such a fixture over the past months. This time, however, they were looking with admiration instead of suspicion.

Amos and Cholok managed to escape from the celebration and found a quiet spot to talk. Cholok was a little calmer, but his eyes were wide, and he couldn't stand still. "We talked of problems in doing this. Did you have many?"

Amos nodded. "Yes, a few. Some were easy to fix, some harder, but I hired the best attorney in San Francisco. They did all the research, prepared the deeds and requests to purchase from the government. It took much, much longer than I thought it would, but there was a great deal of work to do to make sure the title would never be challenged. Actually, we had to buy eight separate properties but together they amount to just over 33,000 acres."

"And it can't be, what did you say...challenged, ever?"

"There was some talk about planning a railroad through the mountains which would connect to the track coming from the east."

"A railroad?" Cholok became agitated instantly.

Amos raised an open palm. "Don't worry, there are many routes to take and most of them are far away from here."

"Railroad." Cholok shook his head.

"Stop." Amos held up the paper. "We bought this land by outright purchase from the U.S. government."

Zuni walked up holding Aponi by the hand interrupting the conversation. "Come my husband." His daughter held out her hand. Cholok took it and together they walked back toward the lodge.

Amos sat down on a rock pile and looked at the fire burning in the common. He felt like something he had done was right. It was new to him.

"Heskym," Cholok called, "Come, we have a gift for you."

Amos stood, his knee creaked, and he rubbed out the stiffness. He took a few steps, and his other knee creaked. *Damn, I'm getting old.*

When dawn came, his body picked up where it had left off the night before. First, he scratched his beard, then his head, as he threw off the blanket. The creak in his knee was followed by a clicking sound as he got up from his bed in the lodge.

The tribe had come a long way since their partnership with Amos. Life in the village was almost the same, but some improvements to daily life were reluctantly accepted by the tribal members. It was still very much a traditional existence, but a few conveniences made life a bit more pleasant. One of the luxuries afforded was the acquisition of feather beds.

Amos's night's sleep had been very comfortable. He slept deep and long. The smell of a cooking fire woke him and despite his body's resistance he dressed and wandered out of the lodge.

"Good morning, Heskym." Cholok greeted him with a smile.

Zuni, also smiling, offered him a hot cup of his tea. Pala, sitting on a bench, was also smiling. The boy was getting tall like his father, and had the wide, kind eyes of his mother.

Amos was immediately suspicious. "What are you all grinning about?"

Pala stood quickly and spoke something Amos could translate. "Let me, let me, father."

Cholok nodded and the boy ran off.

Aponi also smiled—but not like the others, she was always smiling—and ran and sat by Amos's side then hugged his arm. She had developed quite the affinity for the old goat, and was the only person in the world who made him feel vulnerable.

Amos was giving a hawk eye to both Cholok and Zuni, who, still grinning, didn't give anything away.

Pala came back as fast as he left with a female dog following

139

him. Amos could tell the gender because four puppies were running behind anxious to regain her tit. The dog was yellow, big, and seemed friendly, although Amos had learned not to assume anything when it came to mothers protecting their young.

Zuni touched Amos's arm. "For you. One." She waved a finger to the puppies.

"A dog?" Amos shook his head. "I have enough problems."

Another young dog, much larger than the others, approached slowly, apparently wary of the new face in the crowd of humans.

"That one a part of this bunch?"

Cholok shook his head. "No, last litter more than a year ago. Same mother, father unknown. Might even be a wolf. We're not certain. He is called Ta-su which means refuse because he wants no part of any family."

The dog came up to Amos and stood a foot away just looking at him.

Amos looked back for a bit then took a piece of smoked jerky from his pocket and offered it to the latecomer.

Cholok shook his head. "He won't take it."

The dog walked up to Amos, sniffed once, then took the meat.

Zuni pointed to the dog and Amos then said something to Cholok Amos didn't understand.

Amos shrugged towards Cholok.

"Zuni said, 'Two who are alone'."

Amos gave the dog another piece of meat and a new name. "I'll call you Rufus."

CHAPTER 18
CARVERSVILLE, CALIFORNIA
SEPTEMBER 1865

Sid Stull was tired and he needed to get a few hours of sleep, but he was so possessed with formulating a plan he couldn't close his eyes. Every time he thought he had it, he'd find a reason that he'd wind up dead or in prison. The thousand-dollar bounty kept diverting his mind from the crime. A cloud of cigarette smoke filled his hotel room. Opening the window let cold fall air rush in, clearing the grey cloud and his mind.

He wasn't worried about what he and the boys had set up for today. They had done this four times before, and no one suspected a thing, but it wasn't like what they did came off perfect. Twice they underestimated the resistance of the husbands, and once the wife. During the third hijacking, Bite couldn't stop the wagon, so Sid had to shoot one of the horses to act as an anchor. The mistakes made in each of the robberies were because Soapy and Bite didn't listen to him.

Sid decided to rob another wagon, not necessarily because of need, they still had money left from the last one. He wanted to do it this time to find out if he could trust either of them to follow his direction on this next job. The mistakes they made before were ones he couldn't afford when they went to kill Amos Cronin.

Sid and the boys wanted to get out on the trail right after midnight to have time to divert their intended victims from their destination and their lives.

Gold-seekers or soon-to-be farmers from the East used the Oregon Trail until it ran into the Sierra Nevada Mountain range. After that, the trail wasn't just one road anymore. Temporary bi-pass roads were cut to get around washouts, overflowing creeks, landslides, and fallen trees, all caused diversions which made the travelers alter their routes.

The main trail from Carversville to Sacramento was open, so a diversion to redirect the victims into a trap needed to be invented. Sid and his cohorts arrived before dawn and placed a sign at the trail's intersection with an old bypass which read:

WARNING

BRIDGE OUT AHEAD

The sign would cause the victims to reroute up an old, unused path that would be more difficult to navigate. They hammered in the sign, then Sid and Soapy Smith went on ahead. Bite stayed behind to remove the sign after the wagon they were waiting for passed by so no other wagons would follow.

Shortly after dawn, a wagon covered with worn canvas and two passengers, Helen and Douglas Hankel, saw the sign and headed their two-horse team up the mountain trail. Bite waited a bit, pulled the sign out of the ground, then rode up the same trail, offering a polite greeting as he passed by the wagon.

They'd been in position for a couple of hours but were not silent about it. Sid Stull had told Soapy Smith and Bite to stop fooling around several times, but they were paying no mind. His two partners were on the opposite side of the trail and doing a poor job of lying in wait.

"Will you two stop fuckin' around?"

The two laughed as they continued to throw rocks at each other.

Sid Stull stood up and walked across the road. "I swear, if'n you idiots give up our position, I'll gut you both."

Stull's tough guy act rarely worked, and it was having the predictable outcome now.

"Fuck you." Soapy flicked the rock he was holding at Sid.

In an instant, Sid reached and threw his knife. It stuck in a tree beside Soapy's head.

"Uh oh, look out," Bite chuckled, "you made him mad."

Soapy jumped up immediately, his face tight with anger.

The challenge for leadership stopped when a distant sound caused Soapy and Bite to quiet down and hustle to their positions. It was the wagon clanging up the incline, probably a few hundred yards down the slope. Sid judged it far enough away that the settlers coming up the mountain trail couldn't have heard the commotion.

Sid stood for a moment in the road, head turned, straining to hear.

The snap of a whip carried up the hill.

Sid whispered, "Stay quiet until I make my move."

Soapy whispered back, "Yas' sir, boss man."

Sid grabbed his knife then went back to his side of the trail,

Soapy was positioned directly opposite, and Bite was further up the trail on Soapy's side. All were hidden by the brush in the shadows of the evergreens.

The rattle of the wagon got louder. Sid could hear hooves on the trail and hanging pots and pans clanging on the sides of the wagon, but he couldn't hear voices.

Sid signaled to the other two that their prey was just around the bend.

The horses came first. They looked old and tired. Their heads were down, pulling hard, white foam of sweat oozed over the harness and dripped from their mouths. Fifty yards more and they would reach the crest of the hill, and the ambush.

Sid had a short encounter with the Hankels at Goodman's General Store. He heard Mrs. Hankel tell Mrs. Goodman they had set out west escaping from war-torn Fayetteville, North Carolina. They were without work after the North burned the textile mill, and after the South burned all the cotton in the county to prevent the North from laying hands on the only product Fayetteville produced. She said they had no choice but to leave their home and try to find a new life in the West.

Sid also heard her say they had sold everything they owned to set out across the country in hopes their money was enough to get a new start. Sid was also listening when Mrs. Hankel asked if what they'd heard about there being good farmland near Sacramento was true. Mrs. Goodman said she'd heard there was an abundance of good land to farm. She even gave them a bag of corn seed to get them started. Sid watched them purchase flour, salt, sugar, and oats, and pay for their supplies with a pouch that seemed heavy. The travelers were anxious to continue their journey and wanted to move on as soon as they watered and fed the horses.

Sid and the other two bushwhackers were waiting, hiding like the predators they were. Waiting for the Hankels from Fayetteville.

The wagon eased forward and leveled out when the trail flattened. The reins in Mr. Hankel's hands slackened. The horses and the travelers seemed to take a breath.

It was Mr. Hankel's last one.

Sid's knife flashed through the air, hitting Mr. Hankel just below his ear and burying the blade to its hilt in his neck. His hands went to his throat, his body fell to the left, then to the ground.

No sound came from Mrs. Hankel's mouth at first. It was wide open like her eyes. Her silence ended with a blood curdling scream.

Bite appeared in front of the horses who were startled and bucked but came to a quick stop.

Soapy Smith jumped from the brush and grabbed Mrs. Hankel's arm, pulling her off the seat and to the ground. Bite ran around to where she fell, and the two stood over the woman who was white with fear.

They each grabbed an arm and, laughing, started dragging her off the trail.

"We don't have time for that," Sid yelled.

Soapy looked at the terrified woman struggling to get away and said slow and low, "I have time."

A shot rang out.

Blood gushed from her head.

The two men whipped around and reached for their guns.

"I told you, no." Sid had his pistol straight out and pointed at Soapy's head.

The two men looked as if they were deciding on Sid's leadership again. They reluctantly let their guns stay holstered.

Sid started walking back to the wagon. "They have money in a pouch hidden somewhere. We need to find it. Soapy, take care of the bodies. And Bite, get the wagon and the horses."

Suddenly, there was another noise.

A baby started crying.

Soapy and Bite looked at each other, then at Sid.

Sid walked to the back of the wagon and pulled back the canvas cover.

The baby's cry got louder.

Soapy became instantly arrogant. "What you gonna' do now boss—"

Sid's gun fired.

The crying stopped.

Leadership was no longer in question.

Sid crossed the road and stood face-to-face with Soapy. "I'll look for the money in the wagon. While I do that, you search the bodies." He turned and looked at Bite. "Like I told you before, you lead the horses and get the wagon down the trail to the spot we used before on the cliff." He then glared at Soapy. "You, pull the bodies off the trail far enough so they can't be seen, and leave them."

Sid climbed into the back of the wagon and searched while it was moving. He paid no attention to the baby's bloody blanket while searching. Eventually, he found the pouch in a basket. He grabbed a rifle and pistol before he climbed down.

The wagon stopped, and Bite yelled out, "All set."

Stull finished up then helped Bite unhitch the horses and remove their harnesses. The spot on the cliff had been carefully selected and used several times in the past. The wagon was pitched downhill and held in place with the long-handled wheel brake. Bite walked around to the side of the wagon, yanked the brake, and it ran down the slope and off the cliff. It flipped end-for-end twice before it fell through the treetops. It sent an echo up the mountain wall when it crashed into the bottom of the ravine.

Sid signaled to Bite who then led the horses into the woods and shot them both.

The three walked back to the site of the ambush and looked over the trail. Aside from some blood, which would disappear in a day or so, there was nothing that would indicate a struggle. They walked down to a rock formation just off the trail, near where their horses were tied up.

Soapy was picking his teeth with a weed. "There were some bones still there...in the woods...from the last one."

Bite shook his head. "The varmints will take care of all of them soon enough. I think the bears like the horse meat best. Saw some big tracks where I left them two new ones." He looked to Sid who wasn't paying any attention. "Once they start stinking, they'll draw a crowd." He chuckled a little.

Sid had no reaction. He was examining the rifle. When he saw Hankel's name etched on the stock, he walked to the cliff and threw it over the edge.

When he returned, he pulled the pouch from his belt and started counting the take.

"Twenty-five dollars and two bits each."

"Alright." Bite rubbed his hands together. "I'm eaten' and drinkin' tonight."

Sid handed the money over and pocketed his share. What his partners didn't see was, when he was chucking the rifle into the abyss, he put three twenty-dollar coins into his pocket.

"What's next?" Soapy hesitated, then added, "Boss."

Sid hesitated back. "Depends."

"On what?" Both men said almost simultaneously.

"On...if you two assholes will follow my directions."

Soapy laughed. "Sure thing, boss."

Sid spit, then stood and started walking toward his horse.

"Wait, wait." Soapy said. "Okay, yes, I'm in. You're the boss. Whatever you say."

Sid turned, stepped in close, and studied him. "I'll tell you this one time. You fuck me once on this deal and I'll kill you right then."

Soapy, stone-faced, nodded.

Sid looked at Bite who held up his hands and nodded vigorously.

Sid sat back down. "I have come across a job that's dangerous but rewarding."

"How much?" Soapy asked quickly, only responding to the word rewarding.

"One hundred dollars...each."

The two men stood up and almost hurt their necks nodding.

"When?" Bite was grinning.

"Soon. I gotta do some planning."

"Planning?" Soapy looked skeptical.

Sid scowled. "This ain't a couple of farmers."

Soapy snarled. "Or a baby."

CHAPTER 19

CARVERSVILLE, CALIFORNIA

SEPTEMBER 1866

Reginald Cudworth sat behind his desk. It was old and had delicate carvings that spoke to the craftsman that made the piece. Its top was wide and had ancient imperfections illuminated by the only lamp in the room. Heavy drapes covered the windows that overlooked his domain. He occasionally parted them to survey life in the town, but only out of ego, not pride. He sometimes thought of the people who might be walking by his house wondering what life was like behind the closed curtains.

He was passionate about neatness and order, which meant his staff was ever busy straightening books, replacing soiled linen napkins, and dusting every piece of furniture in sight. He changed white shirts twice a day, occasionally three times, and God help the servant who presented him a replacement garment with a missing button.

The bronze-colored chimney of a brass oil lamp lit a corner of the dark oak providing a circle of light that allowed Cudworth to study a map. His attention was intense, a second plan was needed in case his first scheme failed. He was still confident he would succeed, after-all a rewarding Stull with gold was the ultimate argument for committing unthinkable acts. But—a good backup plan would be comforting insurance.

He kept the room dark because he hated the bright light of sunshine and what came with it. He hated people, hated smiles, and hated the warmth a warm sunny day brought to others. He also hated anything that involved doing something that he couldn't get someone else to do— anything that involved physical effort. He was a king in this room, in his house, and in Carversville. And soon he would be king over much, much more.

A small Chinese woman with long straight black hair and a black and red kimono noiselessly approached carrying a silver tray with tea. She emerged from a hidden service door, shuffling with tiny steps, quiet but quick. She halted at the side of the desk, bowed her head, and extended the tray.

He didn't look up, eyes fixed on the map of property that wasn't his.

She remained still.

A minute went by.

The China cup rattled slightly as the strain in her arms mounted.

Finally, he looked up. His white skin, paled from his existence in the dark, blended with the color of his clothes. Cudworth was the color of porcelain, and just as cold. He removed his reading glasses, placed them on the desk, then crossed his arms as he looked up at his servant.

A nervous sound of a small sucking in of air came from the woman.

Cudworth couldn't determine if it was the strain of holding the tray, or fear, but he liked it either way. Her discomfort was a welcome diversion.

There was a knock on the door.

He pointed a dramatic finger at the servant. "Put it down."

She quickly placed the tray on the table and shuffled to open the office door.

His bodyguard, Wesley Strong, entered.

Cudworth's miniature servant slipped behind Strong, her frame disappearing behind his massive form as she closed the door.

He stood, as she had, waiting for permission.

Cudworth looked at him briefly, then picked up the teapot, poured a cup, and put in several teaspoons of sugar. After he finished, he beckoned the bodyguard forward.

Strong approached, stopping at the center of the desk.

Cudworth's voice crackled a bit. "Why is Cronin still alive?"

Wesley cleared his throat. "I've spoken with Stull twice since he agreed to take the job. The first time he said he wanted an advance—"

"Absolutely not," interrupted Cudworth throwing a hand into the air.

"I told him that right off. I told him he gets paid after and not before."

"And the second time you met?"

"He said he was working on a plan."

Cudworth leaned forward almost knocking over his teacup. "You let him get away with that? What if he changes his mind and talks—"

Strong interrupted. "He won't do that. He wants the money, bad. I think he's scared of Cronin, and from what I know of that old man, Stull should be. In fact, I think it's good that he is. If Stull runs at this half-cocked and fails, it will make it harder for us to try again."

Cudworth's rising anger made him start to object—but he stopped and instead took a sip of tea.

Strong remained almost at attention.

"I suppose that there may be some truth to being successful on the first attempt." Cudworth took another spoon of sugar and stirred his cup. "What do you think of Mr. Stull?"

"He is slime, a latrine slithering snake who'd do anything or kill anybody for a dollar."

Cudworth smiled. "So, you have every confidence that he'll kill Amos Cronin?"

Strong nodded. "Reasonable to assume."

"Assume?" Cudworth whispered to himself, then lightly tapped his spoon on the side of the cup. "Would you?"

"Would I what?"

"Kill someone for a thousand dollars?"

Strong hesitated for a second. "Depends."

"On?"

"On who."

Cudworth put down the cup, positioned his elbows on the desk, and leaned forward. "Sid Stull."

Strong smiled. "Abso...fucking...lutely."

Cudworth grunted. "Stull will never keep quiet. Will he?"

Strong nodded again. "No, sir."

"Right." Cudworth waved Strong away as he returned his attention to the papers on his desk.

Strong didn't move, staying at partial attention.

Cudworth was aware but didn't divert his gaze from the map. "What?"

"One thousand dollars for the life of Sid Stull after he kills Amos Cronin."

Without looking up Cudworth smiled at his bodyguard's attempt at negotiation. He put his hands flat on the desk, then peered through squinted eyes while leaning back and crossing his arms.

"Five hundred if Stull kills Cronin, and you kill Stull. One thousand to kill Cronin if Stull fails."

Strong pondered a moment. "Seven hundred and fifty dollars to kill Stull. One thousand to kill Cronin, if I have to kill them both."

Cudworth's amusement disappeared. His eyes squinted a bit, but then he shrugged, relaxing. "Okay, deal."

Strong started to turn to leave.

In a louder voice Cudworth said, "Get it done."

Strong didn't turn around, just turned the door handle and left the office.

Cudworth poured more hot tea.

And then I'll need a new bodyguard.

CHAPTER 20
FEATHER RIVER VALLEY, CALIFORNIA
SEPTEMBER 1866

An unseasonably early snowfall wouldn't amount to more than a few inches, but it would be enough to white blanket the forest floor, make branches sag, and hide impediments on the trail. It also meant Sid Stull's approach to the Old Man's cabin would be slower than he anticipated. He started early, leaving town before dawn, and reaching the fork in the logging road leading down to the cabin before the sun rose above the tree line. He tied up his horse halfway down and walked the rest of the way through the unexpected snowfall. He took careful steps, avoiding ruts and rocks, while being ever vigilant for any movement that would result in being confronted with a set of gnarling teeth. On the positive side, the snow that slowed his progress was also subduing all sound. It was deathly quiet, and any sound wouldn't travel far, but a sharp eye would still see movement. And the sharp eye he was worried about belonged to that damn dog. He'd learned painful lessons from his last experience with the hound from hell, so Sid approached downwind, judged every movement, and remained out of sight.

His hope to be in position before dawn was delayed by the weather. But now, finally an hour after sunrise, he'd gotten to the edge of the forest. When he got close, he'd left the trail and circled around to a spot at the edge of the Old Man's pasture, a couple of hundred yards from the cabin. He found a boulder that had a tree limb hanging over its edge. Stull climbed up, brushed off the snow, and laid flat on the top of the rock. From this position he could watch without being seen. While scanning the pasture, he realized his heart was racing and his breath was short.

It hadn't been a difficult hike, mostly downhill from the logging road. It was the fear of the dog—and the Old Man—that taxed him. His mind went back to how easily the two had bested him. He sat up and leaned back against the tree. He took a chaw of tobacco from a pouch and filled his cheek. After a couple of minutes, he calmed down, and his heart returned to normal. Tapping his boot, he found his knife was still secure in its sheath.

He spit, regaining his confidence, and rested his head on the tree trunk. Cudworth's thousand-dollar fee to kill Amos Cronin had become a literal vision. There were moments when his attention completely diverted from what was going on around him, and he could actually see a sack of gold—gold that he wouldn't share. But he needed a plan.

Bite and Soapy were a liability, annoying and untrustworthy. Soapy had sworn loyalty, and Bite agreed that he too would follow his orders, but Stull knew they were lying. He knew they wouldn't listen to him or follow his plan. It wasn't their nature to obey anybody for any reason. He was tired of their disrespect, their snide remarks, and he really hated it when they looked at each other after he spoke, laughing as they whispered secret insults. He knew he was their joke.

They'll pay.

He had drifted off for that moment, losing his concentration.

Suddenly, in the distance, something moving caught his eye. Stull ducked under the branch and laid flat again, straining his eyesight to see in the morning light. The Old Man was walking across the pasture toward the forest. He was carrying what looked like a long iron bar, and had a sack strapped to his back. The dog was beside him; both were making a path in the fresh snow.

Stull ducked back behind the branch. He had a decision to make. He could go to the cabin and just walk in. It would be easy. The Old Man looked like he was going to do some kind of work somewhere, and he took the dog which meant the cabin was easy pickens'. There were things inside— he knew that— great treasures, and probably gold hidden somewhere.

His vision of the thousand-dollar reward returned, but he spit black tobacco juice on the fresh white snow and the vision sank in the muck.

First, I'll kill him, then get the gold from Cudworth, and still get what's inside the cabin.

He peeked back through the branch. The Old Man was gone, disappeared into the woods and up the mountain. The dog was at the edge of the forest, standing still, looking back across the pasture in his direction. Stull froze.

He must know I'm here.

Stull's heart started beating out of his chest again—panic welling up. His head bobbed back and forth; beads of sweat broke out on his forehead. He put his hands flat on the rock, looking for a landing place to jump off.

Where can I run?

But before he leaped, he summoned every ounce of courage and peeked again. The dog was gone. He scanned the edge of the tree line for movement. There was none. The dog was probably following the Old Man.

He wiped his forehead and cursed himself. *Damn that beast.*

A half an hour passed and the snow had slowed and the temperature started to rise. He jumped down and started walking toward the forest, committed to following the tracks of the Old Man and finding out what he was up to.

The falling snow was hitting his face, so he knew he was downwind from the path the Old Man took. The dog would have trouble picking up his scent. It now also occurred to him that because the temperature was rising, the snow would probably change to rain. He could follow their tracks in the snow, and the rain would wash away his tracks. When they returned, they wouldn't know anyone followed them because his footsteps would have disappeared. He stopped and smiled at his own genius.

What luck.

Invigorated but cautious, Stull didn't cross the pasture, which would have been the shortest route but where his dark form would standout against the fresh snow. Instead, he hurried along the edge of the forest until he came upon the tracks made by the Old Man and the dog that led up the mountain. He followed their trail, stopping regularly to listen and watch. The tracks wound up a narrow path in the forest until they ended at what might have been mistaken for a game trail. It was a wide cutout in the brush where deer or elk might travel to feeding grounds or to where they bed down. But upon closer examination, Stull figured it had other uses. Even with the snow covering the ground, he could make out the impressions of hoof prints and even a couple of wagon wheel tracks.

He continued following the tracks up the game trail but lost them for a few minutes when a creek interrupted his progress. Sid crossed to the other side, then wandered up and down the bank of the creek until he found where their tracks continued. The Old Man's footprints were too far apart for Sid to mirror, and the hound's prints were almost as large as Sid's. All together it looked like a man and a boy were taking a dog for a walk. There was a spray of fresh snow around the front of the prints, which showed Sid the two were not far off. He began paying as much attention to what was in front of him as he did the tracks.

Sid stepped on a fallen branch hidden beneath the snow, snapping it in two. It sounded like a rifle shot. He froze, expecting the charging animal to emerge from the brush any second. A minute went by and nothing happened. Another minute. He waited one more before he started moving forward again.

Everything stopped when he came to a rockslide blocking the path. The evergreen trees ended where a piece of the mountain had slid down a very steep slope. The snow was falling but not sticking to the rocks. The temperature had risen, and the snow was wet and dissolving when it hit the ground. Above him, at the top of the slide, a sheer cliff of grey rock rose into the sky. He looked right then left and finding them impassable, started up. Sid cautiously crept up the rocks being careful not to slip and dislodge something that would give his position away. He didn't know where they'd gotten to, but they couldn't be far.

It took a while to climb the hundred feet to the face of the towering cliff. When he finally arrived at the top of the slide, he was confused by what he saw. He was standing on a plateau which was about forty feet across and deep. In front and to his left, the mountain rose straight up. Ice was hanging off outcroppings on a face that must have been hundreds of feet high and seemed impossible to climb. A short distance to his right, the plateau ended, with a shear drop into a deep canyon.

He scratched his head. There was no snow on the rocks and no tracks anywhere.

Where could they have gone?

He turned around and looked back down. He could see to the

bottom, where the rockslide ended and where he had emerged from the forest. There was no other way out other than straight up or straight down. He squatted, resting on one knee for a minute, the mystery of their disappearance somehow lessening the fear of being discovered.

There has to be another trail.

He walked along the face of the mountain cliff, feeling the rock. He circled around the edge of the rockslide to the edge of the plateau and the precipice of the canyon below. He inched along the edge until it stopped at the face of the mountain. He couldn't see beyond where the grey mountain turned. There was nothing beyond the edge of the mountain but sky. He put one hand on an outcropping and leaned out over the edge of the plateau to get a better view of the mountain face. He regripped and leaned a little farther. When he looked down, he saw a small ledge—a foot or two wide—that followed the curve of the mountain. It was a narrow, treacherous path between the tall granite and the endless sky.

This must be it. It has to be where they went.

He thought about trying to navigate the ledge but stopped. What if the Old Man did go this way and decided to come back while he was walking there? He looked down and couldn't see the bottom.

I'd better wait.

Sid turned and hurried to climb halfway back down the rockslide. He cut across to where the pine trees had survived the slide and found a spot in the trees to hide.

Hours had gone by. Stull didn't know exactly how long he'd been there or what time it was. He didn't know how to tell time, but the sun was starting to set so he figured, late afternoon.

A rock tumbled. He spit tobacco and then heard the faint sound of footsteps. He peered from his hideaway. Rufus appeared at the top of the rockslide, looked around then looked back to the Old Man, who was following behind. Stull watched. Careful and quiet. The Old Man started down, struggling to keep his balance.

This struck Sid as strange.

The dog bounded down, sniffed around, then went back up about halfway, stopped and waited for the Old Man to catch up.

Sid thought he saw the reason why Cronin was having difficulty. It was the weight of the backpack. Something was shifting around. The Old Man eventually took the backpack off and shook it to settle whatever was rolling around inside.

He's carrying gold.

A rush of excitement exploded in his body that caused an involuntary noise to come out of his mouth.

The dog's head snapped toward the sound.

Sid froze, afraid to breathe.

The Old Man, paying no attention, reached the bottom and called out, "Rufus, come on let's go, it's getting late."

The dog stood still a second or two longer then bounded down the rocks and disappeared into the forest following the Old Man.

Gold.

Sid was giddy, tingling, breathless.

Stull waited a few minutes then climbed back up the slide, almost running to the narrow ledge. It was right there in front of him, a twelve-inch-wide path to his fortune. He knew it was true. He knew it.

He looked at the ledge. He looked at the sun.

I can make it.

He hadn't noticed the snow, that had changed to rain, had stopped completely. The sun was now disappearing behind the mountaintop. The problem was now that the sun was setting, and the temperature was dropping.

He took a step out, his heart pounding, his mind consumed with the fever. He got about ten feet before it started to ice up.

I can do it.

His next step almost sent him to the bottom of the ravine.

"God damn it." His voice was loud and echoed.

He put his forehead on the rock wall in frustration then, slowly, started back to the plateau.

After he put his feet back on solid ground, he turned and looked at the ledge. He stuck both hands straight out in frustration. "It's right there."

He put his hands on his hips, shook his head, and started down the rockslide.

When he hit the forest, he suddenly had another rush of adrenaline. This time it was fear.

Oh my God. Can I find my way out?

He looked hard and found a few marks in what was left of the snow. It took hours and hours before he got to the pasture and another hour to find his horse and the trail back to the logging road. It was long dark before he was on the road to Carversville.

The thought of finding the Old Man's gold mine replaced the cold, the wet, and the vision of the thousand-dollar reward for Amos Cronin's murder. But—he needed a plan. Bite and Soapy would be necessary. They would get dead like the Old Man, but they were necessary for right now.

Before he got back to his warm, dry, room—he had a plan, and in it he got it all.

CHAPTER 21
SEA OF CORTEZ
SEPTEMBER 1869

The night sky was putting on quite a show. Henry thought he could have sold tickets to what would be a sellout, standing-room-only crowd. The one thing that he looked forward to, every single day that he was on the steamship, was coming up on deck to see the stars, which, by itself, was worth the trials of the long sea voyage. He didn't think it was possible but, tonight the view was even more breathtaking than what he'd witnessed before.

His expectations for the evening's entertainment were diminished by a suspect weather forecast. There were winds and choppy seas all afternoon and bilious clouds dominated the sky. Toward sunset, the weather cleared, and the wind died down. The clouds retreated, taking the forms of giant children-story characters. The sun slowly dipping under the puffy monsters lighting their extremities with luminous reflections of red, yellow, and orange. They danced together, lighting exploding inside their bodies like they were railing against the darkness. When the sun finally began its surrender to the night, the colors faded, and whisps of granite-grey lace flittered like fingers of cotton candy from the mass of tumbling, rolling clouds. They danced together until the sun disappeared leaving the blue sky to slowly change to purple, then to black.

The clouds had moved in unison toward the west then stopped, holding position on the horizon as if they were waiting for a cue from nature. The blackness rising in the west had become dominant but was penetrated by small halos of glittering yellow and intense white, as the stars began to take center stage.

Henry had seen the night sky many times in his life but never like this. The stars began at the edge of the horizon, rising and engulfing everything, a giant dome, fitted to infinite perfection. Billions and billions of tiny twinkles of light knitted together in streaks and twirls and spirals, like they were once tossed into the sky—now moving ever so slowly but still frozen in place for eternity.

In the randomness of it all, a few brilliant white stars stood out from the rest, dominating and demanding attention, becoming beacons like lighthouses on rocky coastlines. Henry had read the stories of the voyages of Magellan, Drake, and Marco Polo, but now after witnessing the permanence of the night, he suddenly understood how those ancient mariners navigated their journeys.

Clear, cool night air replaced the afternoon rain and what was a humid uncomfortable day. Everything seemed crystal clean. The tops of the small rolling waves of the sea glimmered, twinkling like the stars, making it difficult to see where the ocean ended, and the horizon began.

And then there was the moon.

It seemed to Henry that he severely underappreciated the orb that only provided a night light back in Philadelphia. He was standing and looking at a full moon that was so bright it cast a shadow on everything that protruded up from planet earth. He could see the moon's craters, its mountains, the shadows, and the length and breadth of what he would now and forever more consider a heavenly body worthy of his admiration.

"Good evening, sir."

Henry turned and saw Alejandro had come up beside him to take a position next to him on the rail.

"Good evening, Alejandro." Henry smiled at the steward. "Wonderful night, tonight. Isn't it?"

"Jes, it is. Since the starboard paddle is down and the breeze is blowing portside, we are smoke free." He grinned a wide and very friendly smile.

"Ah..." Henry paused, he almost had complete understanding of the nautical terms and Alejandro's accent. "I got it. Starboard-right...and port-left...but why is the paddle not working?"

"Jes, Mr. Henry. The starboard paddle engine is down—oil pump is rota...," he looked up to the sky for a translation but gave up, "no work. We have only the port engine."

"Is that a bad thing?"

"Jes and no. Not right now, but we have to run with the timon..." again he searched upward, "how you say...rudder...is guiding the boat but only the port engine is...pushing...and keeping us on course, which slows us down."

"And the other problem?"

Alejandro looked left and right on the empty deck the whispered, "Pirates."

Henry's mouth dropped open. "What?"

Alejandro nodded his head. He was a short man, older, Henry guessed fifties at least, but had the thickest, blackest hair he'd ever seen. "Jes, Mr. Henry, pirates. They come out from the Mexican coast and overtake slower ships and rob," he looked down and whispered again, "sometimes worse."

"And we are now slower."

"Jes, much slower. They didn't bother us before because we... all the steamboats...are the fastest ships at sea, but with only one engine, we are not so fast anymore."

"Can they fix the engine?"

"No. We have to put into port at Cabo San Luca to fix the boat."

Henry tried to remember the map and mentally calculate where they were. After a minute he said, "Am I wrong or aren't we in the Sea of Cortez?"

"Jes, Mr. Henry. We are in the middle of the sea, between Mexico and the Baja."

Henry thought a bit, the distraction taking him away from the night sky. "How long will we be in port?"

Alejandro shrugged. "A week maybe two, but I don't know for sure. You should ask the captain. I think he's in the lounge."

Henry took a breath, sighed, and looked up at the stars again. "It is a beautiful sight."

Alejandro leaned on the rail next to Henry. "Una hermosa vista."

Henry opened the doors from the deck, and a gust of wind followed close behind. Tablecloths raised and a napkin or two took a tour of the cabin floor, but no damage was done. No one seemed to pay any attention, except for a man at the bar, who wore displeasure on his face. He had a drink in his hand that apparently spilled on his suit upon Henry's sudden arrival. The other passengers, some seated at tables, some standing, didn't notice and continued enjoying the night.

Aunt Betty, and his new Uncle Gerald, were seated at a small table close to the bar, near a window. They smiled, waved, and Gerald raised a glass while motioning Henry to join. Gerald also signaled to a waiter to bring another glass.

Henry bent and kissed his aunt on her cheek.

She touched his hand and pointed out the window. "Isn't it wonderful? We've been watching from here, but it must be glorious on the deck."

He nodded and grinned wide as he sat down. "I've seen the stars almost every night since we boarded, but tonight was something really special. I can't even begin to describe."

Gerald poured a glass of red wine for Henry and passed it to him. "Was the smoke a problem tonight? It's why we never go outside. It bothers your aunt's sensitivity."

Betty smiled, waving her hand dismissively.

"No, not tonight." Henry's voice changed and his expression became serious as he began looking around the lounge. "I was told the captain was here. Have you seen him? Did he speak to you about our situation?"

"No dear, we haven't seen him. What situation? What's going on?"

"You know the starboard paddle isn't working."

They both nodded.

The man with the spilt drink at the bar stepped closer and was obviously eavesdropping.

Henry noticed and lowered his voice. "We are running on half power, which means we are running slower and consuming more coal than we should."

"That's all?"

"No." Henry leaned over a bit. "Pirates."

The man at the bar chuckled loudly.

Henry gave the man a look of displeasure.

The man took another step closer.

"We have to put into Cabo San Luca where the engine can be repaired, but...I've been told...that there are pirates that prey on slow or crippled ships. We are in the middle of the Sea of Cortez, and days from a safe port."

Alejandro had come into the lounge and started to approach Henry.

"Who told you about this?"

Henry started to speak but then saw Alejandro. "He did, Alejandro. He is the ship steward, and in a position to know."

The man at the bar laughed out loud. "Boy you are young, easily fooled, and just plain stupid to take the word of a common nigger." He laughed again—his time louder.

Henry looked at Alejandro who'd turned and started to walk away.

"Hey." The drunk pointed the hand with a drink still in it at Alejandro. "You, nigger boy. Whatch' you doin' telling tall tales to this little northern blue belly?"

Henry started to get up.

Gerald put a hand on Henry's shoulder. "He's drunk. Leave it be."

The man had gotten on the boat at Guatemala and told everybody every night he was ticketed to San Diego and couldn't wait to get off this smudge-pot of a boat.

Henry sat back down and saw Alejandro continue his retreat to the exit.

The drunk wasn't letting anything go. He took a few wobbly steps toward their table. "So, you richy rich northern nigger lovers haven't learned anything about the darkies yet. They all lie." He staggered a bit. "Lie all the time." He took another step and turned so the rest of the people in the lounge could hear. He stumbled again, awkwardly recovered, and continued to rant. "Pirates...ha...the niggers are the only pirates. They lie and steal."

He leaned over. "It's their nature. I know all about their kind. You Yankees will regret the day you made war with us."

Henry had his head down.

Betty and Gerald were staring at Henry.

The man weaved again, then said, "Pirates, ha. Boy you believed a dumb stupid nigger."

Henry pushed back the chair, which fell over on its back.

The man was startled at first but then squared up with a grin, clearly judging his opponent was no match.

Gerald started to stand but Betty put her hand on his arm and whispered, "Let him handle this."

Henry walked up close to the man at the bar.

Betty nudged Gerald and said in a low voice, "Look at where Henry is standing. The man won't be able to get off a decent punch."

Gerald looked stunned. "Where did you learn about—?"

"I'm Irish. My family got off a boat, just like Alejandro did."

The man was four inches taller and at least twenty pounds heavier, but Henry stood nose to nose. "I heard about the pirates from a man from Columbia, not Africa. Not that his country of origin makes a damn bit of difference. He's lived here for twenty years. He came to San Francisco after his father, a judge, was murdered and his mother beaten, raped, and killed by a gang whose leader was in his father's court charged with murder. Alejandro is his name, and he's sailed these waters for ten years and knows more about the ocean, boats, the weather...and... pirates than you know about being a human being."

A round of applause arose from the crowd that had gathered to watch the floor show. A ring of people, mostly men, had stepped to the front and seemed ready to act should Henry require assistance.

The man, even as drunk as he was, looked around and realized he was outnumbered. "Yeah, well." He finished his drink with one gulp then returned to the bar and beckoned for a refill.

The bartender, who was polishing a glass, shook his head and refused to serve him another drink.

Henry started back to the table.

Suddenly, the drunk leaped forward with a fist raised high above his head.

Another fist arrived before the man's punch landed.

Alejandro appeared, and as small as he was, broke the man's nose.

It wasn't long before the captain, dressed in a starched white uniform and a black-brimmed white mariner's cap, entered the lounge. He used long steps and had a chin sporting a perfectly trimmed grey beard. Following on his right was an appropriately dressed sailor. The captain smiled and waved a royal hand to an audience who seemed disinterested. He leaned to the bartender and whispered something, which gained an immediate answer, and a finger pointed toward the Cronin table.

A few measured steps brought the captain near to Henry, Betty, and Gerald. He bowed slightly and touched the brim of his cap. "Good evening." He had an English accent. "Sorry to interrupt, but I'm of the understanding you experienced a bit of unpleasantness this evening."

Betty spoke for the table. "We did, but it's over now. Thank you for your concern."

The captain continued anyway. "I thought it was proper to come here personally to express our apology for the conduct of the unruly passenger and—"

She held up a hand. "No need, that was settled."

"Yes indeed, but be assured madam, the steward will be disciplined for his unwarranted participation in the affair."

"Disciplined?" Henry immediately became angry.

The captain stepped back a bit, twirling his mustache nervously. "I believe he shared confidential information about our current course and speed without authorization." He grumbled a bit then added, "I suppose it understandable, after all he's not one of us...is he?"

Betty responded before Henry had a chance. "One of us?" Her voice then raised, "Captain, are we running on one engine?"

"Well...yes."

"Are we currently in the middle of the Sea of Cortez, a hundred miles from land?"

His voice lowered again. "Yes."

"Is there a history of piracy in these waters?"

He didn't answer.

"Are we putting into Cabo for repairs?"

He nodded. The sailor standing next to him backed up and Henry detected a small smile on his face.

"Now, Captain, what part of what we were told wasn't true?"

He grumbled, "Well, actually, nothing."

"Were you going to tell us about the danger we might be in or how long the delay to repair the engine would take?"

Again, he didn't answer.

"You didn't think we were deserving of hearing about our situation?"

"No...I mean yes...of course, ma'am."

"Mrs. Margert Myer." Her face was as stern as Henry's when he had confronted the drunk, only she didn't have to stand in close to the captain.

"Mrs. Myer, obviously, I didn't understand the situation." He tried for a comeback. "May I say it was a great pleasure to officiate at your marriage ceremony."

She stayed on course. "Nothing happens to Alejandro."

He started to speak but then nodded and ducked his chin, defeated.

The sailor's smile was now full on.

The captain mumbled. "Enjoy the rest of your evening."

She wasn't done. "If we hear that there were any repercussions to Alejandro's actions to save my son from an attack by a drunk passenger, you will suffer the consequences. And be aware, we plan on communicating with our knight in shining armor for many years to come."

"Of course, Mrs. Myer." He nodded to Gerald and to Henry then quickly exited.

A second round of polite applause rose up from an admiring audience of passengers.

Gerald looked at Henry then nodded toward Betty. "Must run in the blood."

The wait staff was extraordinarily attentive at breakfast the next morning. Betty, Gerald, and Henry had been seated near a window and none of their cups or glasses went unfilled.

"It seems you two are celebrities." Gerald tipped his coffee cup toward his two companions.

"Much to do about nothing." Betty waved him off.

"Babe, you're just going to have to learn to live with fame."

"Stop it." Her face blushed a little and she changed the subject. "It seems we are going to be delayed for some time. I hope there is a telegraph line at the port so we can let the lawyer know of the delay."

Henry acted confident. "I'm sure there is. Alejandro told me there is an American Naval and Army contingent there to help rid the seas of the pirates, so I think it is reasonable to think there is a telegraph."

Betty seemed to accept the information.

Henry looked down and tapped his fingers on the table.

"What is it dear?"

"I've been reading my mother's journal. Going to California was a hard choice to make and getting there was even harder. Now that we are getting close to San Francisco, I've started thinking about my father. I've never seen him, and the only communication I've had were the letters he wrote to you."

She answered quickly. "You were a baby and the more time that went..." she stopped in mid-sentence.

Henry looked at her. "And?"

There were tears welling up in her eyes. "Henry, I don't know why he never wrote to you. I don't understand it either." She wiped away a tear. "I know how it hurt you, and I won't attempt to tell you what he was thinking. He will have to do that, himself. All I can say is the Amos Cronin I knew was a very good man, and he loved your mother beyond measure."

Henry couldn't speak.

She reached across the table and took both his hands in hers. "We'll be there soon, and I'm certain he will answer all your questions."

"I've waited so long...but now that its close...it seems I'll never get there."

She tapped his hands. "Soon, dear, soon."

CHAPTER 22
FEATHER RIVER VALLEY, CALIFORNIA
OCTOBER 1869

Amos arrived in the center of the tribe's village to the usual and happily anticipated fanfare. The children were laughing and yelling, the older ones allowing the younger ones a position up front, near Puddle. Amos, still astride, gently pulled the reins although it probably wasn't necessary. Puddle was coming to a stop anyway, bowing his head slightly to receive the strokes of the youngens' who still, after all the years, were still fascinated by his size.

Rufus came into camp lagging behind Amos maintaining a bit of distance. Normally, the children would stand in awe of Puddle, then mob Rufus with affection. However, during the past few visits, Amos noticed the dog had been avoiding the children, and spending more time with one person, Aponi, Cholok's daughter.

She was, by any definition beautiful. Her smile, her laugh, her sparkling eyes drew admirers, but her intelligence gained her their respect. Rufus followed behind the caravan of children into camp, staying a good distance behind the handing out of rock candy, and sniffed around until he found Aponi. The big dog

173

became a puppy as soon as she saw him and called his name. Amos thought his behavior comical.

Cholok was sitting in his usual place overlooking the river, on a log cut flat on the top so it served as a bench. He had his head down and his fingertips tapping together, keeping a silent beat, and appeared deep in thought.

"Heskym, you look troubled." Amos approached and sat next to his friend.

"I had another dream, old friend."

"You have many years on me...old friend, so I think it's you that's the ancient one...not me." Amos half grinned.

Cholok did not respond. He looked tired. His face had a dark color, like the grey creeping into his hair. "I had the same dream again."

"Is it your prediction of the future? The Sight you insist you don't have?"

"You don't understand. Sometimes the things I dream about... happen."

Amos now hung his head a bit and tapped his fingers together. The two resembled old men in church.

They sat in silence.

Cholok looked out at the sky. "In my dream, all this changes." He motioned with his hand. "The iron horse comes, and our home is destroyed."

Amos's head snapped around and he stood up. "No. No. No." His voice got louder each time he said the word. "I won't let that happen."

Cholok looked up at his friend. "There's more."

Amos tried to make light. "Are you worried something happens to me? Like suddenly, I stumble on a bear in the forest?" He tried to smile.

"No, that would just mean we would have bear meat in the smokehouse for winter."

Cholok looked down. "Listen to me. I had the dream, and you weren't there to help us."

Amos didn't speak.

Cholok's voice was distant. "Neither was I."

Amos looked at his friend, who did not look back and just stared into the clouds.

A bit more time went by.

Rufus came up beside Amos, and Aponi appeared next to her father.

Cholok looked up at her smile.

"You two need to come to eat. Mother is waiting on you both."

"We'll be along in a moment." Cholok patted her hand.

They watched as the two ran back to the lodge. Rufus was letting her win.

"She's the One, Amos. She will lead for me when I'm gone."

"Not Pala? I thought your son would take your place when it was time."

"No," He shook his head. "He's a hunter, not a leader." Cholok looked at Amos. "And I know what you're thinking—ya-ka-he."

"Why do you always call me 'white man' when you think I won't understand your ways?"

Cholok smiled. "Because you always get mad when I do...and it's fun."

On the way back to the lodge, Cholok explained. "Our tribe is very old and has always been led, not by a man, or a woman. Our leader has always been...just the One."

They ate venison stew, yellow squash, and a nut bread made with the flour Amos had brought with him. The gold mine had made a big difference in the Tribe's existence but nowhere more evident than the meals Zuni prepared. The pots were copper, and the utensils were steel. Knives were wood handled, not bone, and the dishes were ceramic from Mexico. There were good things which made life more tolerable, less stressful, but at no point were those things valued more than the way the Tribe chose to live.

Over the years there were those members who decided to go a different way. They packed, said their goodbyes, and left on a different journey. Some chose the white world, others became more traditional, but their lives changed on their own terms. In all the years that Amos had come to the village, there was almost no crime. On several occasions there were altercations for any number of human reasons, but they were all settled, and the parties moved on with their lives. Cholok led by example but was sometimes called upon to settle a dispute. Cholok was respected, listened to, followed, and in turn he had provided a better life for every tribal member using the resources provided by Amos and their shared secret.

The meal had finished and Cholok left the lodge for a pipe of tobacco. Aponi was sitting by the door stroking Rufus, who was as content as Amos had ever witnessed.

"Thank you, Zuni. The meal was wonderful as usual."

"You are too skinny, Amos. You need a woman to help fatten you for winter."

Pala, who had joined them for dinner, laughed, a laugh that was almost as infectious as his sister's.

"What are you laughing at? You have no mate and are as thin as a sapling." Zuni slapped her son on the back of the head. "And... you should say nothing of ill will to the man who saved you from the river. You're being ungrateful."

He didn't quite laugh again but his chuckle was close. "Mother, that was many years ago and, besides, I gave him the fish."

A small commotion coming from outside gained Aponi's attention and she went outside, closely followed by her sidekick.

Amos sat back and looked studiously at Cholok's son. "Your father tells me you want to continue to be the hunter for the tribe."

Pala rolled his shoulders and shrugged. "Because I am the best one."

"You don't want to walk in your father's footprints?"

Pala rose up and beckoned to Amos to follow him. "Come look."

Together they walked outside and saw Aponi walking toward the river. She was followed by a group of children. Behind the children were a few of their mothers and fathers, and behind them were several of the elders.

"See...they follow her. Wherever she goes, they follow." Pala turned to Amos and shrugged. "She's the One."

Amos saw Cholok sitting on the log, grey smoke rising from his pipe.

Pala took off running after the river group.

Amos took his seat next to his friend.

"Tell me you have protected this valley, Heskym."

Amos took a breath and sighed. "I believe so...I think so."

"You have doubts." Cholok's voice reflected his concern.

"If something happens to me, you are protected." Amos tried to sound confident.

There was an awkward silence.

"And if something happens to me?"

Amos looked at his friend. "I didn't prepare for that, but don't worry I know how to fix that. I'll take care of it soon."

Cholok looked at his friend through another puff of smoke. "Amos, I said there was more of my dream. The Thunderbird, the enemy, was not clear to me."

Amos looked at his friend, puzzled.

"Maybe it's not the railroad that takes the Valley from us, maybe it the gold."

The two looked out over the river.

"It's not the railroad...but we have to bury our secret...forever."

Cholok didn't hesitate. "It's time."

CHAPTER 23
CARVERSVILLE, CALIFORNIA
OCTOBER 1869

Amos was staring at the grandfather's clock again. It was the most interesting part of his visits to his lawyer's office, and the only thing he looked forward to in the otherwise painful necessity. He disliked Mr. Clark, Esq., the attorney, but had to deal with him. He tolerated Margaret Dewitt, the secretary, who displayed disapproval of his woodsy appearance and sparse hygiene. However, he really despised the lawyer's wife, Amelia. Her hospitality was a lure, and her sincerity dishonest. She was not to be trusted. Amos thought of her as a viper hiding under a rock. She was a snake—a diamondback, short the rattle.

Rough fingers stroked the polished sculptured wood. Each engraving had a match on the opposite side of the clock, perfectly proportioned and equally as detailed. His eyes went to the clock face and the small key slot that opened a door exposing its innards.

"Can I open this?" His back was to Miss DeWitt and his fingers on the tiny key in the lock.

"Absolutely not." She started to rise from her seat behind her desk. "That is delicate and fragile."

"Thank you." He paid no attention and opened the door.

The sound of the wheels turning intensified. The loudest were the gears holding the two chains that provided the gravity which spun all the gears that incrementally kept time. He'd never seen a clock's inner workings before, and the multitude of moving parts took him by surprise. After only a second or two he found himself wishing he could meet the person who made the fine instrument. About a minute after that, he began thinking of how this gadget reminded him of Cholok's people. Every piece was unique; different sizes, and purpose, some large and powerful like the weights on the chain, some tiny like the delicate hands of the clock, and like the tribe, each part dependent on the other and together—perfect.

"I would appreciate it if you would stop what you're doing."

Amos turned and found Miss DeWitt, arms crossed and an angry puss on her face, staring at him.

She immediately took a half step back, because his angry face was way better than hers.

"Amos." Bogart Simpson Clark, Esquire, rescued her from an imminent demise. "So good to see you."

The lawyer turned to Miss DeWitt. "Why don't you get coffee and bring it to my office?"

She pointed to the clock with outrage still on her face but, before she could say anything, Clark shoulder-guided Amos towards his open door.

The office was as Amos remembered, dreary and musty. The sun was coming through the windows behind the desk and speckles of dust floated in the glare.

Amos cut off the niceties. "I want to change my will."

"Of course. No problem. Whatever you need." The lawyer pulled a file drawer out from the desk and began rummaging.

Amos noticed, for the first time, how the desk out proportioned the lawyer. The piece of furniture looked old and experienced, large and purposeful.

Suddenly, the door opened. "I have coffee and some fresh baked cookies from the café." Amelia entered with a broad smile and a breezy gait.

Amos grimaced as he had hoped for a short, painless visit but most importantly to avoid contact with the Mrs. His face registered his disappointment.

"Just black as I recall." With a little finger extended, Amelia poured from a china pot into a ceramic cup on a matching ceramic tray.

Amos left the cup untouched.

"Milk for me, dear." Clark sat forward in his chair.

Amelia, paying no attention to her husband's request, poured coffee for herself, and sat down holding the cup and saucer on her lap. "What can we do for you today, Amos?" She smiled. "May I call you Amos...of course I can...how silly of me. We are fast friends aren't we Amos?"

"No, we are not friends. I have business with your husband."

His rebuke seemed to have little effect. She chuckled, "Oh Amos, you are such a scallywag."

"Madam, I have business with your husband."

She blinked, but remained seated, taking a sip of coffee.

Amos lowered his voice. "Private business."

That one stung and her cup rattled.

"Amelia, dear heart, would you be so kind to give Mr. Cronin and I a moment?"

She slowly placed the cup back on the tray, brushed her skirt, tucked her handkerchief in her sleeve, and stood. She lifted her chin and slowly strolled to the door, closing it behind her.

"You'll have to excuse my wife, Amos, she's been having a difficult time with some of the women in town which has made her a bit snippy."

"It's probably because she's a—"

"You said you wanted to change your will. I have it right here." He hastily took a document from a file and laid it on the desk. "What would you like to change?"

"Not a change but an addition...a second beneficiary."

The lawyer's mouth puckered as he picked up a pen. "To your estate?"

"No, I'm adding a beneficiary to the land asset on the Feather River. The parcel that I willed to Cholok, the tribal chief of the Maidu Tribe that occupies the 30,000 acres I own on the Feather River."

Clark pondered while looking down, holding the pen, but not writing. "Who are you adding? You said a secondary beneficiary, yes?"

"Aponi, Cholok's daughter. She gets the property if Cholok is not alive to inherit the land."

The lawyer still didn't write anything down.

Seeing that the lawyer seemed frozen, Amos leaned forward. "Do you not understand?"

"No, no, I understand. If the tribal chief precedes your demise, his daughter, Aponi, inherits the land you intended for her father."

"Right."

The lawyer began to write.

Amos sat quiet.

The lawyer looked up. "Amos, if you want to go get something to eat at the café, I'll have the document changed and ready to sign by the time you finish lunch."

Amos nodded and started to leave, but when he opened the door, he startled Amelia who was obviously eavesdropping.

Amos walked past her and stopped at the clock.

"I have noticed you have a special interest in our clock. What do you find so fascinating, Amos?" Her voice was as pleasant as it always was.

He turned and stared at her for a long moment. "Just taking a last look."

Her name was Gloria, and it was appropriate. In all the years that Amos had frequented the café, its owner and chef, Gloria, had never been in a bad mood. She was as predictable as a sunrise, bright, sunny, and always welcoming.

"Amos Cronin, you old reprobate, get yourself in here. I just took a cherry pie out of the oven, but you can't have it until you finish a steak." She laughed a laugh that would make the devil convert.

"Like usual, Glo."

"You bet, Amos. And...," she looked behind the big man in the doorway, "where's your little buddy?"

He looked out the window. Rufus usually was first in the door when Amos came in for a meal, but at the moment he was nowhere to be seen. "Good question. He must be getting into some trouble somewhere."

Amos noticed several townspeople sitting at other tables. He recognized some but had trouble remembering their names, so he just nodded politely, and they nodded back.

Martha Goodman came through the door followed by Rufus who bolted past her and headed straight for the kitchen.

A muted voice from Gloria was heard. "There you are."

Mrs. Goodman approached, hands folded and a look of relief on her face. "Amos. I'm so glad to see you. We've been worried."

Howard Goodman rushed in just then and made his way to his wife's side.

"Sit, please. Have lunch with me." Amos beckoned to chairs at the table.

"Thank you." Howard pulled a chair out for his wife and then sat. "There has been trouble in town, and you haven't been around for a while, so..."

Mrs. Goodman did something very unusual for her. She reached across the table and put her hand on his. "Amos, we were so worried."

Gloria came back into the dining room with a tray of coffee and glasses of water for three. "Saw you come in. Do you want lunch as well, my dears?"

"No. No thank you. We can't stay. We left the store open."

Gloria registered that privacy was warranted and hurried off, saying as she walked away, "Amos, I'll feed your monster back in the kitchen."

"What's wrong?" Amos glanced at both his friends.

Howard looked at his wife then at Amos. "The man you saved from freezing to death last winter is still in town. There are a lot of rumors going around about him and his two friends." He shot a look out the window then whispered. "They are bad men...and...I think they are out to get you."

Amos didn't register surprise, because he wasn't. "What makes you think that?"

Mrs. Goodman acted as if she were committing a sin. She

lowered her head before she confessed her sin of spying. "I overheard the skinny one, I think his name is Sid, talking to Mr. Cudworth's man, Strong. I didn't hear everything, but I heard Cudworths man say...you have to take care of Cronin by the end of the month."

Howard looked out the window again.

Amos patted her hand and looked at Howard. "You are good people and, believe me when I tell you, don't worry about these men."

She clinched her fingers tightly on Amos's. "But Cudworth is very powerful."

"He is, and he's doing this because he wants something I have that he's never going to get."

He patted her hand again.

She rose up slowly. "Please be careful, Amos."

As Howard stood, Rufus bolted from the kitchen and mauled the two shop owners with a wet tongue and smelly fur.

They laughed. The other townspeople also laughed.

Gloria arrived with a plate containing a steak that lapped over the sides and pointed to the dog. "Don't give this one any. He ate one as big as this in record time."

Amos looked at Howard and took a paper from his pocket. "Can you get these things together for me before I leave?"

"Of course, I'll have them loaded into your wagon before you finish your lunch. It will be ready when you are."

Amos then did something very unusual. He stood, took Mrs. Goodman by both shoulders, and kissed her cheek. He then shook Howard's hand. "Thank you and don't worry."

She smiled, somewhat reassured, and together the shopkeepers left, hand-in-hand.

Rufus sat near his chair apparently waiting for dinner plate fallout. "You had yours. Go on, find a place to lay down."

Instead, the dog bolted out the door and disappeared, looking as usual, for some mischief.

He started back to the cabin, bumping along the road, Rufus beside him, the Winchester tucked at his side. He wasn't expecting trouble yet. It was coming, but not here and not now. However, just in case, he had levered a shell into the rifle's chamber before they left town. It wasn't safe, he always traveled with an empty chamber, but he was being cautious and better to be ready than dead.

The wagon hit a big hole that jolted Amos, causing him to almost lose the reins. He winced and rubbed his back with a free hand, then looked around to the load of supplies. He wondered exactly how big a hole he'd have to hit in order for the dynamite to go off, but then that was a question with an answer learned only once.

Rufus had bounced off the seat and was staring at Amos.

"Don't look at me like that. I didn't make the hole in the road."

Rufus continued to stare.

"You can always walk home, you know," Amos grunted.

Rufus climbed back up on the seat.

Amos thought about what needed to happen. He'd given his plan a lot of thought and convinced himself it was the right thing to do.

He shook his head, trying to concentrate on something else.

Henry will be here soon, and I'll make it right.

The sun had dipped behind the mountaintop and, without the sun, it became much colder. He reached under the seat and yanked his coat free, putting on one sleeve at a time. He thought about the boy, wondering what he looked like, hoping he reminded him of Rose. She'd been gone for many years, but in all that time he had always been able to see her when he closed his eyes.

They were one with the decisions they made. Coming west, choosing Feather River to settle, and deciding it was best for her to go back to Philadelphia to have the baby. They decided together the mountain wouldn't be a good place for a while, but she could return after two or three years and together they would make Feather River their paradise.

I'll make it right. I have to make it right.

For her.

CHAPTER 24

CARVERSVILLE, CALIFORNIA
OCTOBER 1869

Cudworth had pushed the chair back and was standing hunched over, with both hands flat on his desk. In front of him was a rectangular piece of yellow paper. It bore a threat to everything he owned.

WESTERN UNION
TELEGRAM

BAO 535 CTD073 1:05 PM OCT 12,1869
CT WWY014 WW13 OCCIDENTAL HOTEL, SAN
FRANSCISCO, CALIFORNIA
REGINALD CUDWORTH. CARVERSVILLE CALIFORNIA.
WESTERN RAILROAD CONSTRUCTION ON SCHEDULE
STOP EASTERN RAILROADCONSTRUCTION FROM SAN
FRANSCISCO BEGAN TODAY STOP FEATHER RIVER ROUTE
MUST BE ESTABLISHED AS CONNECTION ROUTE BY 1
JANUARY OR ALTERNATE ROUTE WILL BE SELECTED STOP

WILLIAM RALSTON PRESIDENT CENTRAL PACIFIC RAILROAD

The telegram had been in the center of the desk since it arrived yesterday. He hadn't slept but a moment or two since it was received. They had given a date and there wasn't any more room for clever responses nor delaying tactics. The clock was counting down and he was no longer in control.

Ralston...you bastard.

Cudworth had set a plan in motion to solve this problem, but it was dragging on and on without resolve, and now everything he had, everything he worked for, was in the hands of someone whose whereabouts was unknown. Every property he owned, every dollar he had, every stick of furniture in his house were in the hands of a no-account thief, and murderer.

He shook his head, hard, driving out the demons of defeat, and slapped the desk. "Enough."

He stood up, his back stiff and aching, and shouted. "Xing, come in here."

The door opened quickly, and the small Chinese servant shuffled into the office. Head bowed; she approached the desk but did not speak.

"Get coffee, run a bath, get me fresh clothes. White shirt. Light grey suit. Black shoes. Grey tie. Then find Strong and tell him I want him here, now."

She nodded and, without expression, and backed up four steps before turning to leave.

Cudworth turned and faced the window, separated the tightly drawn curtains, and looked out to the center of Carversville.

"It needs to happen...now."

Wesley Strong was at the bar in the Saloon and drinking coffee from a ceramic mug. Sid Stull was hours late and Strong's anger was building with every passing minute.

"You want something to eat with that?" The bartender was wiping the bar top a few stools away. There wasn't anyone else in the saloon. It was early afternoon, and serious drinking didn't begin until dusk started to settle on the horizon. If someone wanted food, they ate at Gloria's café. If they wanted whiskey or beer, they came to the Waycross Saloon, an establishment that got its name because it was on the way across California for settlers traveling from Virginia City to San Francisco.

"No." Strong barked quickly, then drew in a breath and added, "thanks," in a better tone.

"You waiting for someone, huh?"

"Yep."

The wiping continued. The spot on the bar top was getting very clean. "Who you waiting for?"

"Stull...Sid Stull."

The bartender scoffed and started to walk away.

Strong's head popped up, the reaction gaining his immediate attention. "Hey, don't walk away. Do you know something about Stull?"

The bartender started cleaning another spot that didn't need cleaning. "Might."

Strong was not in the mood to play. He pushed off his stool. He walked to where the barman was working and slapped the bar with his oversized hand. "Where is he?"

The bartender looked up but was unimpressed. "Twenty bucks."

Strong's fist rolled up.

The bartender didn't flinch.

It was a standoff. Silence ensued and neither man budged.

Strong broke the stalemate. "You have five seconds to tell me what you know, or I'll beat you like you've never been beat before." Strong said the entire sentence slowly, with one breath, and through closed teeth.

The bartender appeared completely unfazed. He stopped polishing and leaned across the bar. "You think this is my first rodeo, bub? Listen pal, I've been threatened by way bigger men than yo—"

Strong's fist hit him between the middle of his forehead and the bridge of his nose. The flat part of his skull made a cracking sound. Blood didn't immediately start flowing, but when it did it was a real gusher.

To his credit, the bartender didn't go down. He remained standing, both feet planted, right there in place. Strong was a little bit impressed. So impressed in fact that he didn't hit him again. Instead, he grabbed the polishing towel, leaned over the bar, and soaked it in a tub of cold water. Strong held it out. "Here."

The bartender was woozy and a little wobbly but held onto the bar with his free hand and reached out to take the towel.

"Where is Stull?" Strong said it calmly.

"He went to Coloma." The bartender held the rag to his nose.

"Where?"

"It's a small town between San Francisco and here, maybe thirty miles."

Strong looked puzzled but continued calmly asking questions. "Do you know why he went there?"

The bartender took the rag away and looked at the blood. He bent over and grabbed a fresh towel. When he turned to Strong, he had a look of defiance in his eye.

Strong waved a cautionary finger. "Don't even think about it."

The bartender put the icy rag back on his head and capitulated. "Stull and his two buddies were sittin' right here a couple of nights ago. I heard Stull tell them he knew a place where they could get a dog."

"A what?" Strong was taken aback and showed it.

"A dog...a fighting dog. They have dog fights in Coloma, you know, where they bet on which dog wins a fight. They have a ring and everything."

"Dog fights." Strong stepped back from the bar, head down, thinking. It didn't take long before he understood.

Strong looked up at the barman who still had one hand on the bar and the other on his nose. The blood had stopped, but both eyes had already started to blacken—they'd be deep purple by morning.

Strong took two gold pieces from his pocket and put them on the bar. He slid the coins across the wood but kept his hand on top of them. "How long ago did he leave?"

"They...left the next morning, so it's been," he paused a second, "two days. I heard him say he'd be back today because he had to meet someone." The bartender's light suddenly went on. "Oh, that was you—why you were here waiting."

"No." Strong took another gold piece from his pocket. "I wasn't waiting for anybody."

The bartender's head tilted.

Strong held out the gold piece. "I was never here, and I never asked about Sid Stull."

The bartender said, "Right, been quiet all day."

Strong flipped the coin in the air. It hit the bar and rolled straight to the barman.

Cudworth had cleaned up and was almost presentable by the time Strong arrived at his office door. He'd washed, shaved, brushed his hair, and put on the grey suit he'd asked for. The clothes were fresh and clean, and his shoes were shined, but there wasn't anything he could do about looking like he'd been through a washer's wringer. Dark bags of skin hung down under red, swollen eyes. His cheeks were drawn, and as white as he was. If he were lying flat, it might be assumed he'd passed away.

Strong was in the office waiting when Cudworth came in. "I have news."

"Better be good." Cudworth walked past Strong without looking at him.

"Stull is in Coloma. He's getting a dog."

Cudworth instantly froze, stunned by something that made no sense. "A what?"

Strong smiled a little at his boss's discomfort and went on. "He went to where they have dog fights."

"Why?" Cudworth recovered and sat down behind his desk.

Strong did something he had never done before. He sat down and crossed his legs.

Cudworth didn't react to the disrespect of an employee sitting without permission. Instead, he sat and waited for an answer.

"The animal that Cronin has following him around is a legend around here. I'm sure you've heard the stories?"

Cudworth didn't speak and remained stone-faced.

"Well, his dog, or as legend has it, his wolf, is a force that Stull obviously thinks he has to deal with before he can get to the old man. Frankly, I might not disagree with that point."

Again, there was no reaction from Cudworth.

"The dog is always by Cronin's side and is an alarm that would prevent Stull from getting close. So, I assume Stull thinks he needs to separate them, kill the dog, then he can kill Cronin."

Cudworth scoffed and spit out, "Shoot it."

Strong shook his head.

Cudworth broke. His voice rose and he spoke quickly. "Why all this planning and plotting? You go get a gun, ride out there, and shoot this bastard. Do you know how many times I've tried to buy that property from him, and he wouldn't even talk to me?" He slapped the desk. "I want him dead."

"Property? What property?"

Cudworth recognized his emotional mistake. "Not your business."

Strong sat without comment, making Cudworth nervously twitch.

A long minute went by.

The dates on the telegram, still in front of his eyes, loomed over him like a heavy, unbearable weight. "I have a partnership with Central Pacific Railroad that is predicated on me delivering a portion of land along the Feather River that Amos Cronin has purchased from the government. I've tried four times to buy it. The last time I offered, through that lawyer, Clark, five times what he paid for it. The lawyer said Cronin refused the offer and said he wouldn't sell, not ever."

Cudworth regained composure and went back to being stalwart. "I have purchased miles and miles of property coming up from San Francisco, but what Cronin owns is key to connecting the western and eastern railroad. If I don't get the Feather River property, everything I already bought will be worthless." He leaned over the desk. "I must have it —at any cost."

Strong stood up and started walking around the office. "And... if Stull kills him then you are above suspicion."

Cudworth didn't speak.

"Stull will probably get it done. But he'll be seen or steal something that connects him to the murder. In any case, whatever he does, nothing comes back to you."

Cudworth nodded imperceptibly.

Strong scratched his chin. "But how do you get the property if it's willed to his—"

Cudworth held up his hand and shook his head. "Not his son. He left everything else to him but not the property I want."

Strong took a second. "How do you know that?"

Cudworth didn't answer.

Strong wobbled his head but continued. "So, if Cronin...goes away, how do you get the ground?"

"When he dies the property goes to an Indian. A chief or something. That won't be a problem."

"But what if—".

Cudworth cut him off, stuck up a hand, and added a menacing stare. "I said, it's not your concern."

Strong shrugged and grinned. He pushed back in the chair and threw a leg over the arm. "So, Amos bites the dust, you somehow get the property, and then you go choo-choo all the way to the bank."

Cudworth was about to get angry with Strong's familiarity but was interrupted by a light knocking on the door. "Come in."

Xing lightly shuffled into the office. "Mrs. Clark is here to see you, sir."

"What does that whore want?" Cudworth grumbled. "Okay, send her in."

Strong started to leave.

Cudworth held up his hand. "No. No, you stay."

Amelia Clark floated in. She wore a dress with a bilious skirt and a frilly top that had lace around a buttoned bodice which was not fully fastened. Cudworth knew her smile was as disingenuous as her intentions.

With eyes directed to Cudworth and ignoring Strong she offered pleasantries. "Good afternoon, gentlemen. Such a beautiful day."

"I hadn't noticed." Cudworth replied quickly. "What brings you here?"

She peeked at Strong then at Cudworth. "I think what I have to tell you might be something better said in private."

Cudworth judged the moment then nodded to Strong. "Stay close. I want to finish our conversation."

When alone, the lawyer's wife became coy and familiar. "Reggie—"

"Don't do that." Cudworth barked rudely.

She continued seemingly unaffected. "I have information that you might find very valuable."

"And what would that be?"

She looked down at her skirt and brushed off imaginary dirt.

"How much?" He said matter-of-factly.

She tried to act offended. "Why, Mr. Cudworth, what I possess comes at a price for which I require only reimbursement."

He repeated, "How much?"

"Why—"

"Tell me or leave."

She dropped all pretenses. "Five hundred, cash, right now." She paused a second then whispered. "Between you and me. My husband is not to know."

"I paid for this information already."

She waved a naked finger protruding from her fashionable glovelet at him. "This is new," then repeated, "five hundred."

Cudworth, feeling rage rising, very reluctantly nodded. "If it has value."

"Oh...it does," she replied confidently.

"Okay, what is it?" His frustration was building.

"Amos Cronin changed his will."

Cudworth leaned forward, a red tint of color rushing to his cheeks. "And?"

She tried again to brush away the imaginary dirt, letting the suspense build.

Cudworth ducked his head, then stood, and walked to a safe on a far wall. With his back to the lawyer's wife, he turned a dial and withdrew a sleeve of paper money. He marched to where she sat and tossed it, unceremoniously, into her lap.

She greedily fingered the stack of bills, then gave Cudworth a report like she was testifying in court. "The Feather River property was in Amos Cronin's will. The beneficiary, unlike the other property he owns, as you already know, is not his son. And by the way, the son Henry, is on his way here and should arrive this week, or next at the latest. There was a mechanical issue on the boat."

Cudworth sat on the edge of the desk, impatiently waiting.

She continued with the court-like testimony. "The change Cronin made was: in the event of his death, he bequeathed the Feather River property to Cholok, leader of the Maidu Tribe."

"What is this? I paid for this already."

"That isn't the change and, for your information, Cholok is not a chief. He has no official position. The tribe just follows him —an elder or some such nonsense."

Cudworth sighed in frustration, "Then what the hell is the change, Amelia?"

She blushed a little and replied coyly. "You've never used my name before, Reggie."

He leaned forward and shouted. "The point."

Shocked, she spoke rapidly. "He added a second beneficiary, his daughter."

Cudworth leaned back. "Cronin has a daughter?"

"No, the Indian's daughter, Aponi. If this Cholok person dies, the property goes to Aponi."

Cudworth instantly rose, walked to the window, and looked out at the bright sunshine. With his back turned, he said, "Goodbye Amelia."

She rose slowly, holding the sleeve of money in both hands. "This stays between us, Reggie? My husband won't ever find out?"

"Please leave."

When the door closed, he turned around, put his hands on his desk and reread the telegram. A smile came across his face.

Now, I've got Feather River, and soon I'll ruin you...Mr. William Ralston.

CHAPTER 25
FEATHER RIVER VALLEY, CALIFORNIA
OCTOBER 1869

Rufus seemed unusually distracted. He was up on the woodpile. There was a fire going, warming the cool fall night air after a day of chasing everything chaseable—all the components for a restful sleep. However, he was sitting up not laying down.

"What's wrong with you?" Amos was concentrating on the task of letter writing but now irritated, looked up from the table. Rufus's panting had disrupted his concentration. "You wanna' go out?"

Rufus didn't move, just stared down at him.

"No? Then lie down and go to sleep. That constant slobbering is bothering me."

Rufus inched his legs forward and lay down, with his head on his paws.

The letter Amos was writing wasn't long because he didn't have the words to put to paper, but he managed some and hoped it was enough. He carefully folded three pages and slid them into an envelope. Using a candle, he dripped hot wax on the back, preventing tampering. The envelope matched the writing paper he'd gotten from the Goodman's store on his last trip into town. It was white and fancy and he handled it carefully. He already had a quill pen and black ink which he used to write lists for the general store, but he had little use for penmanship or composition otherwise. To his surprise, he found that his schooling hadn't totally eluded him, and his letter seemed, at least to him, readable.

He flipped the envelope over and used both hands to square it on the table. He took the pen, dipped in, then held it for a minute thinking about what to write on the front. Without resolve, and a little frustrated, he put the pen down and walked to the fireplace. With both hands on the mantel and the heat warming his face, he closed his eyes and thought of his wife.

Rosey, what do I call him? Henry? Son?

Rufus, for some unknown reason, chose that moment to jump down from the log pile and run to the door.

Amos walked over and opened it, but Rufus didn't run outside. He just stood there looking hard into the night.

Amos then looked too. "What is it? It can't be bad cause you'd be running by now."

Rufus just sat—for a full minute.

Amos, becoming concerned, turned and took the Winchester down from the gun rack. When he looked back to the door, Rufus was gone.

Amos stepped out onto the porch, moving out of the light, and looked for movement.

The night was moonless and only allowed Amos to see halfway across the pasture.

He heard a noise and swung the rifle to his right. Cholok had stepped up on the porch and was standing a few feet away. "Damn, I wish you'd stop doing that."

Rufus came out of the dark and bolted past Amos, running back into the cabin.

"You're getting old, Heskym."

"Not that old. I didn't shoot you, did I?"

They went inside, closing the door behind them and shutting out the world.

"What brings you here at this hour? It's night, the trail back will be hard to follow with no moon in the sky." Amos walked to the kitchen and took two cups down from the cupboard.

Cholok didn't speak at first. He moved to the table and sat down, moving the pen, the bottle of ink, and the unaddressed envelope to the side.

Amos sat down and put a cup of tea in front of his old friend.

Cholok gripped the cup with both hands and after a moment quietly said, "I heard the coyote."

Amos knew what he meant but hesitated to recognize it. "I hear coyotes almost every night."

"You know what I mean, Amos."

"This must be serious. You haven't called me Amos since Rufus was a pup."

"I had the coyote dream again. There is a big change coming. The coyote has foretold it."

Amos didn't respond at first. He sipped his tea. "I think you are right this time. I think we have to destroy the mine, or it will destroy everything."

Cholok nodded without looking up.

Amos got up and walked to the bookshelf. He took a box back to the table, removed the lid, and took out a small rock. "Remember this? This is the nugget I picked up when you took me to the mine for the first time, so many years ago."

He handed it to Cholok who rolled it around in his fingers. "And now, we need what we have and have all that we need."

"All we will ever need."

Cholok nodded again. "Our place is secure because of a yellow rock that means nothing. It is not food. It is not water or crops. It provides no warmth in the winter, or shelter from the rain. It has no purpose."

"It bought your tribe's freedom."

"Indeed, it did. This yellow rock, which is insignificant to everything else in nature, bought our home. It bought our land from people who value something that has no value."

"Never really thought of it like that."

"Gold is a value to man because men say it is."

"So...now...we need what we have and have all that we need. It is enough and time to stop."

Cholok grinned and shook a finger at him. "So, you don't object? Which means in your white man way you heard the coyote as well."

Amos didn't respond because what he was feeling was something different than just closing the mine. He changed the subject. "Something has been bothering me for years. You grew up speaking your language, learned English when you were a kid at boarding school. Then, you escaped and went back to your family. All of that happened when you were just a kid, and you've lived in the mountains ever since. So, my question is...how come you speak so good?"

He corrected, "Speak so well."

"Exactly."

Cholok gripped the teacup again. "I didn't exactly run away from the boarding school. When I was fourteen, they sent me to Kings College in Canada. They thought I was smart, and they were doing 'God's work' by sending me to university where I would learn more than I would have in boarding school. I stayed two years before escaping to go home."

"I have to ask, why did you come back? It sounds like you had a real opportunity there."

Cholok pondered his answer. "The Civil War freed the slaves?"

"Yes."

"And now they are free and looked on as equals?"

"Well, no." Amos shook his head. "Even worse in some places, and definitely not equal."

"But someday maybe, yes?"

"Maybe."

"Well, Indians were never emancipated by a President. No one fought a war for our rights. We still are wards of the government and no matter what we accomplish, or how much money we make, or education we achieve, we are still not equal. And...when anything valuable is discovered on the property that was taken from us then given back as a reservation, we are moved to some other more worthless, and less inhabitable, part of the world."

"So, you've learned your lesson then, and now you a just good Injun." Amos couldn't hold the face long enough and laughed.

"I am now." Cholok smiled. "Since we...you...used that meaningless yellow rock to give us a place to raise our children and live our lives in peace."

"I'd offer you a drink of whisky to celebrate but I know how you Injuns are around alcohol."

Suddenly, Rufus barked once and both men instantly went silent.

Amos blew the lanterns out and the only light in the cabin was the fireplace.

Rufus had moved to the door and was sniffing the gap at the bottom.

Amos took the Winchester and handed Cholok the double-barreled shotgun.

Cholok stood behind Amos and both men followed Rufus out when Amos opened the door.

Visibility wasn't good.

Amos whispered, "Get to the barn. We'll get up in the loft and have the high ground."

They started across, still single file.

Rufus ran in between, tripped them, and they fell on the ground in a heap.

The dog sat down and looked at the two old men sprawled out on the dirt. He barked and ran back into the cabin.

"Damn dog." Amos stood up and brushed himself off.

"When you gotta go, you gotta go." Cholok followed behind his friend back to the cabin.

When they got inside, they saw Rufus had gone back to his outpost and was pawing at his blanket preparing for sleep.

Cholok walked back to the table and sat down.

"You want more tea?"

"No. I'm going to start back." Cholok pointed to the door.

"I need a favor."

Cholok looked up.

"Come with me tomorrow to the mine and help me prepare."

"Are you sure about this?"

Amos nodded. "What I know is I have something that means nothing to nature but has value to men who value nothing."

Cholok grinned. "I'm quotable." He paused a second. "Amos, you haven't answered me. Why now?"

Amos scratched his beard. "I hear things in town...little things...like noises in the woods we hear and know something isn't right. Cudworth has made it clear he wants Feather River real bad. The stranger that showed up here a while back is still hangin' around in town. People are afraid of both of them."

Cholok remained silent.

"We have achieved what we set out to do. We have harvested enough for a generation. It's enough. Will you help me?"

"Of course."

Amos took two blankets down from a shelf. He walked over to a long, wide bench on the far wall and stacked them one on top of each other. "You can bed down here. We'll start first thing in the morning."

"Zuni will worry."

"She'll think you met up with a bear on the trail," Amos grinned, "but then there will be—."

"Meat in the smokehouse for winter." Cholok pointed a finger at his friend. "That joke is getting old."

"Not as old as you, my friend."

"As us both."

CHAPTER 26
FEATHER RIVER VALLEY, CALIFORNIA
OCTOBER 1869

The coyote moved slowly, head down, ears up. He had his nose elevated slightly above his frame. He was crouched over, muscles rippling with tension. He wasn't on the hunt; he was being hunted. The coyote felt the presence of danger. He was a master of stalking a prey and not used to being one. His head turned right, froze, turned slightly left, and froze again. His eyes peered between the branches and twigs, looking not for a prey, but for his predator.

The other mountain killer, the wolf, traveled in packs. Ten or twelve hunting together all moving a victim into a vulnerable position where it would be outnumbered and overpowered. This coyote, like all of the species, hunted, traveled, lived, in isolation. Unless reproduction was involved, he preferred a solitary existence. It had its benefits, there was no sharing of kills, and no fighting for leadership of a pack. So, his survival nemeses were limited to the lack of game, a serious injury, or being in the wrong place at the wrong time.

His careful survey of his surroundings revealed no danger. He saw nothing, smelled nothing, heard nothing.

Suddenly, a movement. A long-eared meal appeared from a burrow that he'd overlooked. His attention was no longer avoiding a predator he couldn't see, but to conceal his approach from his dinner.

The rabbit wouldn't be much of a challenge. It twittered its nose while chomping down a clump of wheatgrass that hadn't yet fallen victim to winter's frost. It would be right to assume the rabbit didn't hear the coyote's slow, calculated approach. The furry long-eared dinner plate hadn't moved except to get a better bite of grass which would turn out to be his last. The coyote was fast, at least faster than this rabbit reacted.

The coyote nudged the fur on the ground. It didn't move. He sat on his haunches, back straight, head raised, nose reaching up into the air about to announce his success. What he was about to do was his one mistake, bragging. It was a hereditary trait. Something he couldn't control. A natural instinct. Had he been more alert he might have sensed the danger an instant before the bullet hit his head.

Now the rabbit and the coyote were both fur on the ground.

Sid Stull made a lot of noise coming through the brush. He didn't have to struggle to be quiet any longer. His prey was down, and he was ready to set the trap.

Sid thought a lot about how to accomplish his task, and had spent many restless nights trying to figure out a way to separate the dog from the Old Man. It took a while, certainly longer than Strong and Cudworth wanted, but he had learned a valuable lesson from his first encounter with Amos Cronin and the dog. There were obstacles to overcome.

He devised several plans only to discard them when he found an unsolvable problem with a scheme. But, one night it came to him. He finally asked himself the right question. What was the dog's number one bad habit? When he figured that out, the plan came together quickly.

It was night and there was a campfire—sort of. Half of it was burning pretty well, the other half had toppled over, tossing a burst of embers into the air. Sid cursed but rose up and pushed the fallen logs back into the fire. Fortunately, the coffeepot remained intact.

He took the opportunity to stretch his back. He'd been crouched over, skinning the coyote. Its hide was all he needed. When he finished, he hung the skin over a tree branch, the night air seasoning its aroma for maximum impact. The carcass would just slow them down, and his horse wouldn't like a dead coyote draped over its backside. He wiped the blood off the knife onto his pant leg, then plopped down on a log by the fire. He hated making camp under the stars, but before they rode out of Carversville, he'd made sure there were provisions just in case. Bedding down for the night in the mountains was wildly uncomfortable, and the food was always undercooked or burnt. But camping out seemed preferable after spending all day on a long hunt, tracking and killing the elusive bait. The sole advantage to sleeping on a rocky bed was they were closer to Cronin's cabin.

Soapy Smith complained loudly that Bite burnt the bacon and beans Sid brought for dinner. The two continued to argue. Their pushing and yelling intensified as they finished off a bottle of whiskey. Finally, Sid's two accomplices went to sleep with their heads on their saddles and trail blankets, keeping them warm. It was peaceful for the first time. The two fought over everything, and it was all Sid could do to keep from shooting one or both just to shut them up.

Sid drug his saddle closer to the fire, threw another log on the blaze, and settled in.

Tomorrow is it.

Sid looked up at the stars lighting the night sky framed by the tops of tall evergreens. All he wanted, at that moment, was to never, ever have to sleep under the cold blackness of the night again.

Light had just begun displacing the night and was greeting the three thieves with cold air and thick smoke from a dying fire. Bite gathered up some kindling to restart the flame while Soapy filled the coffeepot with canteen water. It was the brief moment in time when it was too early for either one of the two accomplices to talk.

"There's no time for coffee. We need to move." Sid had his saddle in his hand and was dragging it to where the horses and the fighting dog were tied.

"I ain't a going nowhere, nohow, without a coffee." Soapy put the full pot on a flat rock near the fire.

Sid stopped for a moment, contemplating the argument that would follow a no-coffee decision. "All right then but make it fast."

Soapy responded without looking up. "Right, I'll tell the water to hurry up and boil."

Bite snickered as usual.

Sid spread his feet, put his hands on his hips, and tried to act in charge. "You know we need to be in place before they leave the cabin." He walked to where Bite was sitting and Soapy was crouched then picked up a stick.

"You'll need a bigger stick than that, if'n you comin' after me." Soapy calmly adjusted the pot so it wouldn't fall over.

Sid, undaunted, used the end of the stick to draw a box in the dirt. "Let's do this again."

"Christ almighty, this is the tenth time we went over this shit." Soapy threw a stone into the fire.

Sid went on without comment. "Here's the cabin." He scratched a square in the dirt. "Here is the line of the forest on the other side of the pasture." He then drew an arrow. "This is the direction of the wind. Comes off the river, up the slope and into the woods."

"Being upwind still sounds risky to me."

Soapy gave a rare answer for Sid. "Nobody asked you, Bite."

Sid continued, "There is a rock formation about fifty paces inside the wood line. It's big and you can't miss it." He scratched the ground again. "One of you take the coyote skin and hang it on a limb." He looked at both of them, shifting from one to the other. "Soapy, you should get up on the top of the rock, so you can see them when they leave the cabin and then you'll be able to see the Old Man's dog comin'. Bite, you stay with the fighting dog, and remember, don't take the muzzle off till Soapy gives you the signal. I think Cronin's dog will get the coyote's scent pretty quick and leave the Old Man to investigate. When it shows up and gets close to the skin...pull the muzzle and stand back."

"What if the Old Man hears them fighting?"

"He'll most likely be halfway up the mountain by then and won't hear them, but even if he does, he'll most likely think it's the dog dispatching another coyote and keep going."

"I don't understand. Why wouldn't he come runnin'?"

"The dog has gone after coyotes before. I've heard the stories in town. According to a bunch of locals, the dog is invincible."

Soapy leaned back. "Invincible? So, you think this other dog will—"

"We got us a killer dog." Sid became aggressive. "That's all that dog knows. He was raised to kill, and that's all he wants to do. It's a straight-up fight to the death."

Bite jumped into the mix. "And if our killer loses?"

"Won't make a difference. Most likely by the end, Cronin's dog will be so beat up it won't be much good anyway. Just let it die out there in the woods and remember..." he pointed at both of them, "don't shoot. A gunshot will travel miles. It will spook the Old Man, and the whole plan will go to shit."

"What about the other dog—our killer?" Soapy asked.

"We hadn't talked about that before. This is why I did this ten times. We can't make any mistakes."

"Well?"

"Kill it. Use a knife, or a rock, or a stick, I don't care, just don't use a gun."

There was silence for a bit.

Soapy took the pot off the fire and poured a cup. "And after that we meet up with you."

Sid scratched out the dirt. "You leave the horses tied on the trail and walk up the mountain to the clearing I showed you yesterday. You wait there and I'll come get you once I find the mine. Then we will go together and get the gold." Sid's eyes darted for a second.

The two thieves looked at each other.

Soapy finished his coffee then asked again, "Where's the mine?"

"Are you stupid? I don't know where it is. That's why we have to go through all this. A while ago, I followed him up to a rocky plateau and then lost the trail. I couldn't go any farther because of the dog. He'd see me coming, warn the Old Man, and we would never find it."

"So, what's different this time?" Bite spoke.

"Cronin will be alone. He has no lookout. I'll be there watching where he goes."

"I don't know."

"I'll find the mine." Sid stood over Soapy. "I'll find the mine."

There was a decision being made by Soapy and Bite. They looked at each other and remained quiet.

Sid shook his head in frustration. "This ain't no 'panning the river to find a couple of nuggets and some dust. This is a mine, like Sutter's Mill, up in the mountain with hunks of gold stuck in the rock. All we have to do is shuck it like a walnut."

Soapy laughed. "How do you know that's a fact?" He stood up. "You're guessing."

"Think about it. He's rich, right?"

Soapy shrugged.

"You see any sloosh boxes in a river anywhere? You see any wagons hauling ore to be sorted or screened? You hear of anybody ever working a dig for him?"

"No." Soapy looked like he finally figured it out and his voice changed. "No, I haven't heard of nothing like that."

"Then where in hell did that Old Man get enough gold to build the best cabin and the best barn you ever saw? Ask yourself where did he get enough to buy property that Cudworth wants us to kill him for?"

Soapy turned around and poured what was left in the pot on the fire without offering it to his thief-mates, then turned to Sid. "Alright there's a mine, but if you don't show up..." He paused and looked hard at Sid, "I'll find you and kill you dead."

Sid didn't act the slightest bit scared. "Any other way to be killed, than dead?"

Soapy started walking to where the fighting dog was tied up. Bite followed.

Sid stood still for a minute then kicked the logs around in the fire.

Yeah, I'll meet up with you, Soapy, when I see you in hell.

CHAPTER 27
FEATHER RIVER VALLEY, CALIFORNIA
OCTOBER 1869

Amos, Rufus, and Cholok came out of the cabin one after the other, walking a little slow and shaking out stiff joints. Neither man could deny his age was showing. Rufus, on the other hand, bounded out of the cabin, ran full blast for a stretch, then returned to the slow-moving pair, tongue wagging, anxious to get started.

"Sometimes, I really hate this dog." Amos patted Rufus's head who then bolted toward the barn.

Amos opened the barn door and was greeted with a snorting and grunting orchestra. "I'm coming. I'm coming." Amos threw up the cover to the oat bin and shoveled the morning ration to Puddle and his three buddies.

"You want me to feed the cattle?" Cholok was already walking to the hayloft ladder.

"You sure you can still climb up that high?"

Cholok who had a hand on the first rung said, "You know sometimes I really hate you, Heskym."

Six head of cattle rumbled into the paddock from the field and stood like kids at Christmas waiting for the hay from the loft. Puddle finished his oats and pushed out of his stall to gain his helping of sweet hay.

They waited until the domesticated herd was satiated before closing up the barn, securing the cabin, and checking their weapons. Amos, as was his custom, carried his Winchester rifle, while Cholok selected Amos's Peacemaker.

The Indian didn't often have a need to carry a gun. He'd left that to Odina and the other hunters of the tribe. He rarely traveled alone these days—Zuni saw to that. This trip was different. There was danger. The coyote had told him.

Amos packed two cloth bags with the tools and supplies they needed in one and the rest of the dynamite he'd gotten from Goodman's store in the other. Both had leather shoulder straps, and he gave the bag with the tools, dried beef, and cornbread to Cholok. He slung the bag with the explosives over his own shoulder.

The sun had been up for a bit and the frosty dew covering the pasture grass had started to melt off.

"It takes me an hour to the mountain then another to get to the plateau."

Cholok shook his head. "Don't say it."

"Naturally, it will take a lot longer with you tagging along."

"What did I tell you? Now, I'm going to have to push you off a ledge."

"You can try." Amos started off with his rifle nestled across both his arms like a newborn.

Rufus bounded ahead—his footprints visible in the dew.

From his vantage point atop a big rock outcropping fifty paces off the wood line of the pasture, Soapy watched Amos, and an Indian, do morning chores. Stull never talked to them about anybody else being there, especially some stinking Indian. For a half a minute he thought maybe they should pull out. This Indian showing up might blow Sid's whole plan. But the other half of the thought dismissed that idea. Soapy knew Stull was a heartless bastard and he knew Stull would kill the Old Man then throw in the Indian for free.

He glanced through the low hanging branches to where Bite was sitting nervously with the killer dog. The animal had short black and brown hair, a body that bore numerous scars, and weighed at least eighty pounds. Its head was huge and disproportionate to the rest of its body. The back legs were almost scrawny compared to the muscular front legs which looked like tree trunks. Bite held a thick leather strap around the dog's wide, thick collar. A muzzle made up of chain links prevented it from making a lot of noise and from removing body parts from Bite.

Bite had wrapped the leash around a tree and positioned himself on a limb above the dog so he could pull the muzzle off, then release the leash with two quick moves, while staying out of harm's way.

The only thing they needed was for Cronin's dog to get the coyote's scent. Soapy could smell it. It stank. He'd been sitting there since dawn and was certain that the awful smell could be picked up in Carversville.

The trio hadn't gotten that far. They'd barely climbed the first slope past the wood line when Rufus abruptly stopped in front of

Amos. He stared off into the woods, watching, nose in the air searching for scent. He looked left, his head moving slightly back and forth.

Amos and Cholok stopped as well.

Amos slowly levered a round into the rifle's chamber and Cholok flicked the strap holding the Peacemaker in the holster.

Rufus then turned and looked in a different direction, back the way they came. His nose twitching.

Amos looked at Cholok and signaled for him to watch their backs.

Rufus then turned forward again staring into the woods. Suddenly, he bolted forward and leaped into the air, his front paws landing on the shoulders of a man who'd magically appeared out of nowhere.

Odina caught Rufus on the fly, and the dog proceeded to sloppily lick the Indian brave's face.

Cholok hooked the strap back on the gun's hammer then approached and spoke in Maidu to the man whose name meant 'mountain.'

Amos shook his head, wondering how a man whose name was a description of his size could have possibly gotten this close to them without being seen. He was then really startled when a second, thinner, smaller brave emerged from nowhere.

"Let me guess, this one's name means foothill."

Cholok shook his head. "No, Togquos means twin."

Amos chuckled, "There is no way he is Odina's twin."

Cholok shook his head again. "No, not Odina." He pointed to the path. "This is his twin." He pointed to Togquos's brother, who also had appeared like a ghost and was now standing in the path in front of them.

Amos held up his hand. "Okay, never mind."

Cholok continued a conversation with Odina.

Rufus ran back down the trail and was now giving his full attention to the way they had come.

Amos watched as Rufus started moving slowly, nose in the air, as was his way, searching for scent.

Cholok stopped talking and all of them turned to watch Rufus.

The dog took a step, then another, then froze. Surprising the group, he suddenly bolted back down the slope, disappearing as quickly as the three Indians had appeared.

Amos walked to Cholok and nodded toward the new arrivals. "Why are they here?"

"Zuni sent them to watch over us."

Amos almost whispered, "You know they can't follow us to the mine?"

"You don't have to whisper. They don't speak white man."

Amos looked at the three protectors who were razor focused on the path Rufus had taken.

Cholok held up his hand to Amos, then spoke to Odina.

Mountain looked at him and started to object but Cholok apparently overruled him, loudly.

Mountain looked at Amos then gestured to his two companions, and they took off after Rufus.

"I told them to see what Rufus ran after."

"Good. It's probably just a coyote again, but that will give us time to get up to the mine without your protection."

Cholok nodded and pointed. "Move on old man."

"Now, I'm definitely pushing you off a cliff."

The wind had picked up and a steady breeze was blowing the leaves that were still hanging from branches into the air. The leaves soft landings, the gentle knocking of the bare branches, and the swaying of the evergreen treetops provided the normal background sounds of a fall day in the mountains. However, the two predators were listening for the odd noise, the out of the ordinary, something that would indicate the approach of their target.

Soapy was impassionate about the task at hand. It seemed easy to him. Something Bite could do on his own. He should be with Stull looking for the mine, not here on this fool's errand.

I've killed at least a dozen people, and here I am on a rock waiting for a dog.

Soapy trained his attention to a clearing in the distance. It ran just inside the wood line, and he thought that if something was coming this way it would have to pass through that opening in the woods. He was distracted and it was hard to keep focus on the job. His mind wandered to the gold and how he would dispose of Stull and Bite when the time came. He was definitely faster than Bite, and Stull's gun hand was equally as slow. However, Stull had that knife. Soapy had seen him use it several times and each time he had to admire how fast and how accurately the knife found its target.

Something brown moved from one tree to another in the clearing. Soapy strained to see, but it didn't happen again. He struck a stick on the rock, and Bite looked over at him. Soapy pointed and nodded.

He saw Bite reposition himself on the limb and reach down to test the collar of the killer dog.

The brown thing moved again, but this time it was right at the edge of the woods. For a second, he wondered how it got there without him seeing it move.

Soapy snapped the stick again, and Bite held his hand just above the collar in ready position.

Rufus appeared about fifty feet away. He emerged from behind a boulder and stood with his nose in the air, sniffing the stench of the coyote skin. He stepped forward, ducked down, sniffed again then moved sideways back into the brush. He was now only thirty yards away.

Come on dog. Ten more feet.

Rufus emerged from the brush, and Soapy heard him growl.

Soapy snapped the stick hard.

Rufus looked up and immediately stepped toward Soapy.

Bite unhooked the muzzle and released the killer dog.

Rufus instantly reacted, taking a defensive stance, front feet spread apart and head down.

The killer dog was charging like a freight train, his front legs churning like pile drivers on a steam engine's huge wheels. His mouth was open, his tongue flapping, and streams of spit were flying in the air.

Soapy sat up and smiled.

Bite dismounted, seemingly pleased he did what he was told and wasn't mauled.

The killer dog ran straight at Rufus. At the last second, Rufus dodged, and the dog flew past him. Rufus whipped around and pursued his attacker. He leaped into the air and came down on the dog's back, knocking it flat on the ground. Before it could right itself, Rufus had it by the neck and was shaking it with all his might.

The killer dog seemed undaunted and pulled with its front legs until it was standing. It shook and turned, spinning around and around until it loosened Rufus's grip. With one mighty spin, Rufus was launched into the air and the dog was on him instantly.

Rufus yelped loudly in pain when teeth bit into the muscle of his leg. He was being spun around, his blood spraying a circle on the fallen leaves. The killer dog had a grip Rufus couldn't shake loose. He tried to gain a position to get his teeth into the predator but couldn't get far enough around.

Bite came out onto the path.

Soapy had climbed down from the rock. "This will be over soon."

"Yeah, Stull was right. Cronin's dog is no match for this animal."

There was a sound. A woosh.

It wasn't a leaf falling.

An arrow went completely through the killer dog's neck.

Bite and Soapy were stunned and didn't move.

A second arrow hit Bite in the chest. His eyes went wide and black with shock. Slowly, he looked down and grabbed the feathered shaft with both hands, then fell flat on his face, driving the arrow almost completely through his body.

Soapy grabbed for his gun but could only fire a shot while it was still in the holster because Odina had grabbed him from behind.

There was no chance for Soapy to repent for his sins.

CHAPTER 28
FEATHER RIVER VALLEY, CALIFORNIA
OCTOBER 1869

The sound of the gunshot rolled up the slope like a long cylindrical form. It was loud at its head, and soft at its tail, however it came to an abrupt end when it impacted the stone face of the mountain. It also stopped Amos and Cholok in their tracks, who at that moment, knew Rufus hadn't been chasing a coyote.

Cholok considered the sound thoughtfully then said, "That wasn't Odina. We hardly ever hunt with rifles, and never with pistols, and that, definitely, was a pistol."

Amos nodded, agreeing, "It wasn't a random hunter either, same reason...pistol not a rifle."

"But why only one shot?" Cholok turned to Amos with a curious look on his face.

Amos didn't speak right away. He leaned back against a tree, then slid to the ground.

"I've broken my routine over the past week or so." He gestured up the slope. "I've come up here almost every day and didn't take my usual precautions about being followed."

Cholok squatted next to him.

Amos looked up at the sky then at his friend. "I think I must have been seen going up to the mine. I kept an eye out, and Rufus was with me most of the time, but every once in a while, I had a feeling I was being followed."

"How sure?"

"I'm not certain, I just felt like there were eyes on me." He picked up a stick, thinking. "If there was someone watching me, I think I know who it must have been—Sid Stull."

Cholok looked a little surprised. "That wanderer you took in last winter?"

Amos nodded. "He's still staying in town, and there's gossip he and two other low lives have been going after single wagons traveling to the coast."

"Why do you think this guy is coming after you?"

Amos's eyes narrowed and his face tensed. "He's been inside the cabin, and I know he thinks I'm rich." He tossed the stick. "Living alone out on the mountain makes me easy pickens'. It's just plain greed, Cholok—avarice and greed. I think he's doing it because he's just plain evil."

Cholok sat down beside his friend. "Which makes him very dangerous."

"He's a thief and a cold-blooded killer," Amos grimaced, his expression hard and tough, "but he's a coward and would never come after me head-to-head." Amos paused and took a breath. "I've had a feeling that comes to me like a cold rush up my spine. I know about Stull." He stopped abruptly.

"What else is worrying you?"

"It's possible something else is going on. I think Cudworth might have hired Stull."

"The railroad?"

Amos nodded then started to stand and said quickly, "But that's not important now. What matters is getting rid of all traces of the mine. If it is Stull and he finds it, he'll start living like a king and your valley, the river, and the tribe will be overrun with prospectors. We have to fix this first and worry about Cudworth later."

"Are you worried about the gunshot?"

"Stull couldn't get near me if Rufus was around. I think he must have come up with some kind of plan to get Rufus off on another trail then maybe kill him."

"Possible...but do you think Stull was good enough or smart enough to surprise Rufus on the mountain he lives? I don't."

"Maybe." Amos tried to be hopeful.

"Even if Stull tried something, he couldn't have expected Odina to be there." Cholok pondered his words a minute, then said confidently, "Rufus wasn't alone. He had three of the finest Indian hunters right behind him."

"So?"

"Stull got off only one shot, which I think means whatever he had planned...didn't work."

Amos looked at his friend and shrugged. "I hope you're right." Amos then added, "But I don't think it was Stull who fired the gun. It had to have been somebody else, maybe one of his outlaws. No, he's waiting for me up there." Amos pointed to the mountain trail in front of them. "He's up there. Waiting for me... but just me. He doesn't know about you yet."

Cholok stood.

Amos picked up the bag of dynamite and beckoned to Cholok. "We are on our own. Once we get to the mine, Odina will not be able to find us."

Amos started walking up the mountain. "You coming?"

Cholok picked up his bag. "You have to ask?"

At the same time, farther up the mountain, Sid Stull heard the gunshot then cursed a stream of every foul word he could think of. It was the one thing he had told those two idiots not to do under any circumstances. He figured they must have fought over something, and one shot the other one, or they had to shoot one of the dogs, but it didn't matter now. The only thing that counted was seeing the Old Man walking out onto the plateau.

He'd been stalking Cronin's trips up the mountain but lost him every time. He marked the spot where Cronin disappeared, found a hiding place nearby, making sure he was out of sight and upwind, then waited for the Old Man's next trip. Stull got one step closer each time until finally he was convinced that, this time, Cronin would finally lead him to the mine.

The last place he lost track of the Old Man's journey was this plateau, where he was now perched and ready. He found the perfect position to watch the Old Man approach. He could see where Cronin would come out of the forest, cross onto the flat rock plateau where he disappeared last time.

The plateau was wide, flat, and just beyond the path from the forest. It was surrounded on three sides by columns of unclimbable rock towering up into the sky. The fourth side of the flat rock space was a thousand-foot drop to a boulder-filled crevasse. He couldn't figure out where the Old Man had disappeared. He searched for loose boulders or hidden passages but found none. He was convinced, this time, Cronin would reveal the secret. His only concern now was whether or not the gunshot scared Cronin off.

Stull was peeling a branch with his knife. Fine strips of bark sliced off the stick like it was butter. He'd spent an hour the night before honing the blade to a razor-sharp edge. In mid- slice he saw Cronin come out of the woods, but the brush behind him kept moving.

It can't be that damn dog.

Cholok emerged.

An Indian?

Stull had seen him before, once at the cabin, and once in Carversville, but him showing up now caught Stull completely off guard.

Cronin crossed the plateau quickly, coming to a stop at the rock column at the far end.

Where's he going?

The Old Man deftly reached around the buttress of solid rock. Sid saw him swing his leg out and around, then place his foot on what looked like a narrow rock shelf. Cronin's body followed his foot around the edge of the mountain then started inching along the narrow passageway. The ledge wasn't very wide, and Stull scratched his head wondering how he'd not seen it before. It was narrow and hung out over a long drop into the canyon below.

The Indian followed, appearing equally sure of step. They walked slowly, carefully, one behind the other, along the ledge for about fifty feet until the ledge ended at another immense column of rock.

What now?

To Stull's surprise, the Old Man did something that made Sid expel, "Oh."

Amos bent down to what appeared to be a black shadow at the bottom of the wall. He took off his pack, got down on all fours, then disappeared into the black space. Stull could now see it was a tunnel.

A tunnel. Bingo. That's it.

He had what he needed. The rest of his plan, which now included adding a dead Indian, was going to happen today.

Amos and Cholok moved quickly through the narrow tunnel and stood when they got to the great cavern. In spite of the countless bags of gold Amos had removed from the walls over the years, the cave was still a thing of beauty. The light beams streamed in from the fissures high above, and the small stream of mountain water was still flowing uninterrupted by Amos's excavation. The smell of evergreen the creek brought with it on its long journey to the sea was now mixed with the odor of kerosene from the hurricane lanterns Amos had rigged to help illuminate the cave.

"You like coming here, don't you?"

Amos grinned. "I have to admit I do. It's peaceful and the work is easy. I mean...look at it."

Cholok turned his head in a circle, looking at the streaks of gold rock embedded into the face of the mountain. "How long has it been?"

"I've been coming up here for more than sixteen years."

"It looks like it's never been touched."

"Something isn't it? I just hit the deposit a couple of times with a hammer, and a rock the size of my hand comes loose. Every trip I collect fifty or sixty pounds of gold and yet it looks like I've never been here."

Cholok bent over and drank from the stream. "What do you need me to do?"

Amos picked up the bag of dynamite. "The tunnel. We need to rig the entrance. Look here." Amos pointed to a roll of fuse wire on the ground. "We connect the fuse from the charges I planted on my last trip with this new dynamite above the tunnel, light it, and get out."

Cholok looked at Amos who was glancing up at the rock wall above the tunnel entrance and then at him. Cholok shook his head.

"What's the matter? I thought you could still climb up high."

Cholok grimaced. "I can climb, old man." He grabbed the bag and walked to the cliff. "I'll do it because I don't want to have to carry you after you fall."

"I just need to run the fuse. If you don't want to do it, I'll go get Zuni. She'll do it."

"That is beneath you, even for a white man."

Amos chuckled and pulled the coil of fuse from his pack and tossed it to Cholok. "Throw this down after you set the charge."

It wasn't a long climb or even very high for that matter. About ten feet above the entrance, a small fissure was the perfect place to set the sticks of dynamite. He stuck the fuse in one end and tossed the roll down to Amos.

Near the creek lay a second wheel of fuse that would burn long enough to allow Amos and Cholok time to get through the tunnel, get across the ledge and out onto the plateau before the explosion was triggered. Amos took the end of the fuse and bent down to tie it to the other fuse.

Amos had his back to the tunnel when he heard a gun hammer click.

Sid Stull came out of the black shadow of the tunnel with a pistol pointed at Amos. He stepped out and stood up straight. He wiped his eyes, blinking, adjusting to the light. The tunnel was black, and the cave was lit by the lanterns. It wasn't a morning sun, but it was enough to cause a hesitation which was all Cholok needed.

Sid's eyes were blinking almost as fast as they were darting around the cave. "Where's the Indian?"

Cholok made him aware of his presence when he dropped off the wall and onto Stull's shoulders.

Both of them fell forward. Cholok had a knee in Stull's back who yelled out in pain when they hit the ground.

Amos ran to the two, who were now wrestling on the ground, and grabbed Stull's gun arm.

Stull rolled over, causing Cholok to wind up on his back.

Amos held the gun in a vice grip, but he didn't have Stull's knife hand.

Stull's blade penetrated Amos's side below the ribcage. Incredible pain caused him to instantly grab the wound and release his grip on Stull's arm.

Sid stood quickly, getting the drop on the unarmed Cholok. He grinned then laughed. "Sticking you in the belly was one of the best moments of my life...Old Man."

Cholok took half a step but stopped when Stull trained the barrel of the pistol on his head.

"Good injun." Stull waved the gun. "You speak English, you red bastard?"

Cholok didn't answer.

"Well, you don't have to. You know this is a gun and I'd kill you as soon as spit."

Cholok showed no sign of understanding.

Stull turned to Amos, who was lying on his side, his hands over the wound, blood seeping through his fingers. Stull held the gun on them, but his eyes diverted from his two prisoners to look around the cavern. He was dumbstruck by the gold locked in the purple granite, glistening in the lantern light. He reached up to wipe away a small stream of drool that had leaked out of his mouth.

Cholok moved an inch.

Stull started laughing gleefully, slow at first then louder, then hysterically, the gun now waving in the air. "I'm the richest man on earth." He took a few dance steps, lifting his boots high and threw a hand in the air. "Gold, so much goddamn gold."

Cholok mustered up every bit of energy he possessed and threw a stone. It was round and half the size of his hand.

It hit Stull just below his jaw. His pistol fired. The noise it made was deafening, bouncing around the cavern over and over again.

Cholok was propelled backward, his arms and legs flying in the air.

Stull was still standing but hunched over, gun arm bent, barrel smoking, blood running down his neck.

Amos rolled over and saw his friend lying motionless on his back, a red stain swelling on his shirt from a hole in his chest.

Stull, still holding his neck, hobbled over to the lifeless Indian and kicked Cholok in the side.

Cholok made no sound.

Stull glanced at Amos then walked to the creek and still holding the gun in one hand, dipped the other into the water, splashing it up on his neck and face.

He stood, walked back to Amos, and bent over. "He missed me." He kicked Amos who yelled in pain. "I didn't." He waved his gun in the air then holstered it. "This was too easy." He shook a finger in the air. "It took a while," he bent over Amos getting close to his face, "but I beat you. I got rid of that damn dog and now you." He smiled, stood up, and started strutting. "Cudworth is paying me a thousand dollars to kill you. And the funny part is all you had to do is sell him what he wanted, and I probably wouldn't be here right now." He squatted down near Amos again and gloated. "Oh...by the way. He knows all about you leaving the ground to an Indian." He was suddenly inspired. He stood and pointed to Cholok. "Would it be this one?" He then laughed again. "Doesn't matter, he knows all about your will—the chief and his daughter. Your lawyer's wife told him all about it. He sent me to kill you, and Strong was supposed to kill the chief, so, I ask you, how long do you think that girl will live after you're both dead?"

He picked up Cholok's empty bag and walked to the purple granite wall of gold. He grabbed a hammer from the ground and hit the wide streak of yellow rock. The gold fractured—pieces fell to the ground. He picked up hunks of gold and stuck them in the bag. He was giddy. "Look at this...gold."

He lifted the bag in the air and bounced the rocks he'd collected. "What's this, five, ten pounds of gold? And it's all mine." His mouth dropped open, and his eyes got wide. "Mine... get it... a mine that's mine."

"All I have to do is drag your bodies out to the plateau and its done. One dead Indian and one dead Old Man. Who killed who first? Why, no one will ever know or probably care."

Cholok opened his eyes and looked at Amos.

Amos somehow understood what had to happen. "You're nothing but an animal. A low-life, stinking animal. You'll never get away with this."

Stull spun around, like a snake ready to strike its prey. His head was bent forward, and he hissed. "Get away with this? I'm not only going to get away with this, I'm gonna' dance on your grave." He pulled out his knife and started forward, one hand on the knife, the other still holding a steel grip on the bag of gold. He took a step, then another, then he started to run, gaining momentum, raising his arm in the air, anticipating plunging the blade into Amos.

Cholok grunted, then reached out and caught Stull's trailing heel with his hand. Sid lost his balance.

The knife came loose when Stull hit the ground. Sid and the knife slid across the rock and stopped near where Amos lay.

Amos grabbed the razor-sharp blade, rolled over, and gave it a new home—in Sid's left eye.

Stull spasmed for a while until all of his life left his body.

Amos got up on all fours and crawled to Cholok who was breathing fast, some blood mixing with his exhales. "I'm dead, my friend."

Amos took his hand his voice breaking, "No."

Cholok shook his head slightly. He choked. His dying breaths coming. He looked at Amos, "You saved my son, now go...save my daughter."

Amos held his friend's hand as he died.

CHAPTER 29
FEATHER RIVER VALLEY, CALIFORNIA
OCTOBER 1869

Amos cut a length of fuse cord and used it to secure his shirt around his belly, compressing the wound. It took every ounce of energy he had. The effort caused everything to spin. He put a hand on the cold stone wall trying to regain his center. Taking a breath, he cinched the cord tight— excruciating pain followed. Light disappeared as he slipped into unconsciousness. His mind shut off the pain, and his body forgot how to stand.

Something cold and hard was digging into his face.

Cholok's voice spoke from the darkness.

Wake up.

Amos blinked, then opened his eyes, his vision was clouded and out of focus. He lay on his stomach, arm hurting and his head bleeding from hitting the ground when he collapsed.

He blinked again, vision clearing. He saw his friend, a few feet away, lying face up on cold rock. Cholok's face was ghostly white and frozen in death.

Amos pushed himself up and sat staring at his friend.

"I'm so sorry, Heskym." Tears ran down his face. "I know

you'd be laughing right now...me crying would be a real treat for you."

He tried to stand, and pain shot up his arms and down his legs, but he shook it off. He made it to his feet and checked the bandage. It seemed to be holding. Wobbling, he stumbled to the fuse but had to stop. He sat down, but too quickly, and pain shot up his spine.

"Ahhhh." His scream filled the chamber.

It took a few minutes, but he gritted his teeth and fought through the pain. Standing was difficult but he needed to get to the fuses. Grabbing the ends of the two fuses, he checked if they were still connected to the dynamite. One led up the far rock wall, disappearing into the shadows and the other hung loosely from above the tunnel. With shaky fingers, he took the two ends and connected them together. Exhausted again, he had to sit for a minute. However, this time he didn't black out.

After a few minutes of rest, he found a stick match in his pocket. He dragged the fuse to the tunnel entrance. He wasn't sure how long it would take for the fuse to burn. He didn't know how long it would take him to crawl out of the tunnel and get across the ledge either. What he did know was it was the only way to save the village and Aponi's life.

He sat for a minute, storing up energy when his mind went to a very dark place. Anger was added to his determination.

The lawyer's wife.

He gritted his teeth, got up on his knees, crawled into the tunnel and pulled the fuse behind him as far as it would reach.

The flame on the match, surrounded by blackness, allowed him one last look at the peaceful place that gave and took so much.

As soon as the fuse flared, he started crawling. The blood didn't start seeping again until he got out of the darkness and onto the ledge. He stayed on all fours, crawling along the narrow edge. His knees and hands were now bleeding. The pain in his side returned. He tried to fight through it. Part of him contemplated letting go and allowing gravity to take over, but Cholok refused to let him.

Save my daughter.

Drips of red blood on the ground marked his progress at first, then smears of red from his knees painted the surface. He inched along the narrow ledge until he reached the face of the buttress which stopped him from getting to the plateau. He laid down to rest, wondering how much more time he had before the dynamite blew.

Help her.

With new determination, Amos rose up from his knees, stood and reached out, locking his fingers on a protruding rock. He pulled himself flat against the buttress and started to lean out to move around the column of rock to the plateau.

The explosion was massive.

Before he could react, he found himself in the air, connected to neither the ledge nor the buttress. He was flying. It only took a moment, but it felt like a lifetime.

He was surprised when instead of a thousand-foot fall to a rocky death, he bounced. The explosion had blown him forward to where he landed just on the edge of the plateau. His feet were hanging over the edge but nothing else. He shook his head—legs felt cold—the shirt was wet. He reached down and cinched the bandage again. Air instantly left his lungs, and he blacked out.

He awoke not knowing how long he'd been unconscious. He stood and hobbled to the buttress and saw that the ledge and the tunnel entrance were gone. A slope of the mountain had collapsed, and clouds of dust were rising up and dissipating into a clear blue sky.

It's gone.

He began walking across the plateau. One step, then another, all the while holding his wound with both hands. He got to the forest, found a stick to use as a crutch and started down.

Eventually, walking became an involuntary muscular reaction. It was all instinct, determination, and sheer grit. He kept pulling on the cinch and the pain it caused kept him conscious. Time became unmeasured, steps replaced seconds.

Then, between the trees, in the distance, he saw the cabin— the barn, Puddle in the paddock. He was still deep in the forest, but his seconds had run out. He had no more steps.

The blackness took him away.

His tongue was cotton dry, and too big for his mouth. He could feel his toes, but little else. Cold was breezing across his forehead, it was wet. One eye slit allowed a tiny amount of light to enter. There was movement.

Then the darkness returned.

He felt warmth. A fire crackled somewhere. Both eyes opened slightly, and his blanket came into focus. He looked up.

Odina stood like a statue at the foot of the bed, arms crossed and face grim. Amos saw the Indian's leather shirt was covered with blood.

Amos tried to speak but nothing came out.

The Mountain didn't move.

Amos used his hand to indicate he needed water.

Odina immediately went and got a cup, bent his enormous frame over the bed, and assisted Amos in taking a sip. He held his head with one hand and the cup with the other.

Amos's voice cracked, "Hetch" came out. It was the word for thank you, one of the few he'd mastered.

As time became restored, he started taking inventory of what body parts were working. One arm responded, and its corresponding leg. His other leg moved but not the arm, however all the fingers wiggled.

Another, longer sip of water helped.

The cabin door opened and Togquos stepped inside. He looked as serious as the giant who was now standing facing the brave, holding a tiny cup of water in his giant paw.

Togquos, the twin, stepped aside and Zuni, shoulders wrapped in a blanket, came through the door.

The three stood aside, speaking softly as if Amos understood. He heard many words he didn't know, but a few he did. The native tongue wasn't mastered but their body language helped him understand. It seemed Odina had tracked him from the blood trail then carried him here.

Zuni looked at Amos then asked Odina another question.

Odina shrugged while shaking his head. He made a gesture to his chest then another indicating something got away.

Zuni brought a wet cloth and wiped the dirt from Amos's face. She was half the size of Amos and Odina made Amos look small. However, when Zuni spoke, the Mountain moved.

She continued to wipe the dirt from Amos's face and arms. "Momin." She beckoned to the two braves who collided trying to get more water.

She leaned to Amos's ear. "Cholok?"

Amos still couldn't speak but his tears answered.

A sudden small inhale of air was her only response.

Odina arrived with another cup.

She took it and put it to his lips. He sipped, then she put the cup down and pointed to Amos's chest. "Takini."

Amos shook his head as far as it would go. He couldn't say he didn't understand.

Zuni leaned to his ear again. "It means, one who has been brought back to life."

Odina approached with a clean cloth.

Zuni untied the fuse cord and everything became blurry. Time started to stretch. Sounds were distorted and blackness edged his vision.

He heard a voice.

You cannot die.

But he didn't know if it was Zuni or Cholok.

CHAPTER 30
CARVERSVILLE, CALIFORNIA
NOVEMBER 1869

Wide eyes and expressions of hopeful anticipation were on the faces of all three of the travelers, but one of them was barely able to keep his seat in the stagecoach. There wasn't a single thing that wasn't a brand-new experience for Henry, for all of them actually, but Henry's enthusiasm exceeded that of Betty and Gerald by a country mile. He was nineteen and resembled an adult, tall, muscular, even the beginnings of hair on his chin, however Henry's curiosity was that of a child.

When the coach cleared the edge of the forest, the first view of Carversville marked the end of the journey and a welcome sight after more than two months of travel from Philadelphia. This last leg, a rut-filled dirt road from the port, caused much discomfort even while offering the most spectacular views of the Sierra Nevada Mountains. The long vistas, blinding blue sky and every spectrum of green nature could muster was now replaced by the view of a picture-perfect town with a mountain backdrop. The rocky road was replaced by the staccato thumping of the wagon wheels on the town's new cobblestone street. Henry had his head out the window and fingers tightly gripping its frame.

"Beautiful." Aunt Betty sighed and patted Gerald's hand.

"I'm surprised," Gerald responded. "Honestly, I didn't know what to expect but a town like this, so far from the city...why, it's just completely unexpected."

Henry wasn't paying attention, the bumps, thumps, and bouncing coach of the fifty-mile two-day journey from the port became a quickly vanishing memory.

Gerald leaned back. "I want a steak, a bath, and a soft bed."

"The bath sounds dreamy." Betty smiled.

Henry remained silent, still focused on the view of the picture-perfect town.

"Henry?" Betty said, demanding attention.

He whipped his head around. "What? Oh, sure...do you think my father will be here?"

"Maybe, but in any case, I'm certain you'll see him soon." Betty now patted Henry's hand.

The stagecoach passed several houses and stores and pulled up at a building with a long wooden porch under a cedar roof and a sign that read *California Stage Company.* The horses grunted and the wagon master jumped down to open the carriage door.

Standing up straight required stretching and the adjustment and dusting of clothes.

The stationmaster came out through double doors. He wore a starched white shirt, red suspenders, and a grey mustache that took up most of his face. "Afternoon folks, Frank Stebbins is my name, and I hope you had an uneventful trip."

"We did, thank you, Mr. Stebbins." Gerald stepped up to take charge. "Is someone here to meet us?"

He shook his head and there might have been a grin under the facial hair, but it was difficult to tell. "Please, call me Frank, and you must be Amos Cronin's relatives."

Henry burst forward his head spinning like a top. "I'm his son, Henry Cronin. Is he here?"

The mustache shook his head. "No, Amos hasn't been in today." He hesitated then continued, "Actually, we didn't expect you until tomorrow...but...I'm sure he'll be along." Something black dripped down his chin.

Gerald, still in leadership mode, spoke up. "I think then we'll need a room and a meal."

Frank pointed down the road. "Red lettered sign, long porch, other side of the street. Hotel Ramona. They're expecting you. I'll get our boy to deliver your luggage. You all go on down and settle in. Amos took care of everything already." Suddenly, a black thing exploded from the face hair and hit the cobblestones with a splat. "Amos is a real big deal in these parts. A good man...but his dog is a little crazy."

The three started toward the hotel, exchanging a variety of glances each apparently trying to decipher what the stationmaster had spit.

"Mr. Henry Cronin." An excited voice came from a small man wearing a black vest and matching suitcoat and sporting slicked down hair. He was hurrying across the street, a woman in a beaming yellow dress and carrying a small, useless, matching yellow parasol, trailing behind.

He shouted again, "Mr. Henry Cronin."

Henry raised his hand. "I'm Henry."

The lawyer, a little breathless, huffed out, "Bogart Simpson Clark. I'm your father's lawyer."

The woman arrived, without the heavy breathing. When the lawyer, still grinning, didn't introduce her, she kicked him in his shin with a fashionable shoe.

"Ow...Ahhh...Please allow me to introduce my wife, Amelia."

The wife curtsied.

Betty and Gerald glanced at each other.

"Is my father here? Is he coming?"

The lawyer continued to smile and put one hand on Henry's back while starting to guide him in a different direction. "I haven't seen him yet today, but I'm certain he'll be along, soon."

There was an almost imperceptible sound from the wife which caught Betty's attention.

The man's new direction seemed to be a door under a sign bearing the lawyer's name.

Betty nodded her head toward Gerald, but her husband had already moved to intercept Clark. He put his hand on the smaller man and separated him from Henry. "We will be going to the hotel. Anything you have to say will wait," he gave the lawyer his best stare, "will it not?"

The lawyer didn't speak again but Amelia was undeterred. She fluttered her hand like a fan. "Of course. You all get settled and we will meet you for dinner. They serve quite an acceptable pot roast."

Betty, short on patience and long on instinct, possessed a much better stare. "How about, we settle in, have dinner by ourselves, and call you when your services are required."

Henry was shocked out of the unfamiliar state he had drifted into.

Gerald smiled and guided his charges to the Hotel, leaving the lawyer in the road, head down and obviously disappointed his fortune was walking away.

The interior of the hotel was, like the town of Carversville, unexpected. The lobby they entered was bright, well furnished, had draperies on all the windows, and what might have been Oriental rugs on a polished wood floor. They could see the dining room and it was similarly decorated. It wasn't downtown Philadelphia, but it was, for a hotel a hundred miles from a major city, elegant.

"Good afternoon." He could have been from England, tall, thin, long nose, big ears, and a bit of posh attitude. "May I be of service?"

Betty stepped forward. "We are the family of Amos Cronin. I believe you have rooms for us."

The accent of the man behind the desk slipped a bit. "Yes ma'am...I mean...Yes, Mr. Cronin made arrangements, and we are prepared for your arrival. Three rooms. Henry Cronin, Elizabeth Nichols, and Gerald Myer.

"Two rooms," corrected Betty.

"Of course." His eyes darted a bit, but he overcame his curiosity quickly. "Two rooms." He opened the register and began to write. "Mr. Henry Cronin and—" He paused, head down, pen on paper.

"Mr. and Mrs. Gerald Myer." Gerald's voice was polite.

Betty's look was not.

The clerk nodded, jotted, then looked up. "My name is —"

Gerald didn't wait for the introduction. "When our bags arrive, send them to our rooms immediately. We'll want to bathe, dress, and have dinner in an hour. Can you manage that?"

The nameless man nodded. "Rooms 102 and 104. Up the stairs to the right."

Henry watched Betty take the keys and walk with an authority he hadn't witnessed before. He heard her mumble, "Mr. and Mrs.

..." there was something else she said he couldn't make out and was glad he didn't.

An hour later, almost on the dot, the three now refreshed travelers arrived ready to devour an entire cow. Three other tables had diners who all instantaneously raised their heads and halted their meal. The town folk were polite, nodded, then continued on with their meals.

The three hurriedly chose a table near a long window with a view of Main Street.

A bifold kitchen door suddenly parted in the middle and swung open. A portly man wearing a stained kitchen apron, showing off a head full of red hair, and carrying a long metal spoon headed for their table.

Henry momentarily feared the man had already eaten the steer.

The man walked up, pulled out the odd chair, and plopped down.

The pretend Englishman appeared, suddenly looking horrified.

The red-haired man pointed the long spoon. "Go back to the desk, you pompous ass."

Betty grinned wide. "I love this man." She stuck out her hand. "I'm Amos's sister-in-law, Betty. This is my husband, Gerald. And—"

"Don't tell me. This has to be the infamous Henry Cronin." He laughed a belly laugh. "Sweet Jesus, you're a spittin' image lad."

Henry smiled but looked at his aunt. "Infamous?"

She leaned over, "I wrote a lot of letters."

Henry was more than surprised by her revelation.

"We'll talk later."

"You three have had quite an adventure." He slapped the table with authority. "Whatever you want is my pleasure. Name it, I'll make it." He laughed again and the three followed suit.

Gerald leaned over a bit. "What about..." He made a hidden finger point toward the desk.

"Ha. Don't pay any attention to the fop. This is my hotel. He works for me."

Betty took the lead. "I'm afraid you have us at a disadvantage. We don't know your name, kind sir."

"Angus." He belly-laughed again. "Anything you want or need; you just have to ask. My friend Amos has been there for me countless times and I finally have a chance to give back a little. Now, what do you starving travelers want for dinner?"

Betty looked at her partners. "Angus, dear man, we would be very happy to enjoy whatever you would like to make for your friend's family."

His eyes twinkled and he was momentarily silent. He rose up like he entered the room, quickly, then started shouting before he got back to the kitchen door. "Miguel, we have a special order coming up. Get me the big pot."

It took the next hour for the food to stop. At the end, the three sat completely full and thought they were absolutely incapable of another bite, but that was when coffee, liquor, and a chocolate dessert arrived.

"No...no more." Betty protested then drank a glass of the golden syrup and ate a few forkfuls of cake. After the third bite, she tossed the fork to the table and waved her hands. "No more. That's all, really. No more."

It could have been a perfect moment, but it was interrupted.

The lawyer and the wife arrived. He still wore the same suit, but she had redressed into blue, with matching shoes and hat. As if they were arriving in court, the pair started across the room towards the family.

The kitchen door swung open and, Angus entered like a Norse Viking. At first, he looked as if he was going to ask if they wanted anything else, but Henry saw the look on his face change when he saw the pair of interlopers.

Angus altered his trajectory a few degrees and the lawyer abruptly stopped walking. The wife did not.

"Angus, how lovely to see you. Bogart and I are here for dinner." Her eyes diverted and then she pretentiously waved at the clients. "Oh, look. Our friends. I'll just pop over and say hello."

"No, you won't. You want dinner? Sit over there." He pointed to a table across the room. "You say a word to any of them and the kitchen is closed to you for a month."

She blushed and took a step. "I just—"

He matched her step. "No, you don't just. You go sit over there or leave."

The lawyer started walking toward the table and the wife, apparently unaffected, followed her husband still maintaining a frozen grin. Henry thought it must have been part of her makeup.

Henry could see Betty watching the drama unfold and her expression revealed the pair's actions were confirming her suspicions. "That was interesting." She stood up as Angus approached. "That was just magnificent." She glanced over at the couple now sitting far away. "Is confronting them a problem for you?"

Angus chuckled, "Not a chance. They're used to it. Besides, nothing gets through their pompous, but I will say this," he stopped a moment apparently considering his next remark then addressed Henry, "be very careful around them. He is a lawyer who does some work for your father. I think it's mostly because he's the only lawyer in town. He's not terrible, but...not a soul trusts the wife."

They all got up slowly and Betty stepped back from the table, groaning, "I've never eaten so much. It was so good." She pushed up on her toes and kissed Angus's round red cheek. "I think I need an elevator to get to my room."

"No problem," Angus immediately swept her off her feet and started to carry her.

Betty started laughing and kicking her feet.

Henry also started laughing.

Gerald chuckled but said, "Hey, big fella, that's my job."

Angus put her down. "Well, if you need any help let me know. Remember," he looked at all of them one at a time, "whatever you need."

CHAPTER 31

CARVERSVILLE, CALIFORNIA

NOVEMBER 1869

The morning had arrived none too soon for Henry. He'd been at the window of his room peering out at the morning activity since sunup. Some wagons were transporting wooden barrels bound with wide metal hoops. Some had stacks of bags laden with grain or flour. Some had large wooden boxes tied down with thick corded ropes. Others had open crates with chickens poking their heads out between the slats. The birds also seemed to be watching everything that was going on, but they had less than a rewarding future outcome.

Several boys, who looked to be his age, were walking along the porches, some carrying tools, others carrying boxes. A few children were running in the opposite direction carrying schoolbooks. Two women were busy sweeping the porches in front of open store doors and a man with a funny-looking peaked hat stood with his hands on his hips admiring a tower of apples on top of a table in front of his grocery store.

Henry considered this activity was not unlike what he'd witnessed back in Philadelphia on any normal working day.

Sundays, of course, were much different, but today, like every Tuesday in his hometown, was going to be a day just like any other.

Or so he thought.

A knock sounded at his door. "Henry, we're going downstairs for breakfast. Are you coming?"

His aunt's voice startled him momentarily. "I'll be right there." He bolted from the windowsill, pausing to look back to an unmade bed, something he would normally never leave undone, but shrugged off the instinct and dashed down the stairs after his aunt and uncle.

Breakfast was not unlike the dinner they feasted on the night before. It was more food than they were used to, but this morning they managed to dine with fewer remarks.

Between bites of pancakes, Henry noticed Mr. Stebbins, the moustache from the stage office, had entered the hotel and received a directional pointed finger from the desk clerk and was now headed toward their table.

"Good morning." The words apparently came from the hair-covered mouth. "I haven't received any word from Mr. Cronin about his arrival and..." he scratched his head before he continued, "and frankly, it's not like him. I'm concerned."

Aunt Betty queried. "Concerned?"

"I saw Amos a week ago Wednesday, and he was very specific about the details of your arrival. He didn't...we didn't...know exactly when you would get here so he paid the hotel for rooms for three days."

No one at the table added an "and" to his sentence.

Mustache did. "And...I don't understand why he hasn't shown up yet...so, yes, I'm concerned."

"Okay." Betty promptly put her fork on the table and wiped

her mouth with a napkin as she stood. "When can you have a carriage ready for us?"

"One hour...less...I'll run back now and hitch a team. I'll have it ready to go in front of the stage office when you're ready." He started away but stopped and turned, mid step. "Ah...I should also tell you that Mr. Clark, the lawyer, made an inquiry about a carriage this morning. I'm thinkin' he'll be headed out that-a-way too."

Gerald pointed at the man. "Make sure we get ours first. He's not to leave before we do."

The mustache nodded and Henry would have sworn he was smiling but he couldn't be certain.

As they left to ready for the trip, Henry heard Betty mumble again. This time he understood what she said under her breath and agreed.

Gerald was handling the team well. Driving a carriage wasn't anything even remotely new for the Philadelphia expert horseman, but the team pulling the wagon and the road were unfamiliar, so he was being careful.

The carriage that was following behind them containing the lawyer and the wife were not fairing as well. The horses pulling that wagon were not responding to a whip and the ruts in the road apparently were causing the wife to reprimand the lawyer constantly.

Mr. Stebbin's directions were simple, drive out on the north road until the road forked, then take the right divide down the slope until one sees Amos's cabin and barn. The trip should take about three hours and, given the fair weather that day, should be uneventful. The directions were true and the sight that appeared when the wagon emerged from the forest was as impressive as when they first saw Carversville. They were stunned.

"Oh my." Betty uttered. "This is…"

"Like a painting in a museum." Gerald finished her thought.

Henry tried to stand to get a better view, but the rolling carriage forced him back down. The sun had risen above the mountain behind the cabin and the river flowing past the back of the barn was glistening with reflected sunlight. Several steers grazing peacefully in the pasture had paused to watch the arriving visitors. There were three horses in the paddock. Standing side-by-side, they looked up in unison, then went back to grazing, apparently their curiosity satisfied. Another horse, one of great stature, stood alone in the field. The big black had his head up, watching, ears twitching, tail occasionally flapping. He, unlike his counterparts, appeared to be much more interested in the approaching wagons than what was growing in the field.

The wagon turned the corner of the fenced pasture, and the passengers saw a smaller horse with a brown body and white backside covered with dark spots. It was pawing the ground and standing untended in front of the cabin door.

The three looked at each other curiously.

"That's an Appaloosa." Gerald pointed. "Their ancestors are from an ancient breed and now have become a breed of their own." He paused a second. "I've read about them." He looked at Henry and Betty. "They've become indigenous to the plains Indian Tribes here in the West." He had pulled up on the reins a bit but then snapped them lightly and the carriage continued its journey.

The lawyers' carriage, just catching up, made a loud thud as a wheel found another rut.

Amos's family traveled the distance to the cabin along the dirt road which was fenced on both sides. The cattle and horses in the pasture started to drift away, but the big black stood his ground, his chest out, head up, front leg thumping the ground.

At the end of the fence and near the cabin, the Appaloosa, standing alone with no bridle or rein, began backing up as the wagon approached.

No one spoke.

When they arrived, the noise from the wagon was replaced with the sound of the river's current splashing on rocks, thousands of insects twilling to their own songs, and from above, a bird calling out from somewhere in the distance.

Gerald tied the reins to the wagon break, the carriage now just short of the cabin door.

Zuni stepped out of the cabin. She had her arms crossed over a woven blanket that was draped over her shoulders, and a portion of it covered her head. She bowed her head slightly to the arrivals. "My name is Zuni."

Henry was first off the wagon, both feet hitting the wooden porch with a thump. "Hello, I'm Henry Cronin. Amos Cronin is my father. Is he here? Is he inside?" His eyes were darting back and forth.

Betty, starting to climb down, immediately said, "Henry, stop. Wait there." When on the porch, she moved to stand next to Henry. She put her hand on his shoulder while looking at Zuni. Zuni's lack of expression confirmed Betty's intuition.

Zuni stepped to the side and gestured with an open palm toward the door.

The second wagon arrived with the lawyer. The wheels had barely stopped turning when he jumped down, leaving the wife seated, unattended, and clearly unhappy.

Gerald blocked the lawyer's approach.

Betty stepped in front of Henry and entered the cabin.

Amos was lying face up on his bed, a blanket pulled up to his chin. His feet stuck out from the bottom of the bed, hanging white, and lifeless.

Henry took a step to get around from behind his aunt when he heard her suck in some air. He shouldered past her.

She didn't stop him.

"Dad?"

Gerald came into the cabin followed by the lawyer and the wife, who coughed, apparently to let her presence be known.

What no one saw was Odina standing against the wall in the shadow of the open door. Being almost as wide as the opening, it was the one place in the cabin where he might have been, for the moment, overlooked.

Betty looked at Zuni. "How?"

"He and my husband, Cholok, were in the mountain. They were attacked by evil men. My husband was killed also killed." She pointed out toward the mountain then back to the bed. "Amos died here."

Henry was frozen, everything he thought he would find out about himself, and his father, was vanishing before his eyes.

"Do you know why?" Betty asked, her monotone voice speaking almost by rote.

"I do not," Zuni paused a second, "and I fear the evil is not done."

Gerald reacted instantly. "You mean there is danger here...for us, now?"

Zuni shook her head and pointed to Odina, who stepped forward out of the shadow. "No, not now."

Henry recovering, looked at the petite woman. "Did he say anything before he—"

"Odina found your father on the trail and brought him here. He lost much blood, but he was strong and gained some strength back. But the blade that cut him injured too much. Poison from inside made him weak and he couldn't live."

Betty stepped toward Odina and put her hand on his arm, her eyes appreciative of the mountain's help.

"Your father left a letter for you. He wrote it before he went off with Cholok." She pointed and all looked at the kitchen table where a sealed letter lay carefully centered in its middle.

Henry's voice was unsteady. "Did he say anything before...?"

Zuni shook her head. "He couldn't talk but he wanted to write note. I gave him paper and he used his last bit of energy to write something for you." She pointed again to the table. On top of the envelope was a small, folded paper marked with a red bloodstain.

Zuni moved to Henry and took his hand. She examined it closely, then she looked in his eyes. She smiled for the first time, then patted the back of his hand. "You need to honor your father's wishes."

Henry thought she wasn't telling him, she was pleading.

While this moment was happening, the lawyer's wife edged closer to the kitchen table. She got within a few feet. Ever so slowly she started to reach a hand toward the folded paper.

Betty, as quickly as she had ever moved in her life, pulled Odina's knife from the sheath on his belt, took three quick steps, and stuck the blade in the tabletop. "You reach for that note again and you'll bring back a bloody stump."

The lawyer's wife grunted in surprise, pulled her hands to her face, and backed up. "Well, I never."

Clark took half a brave step and with kind of a stiff conviction started a sentence he didn't have a chance to complete. "I'm your father's lawyer and in that capacity, I believe I..."

Betty's stare was backed up by Odina's.

The lawyer and the wife, defeated, backed up and exited the cabin.

Betty picked up the folded paper and without opening it, handed the note to Henry.

Henry took it and turned it over, avoiding the blood. His name was shakily written on its face.

Zuni stepped away, pulled the blanket off her head, and she and Odina left the cabin.

Henry looked at Betty and Gerald while holding his father's dying words in his hand.

He unfolded the paper.

Cudworth killed me and Cholok.

CHAPTER 32
FEATHER RIVER VALLEY, CALIFORNIA
NOVEMBER 1869

A day before the funeral, Aunt Betty took a two-hour walk about. When she returned to the cabin, she announced she'd found the perfect place of rest for Amos. "It's on a hill, near the cabin, overlooking the river."

Henry walked with her out to the spot then sat on a log. He stayed quiet for the longest time. Eventually, Betty left him there alone and returned to check on her husband.

Gerald, who was well acquainted with the duties surrounding the care of livestock, had fed and watered the other residents of the Cronin ranch, taken care of their stalls, and secured the barn. He'd looked after all the stock except the big black horse whose name Betty discovered on his stall. She had taken a shine to him, or rather Puddle, had friendlied up to her.

Henry had been gone a long while, but they waited patiently. He hadn't said much over the past days but when he finally arrived back at the cabin, shortly before sundown, he started talking. With a pleasant voice he said, "I think the place you picked is perfect."

She smiled, then hugged him.

He stepped back after the much-needed comfort hug and looked at her with a puzzled look on his face. He chose that moment to let her know he hadn't forgotten the dinner conversation with Angus. "The legendary Henry Cronin? You wrote a lot of letters about me to my father?"

She was momentarily stunned, then laughed a little laugh. "Yes, I did. I guess I owe you some conversation about that."

"You do...and fortunately, it's a long ride back to town. Meanwhile, you two have kept us here long enough. We'd better get started. We have a big day tomorrow."

Henry started for the door, and Betty and Gerald started the game of following the new leader.

They were in front of a long line of horse-drawn wagons, carriages, and buggies, a procession of Amos's friends, well-wishers, and the curious. The road had never seen this much traffic before. It was slow going and there were frequent stops to help move a fallen something or lift a rutted wheel. The pace was slow, but patience was long. Everyone seemed to manage the problems while keeping their Sunday-go-to-meeting clothes clean.

Henry was looking out the carriage window, but his sense of wonderment had changed. The trees seemed taller than before, the road steeper and had more shadows. Even the distant mountaintop covered with snow seemed farther away. He thought it to be much quieter than before. He hadn't heard birds calling, or tree branches rattling, even the insects had stopped their incessant twilling. He only heard the sound of the horses' hooves thumping on the drum-tight ground.

Gerald handled a team again, but this time the horses were hitched to a finely polished covered carriage. Betty sat beside him up on what Henry learned was called the box seat. Henry was in the coach of the brass-adorned carriage, complete with a roof, two doors, windows and enough space for four. He was alone.

In his pocket was the still unopened letter from his father, and the blood-stained note.

He had a lot of questions.

The caravan behind them had many different types of wagons, all filled to capacity with townspeople. To Henry it was unknown if they be friend or foe, but he did know for certain, some of them had answers he needed.

There was little doubt that all the decisions regarding his father's burial were his to make. Aunt Betty unobtrusively helped him make them in a timely fashion, especially since his current state had him completely incapable of doing so. She made suggestions, not decisions, about arrangements, all of which he found to be, as all new thoughts always were, new. There was enough confusion in his mind and soul that deciding what the next logical or necessary thing to do was as if someone was speaking a foreign language, but Aunt Betty carefully guided him through what he needed to understand about burying the man he'd never met.

Angus was there every step of the way, like a true friend would be, helping all of them with their life needs, and most importantly with the who's-who issues.

Angus supervised the first of the long line of people with interests in Amos Cronin's death. It was, naturally, Sheriff Mitchell who did an investigation because it was, obviously, a murder. The lawman's first jump to a conclusion was to suspect the Indians, all of them. His immediate natural-born instinct was to question and mistrust anybody who was not white.

Angus quashed the sheriff's suspicions when he handed him the bloody note. Upon reading Cudworths name, the sheriff went into a prolonged coughing fit, followed by an exceedingly long drink of water that gave him time to think. When he returned to his authoritative self, he pronounced that although the Indians were not suspects, a note of suspicious origin wasn't enough to make an arrest of a prominent member of Carversville. He said more evidence would be necessary and he would look into the situation promptly.

His in-depth investigation lasted ten minutes.

If Angus was the soul of the community of mourners, then Howard and Martha Goodman, the dry goods store owners, represented their heart. They were the silent right and left arm of Betty and Gerald. They handled the details necessary to conduct a meaningful service. They arranged for flowers, refreshments, the Reverend O'Neil for a few words, and even a small chorus to sing a spiritual remembrance. As it turned out, however, the song became unnecessary.

Two other friends of Amos teamed up to handle the more delicate arrangements. Doc, a man who had a first and last name nobody ever used, and old Tom Hardy, the barber, made all the burial arrangements. A nice respectful coffin was procured in record time, and they engaged a few other volunteers to excavate what would be Amos's forever home.

All the travelers, including many unknown but sorrowful onlookers, arrived at the cabin that day. Two not of that group, were Bogart Simpson Clark and the wife, Amelia. The lawyer was in his normal black suit, but she outfitted herself in a flowing black dress complete with a veil. If it was anybody else's funeral, or if they weren't just so incredibly desperate, it would have made Henry laugh.

Angus selected six strong and true to carry Amos. They led the procession to the hill. Reverend O'Neil was there waiting. He wore an official looking cloak of some kind over a starched collar and bow tie. He was skinny, bald, and clean shaven and had a friendly smile and calm demeanor. The sun was out which made his head glow, but it bore no resemblance to a halo.

It took a few minutes for the crowd to jostle around. Several women from the town, who were carrying truly lovely arrangements of flowers, spent some time placing them with great care. There were even a few older children there, all of whom were remarkably quiet.

"Friends today is a very sad occasion. We are here to lay a great man to rest. I did not know Amos Cronin well…" he paused a second, "actually, I didn't know him at all. He never set foot in our church."

A small chuckle went up from the crowd.

"But I can say with authority and with righteousness of heart, that Amos Cronin was a good neighbor, a good friend, and a good man." He was carrying a book in his hands, presumably a Bible, but he chose at that moment to put it in his pocket. "I have no idea what he believed in. But from what I know of him and his… antics…"

Another chuckle from the crowd.

"I can say he was a righteous man. I can say with certainty there isn't a man or woman here today who didn't know that to be a fact."

The lawyer's wife did not burst into flames.

"I won't disrespect him by saying words I have lived by over him. I will say only, despite what some would call a reclusive nature, I have never once heard a word against his character. In fact, I have heard the stories of how when one of us was in need, somehow the need mysteriously became diminished."

Heads nodded.

"There was of course the crazy dog."

The children giggled but were shushed.

"In conclusion, if there was ever a man who could show you how to live by example, it was this man, Amos Cronin...may he rest in peace."

The reverend nodded to Henry, then to Betty and Gerald, and started away.

Henry approached the coffin and put a wildflower one of the ladies had given him on the coffin.

I wish I had known you.

A whinny from a horse interrupted the silence and made heads turn.

Approaching in numbers equaling the townspeople was the Maidu Tribe. Eight fine steeds with eight braves led the procession. Zuni, flanked by a young woman and a young man walked behind the horses and in front of men, women, and children, all approaching silently in double file. The women were on the right side and men on the left. The children were together walking in a group between the two lines and carrying a long rope vine intertwined with beautiful purple flowers.

The townspeople, many of whom had never seen more than one Indian at a time, parted as they approached.

As Zuni passed Angus, she put a hand on his arm.

Henry was still in front of the coffin and Zuni walked to him then beckoned to the children who formed a ring around Amos. They began singing a native song that had no resemblance to anything ever sung in a church but was as holy as the Ava Maria. They held the flowers up in the air, then down, then up again. It took only a minute or two but when they finished, they circled the flowers around the coffin then ran back to their mothers.

The lead horses turned and started back the way they came, the Tribe in tow.

Zuni, flanked by her son and daughter, remained.

She addressed Henry and pointed to the young man who appeared older than Henry by a few years. "This is my son Pala. Your father saved his life."

The boy nodded then stepped back.

"This is my daughter, Aponi."

The girl was looking down. Her face was partially hidden by long black hair parted in the middle. She looked up. Her eyes were green, like jade.

Henry hadn't spoken. He wasn't sure why. He hadn't or couldn't.

Zuni looked to Betty and Gerald. "My husband is dead. He was our guide, our elder, and wiseman. He has gone to Galvloi, what you call heaven, and Aponi is now the leader of our Tribe. She is the One."

Betty embraced Zuni.

The genuine emotion was a complete surprise to the Indian mother.

Betty then guided them toward the cabin.

The Doc, Howard Goodman, and old Tom Hardy funneled the onlookers to tables set up by the barn. Food and drink replaced curiosity.

The cool cabin was a relief. The sun had blessed them with a pleasant day, a surprise given the month and normal weather pattern. Even so, Gerald had a small fire going in the fireplace. Betty poured water for everyone including Zuni and Pala who had started to tell the story of him, Amos, his father Cholok, and the fish.

Henry stood alone near the wall. Aponi walked to him and handed him water.

Half a "thnk u." came out.

She smiled.

Years later Henry would tell his granddaughter about that moment.

The sun was almost at the mountaintop. Most of the townsfolk had left and the last few were mounting up. The lawyer and the wife had left immediately after the service at Angus's suggestion which was more insistence than suggestion.

Henry and Aponi had left the cabin together and walked silently down to the log by the river. It seemed like a place where his father would have come to sit, perhaps even with Cholok.

He spoke. "You knew my father well, then?"

She shrugged. "Not really. He visited us often, but I knew him because my father spoke of him all the time."

He looked at her curiously. "I'm sorry but I have to ask—"

"My father. My father, Cholok, taught me English."

Henry nodded.

There was quiet again.

She suddenly looked up and pointed. Odina had appeared. "He has returned to escort us back home."

"He is as big as a—"

"Mountain. Odina, that's his name, mountain."

Odina was riding a large horse, and it seemed he had been hunting because it looked like a wolf was draped over the mount. However, Henry saw it was still moving.

"Is this the legend I've heard so much about?"

Aponi nodded. "Yes. Rufus was attacked by a fighting dog, rescued by our braves, and is recovering from his wounds."

Henry watched as Odina dismounted and took the big dog down. A large patch of hair was missing and a crude row of stitches stretched across his side. Rufus took a second to right himself then walked slowly to the now-covered-over grave and lay down.

"Come, I'll introduce you." She stood and took his hand. Hers was cool and warm at the same time.

Henry thought, for a second, she was talking about the giant man standing in front of them, but she wasn't.

They walked together to Rufus who had his head on his paws.

"This is Rufus. He was your father's best friend...beside my father of course."

Henry remained standing for a moment, then sat down next to the big dog. He didn't say anything, he just stroked the dog's back.

Rufus lifted his head, sniffed Henry, then put his head back down.

"I'll wait for you in the cabin." She and Odina walked away in the fading light.

He was still stroking Rufus. "So, I'm told...she's the One."

Rufus grumbled a dog sound then put his head on Henry's leg.

CHAPTER 33

CARVERSVILLE, CALIFORNIA

DECEMBER 1869

Henry, Aunt Betty, and Gerald came down from their rooms early, but none of them were interested in breakfast. It had been a long couple of days and sleep didn't seem to come easy to any of them. Henry was still recovering from finding Amos dead and, although he rose to the occasion, when necessary, he reverted to a remote isolated state that made it difficult for him to function.

Betty and Gerald had coffee cups in front of them, something Henry declined. He sat with his hands in his lap, not being rude, just not present.

"This has been a lot," Betty finally broke the long silence, "and, I have to say this sudden meeting to read your father's will is very strange. I don't understand why this lawyer thinks it's so important for it to happen this morning."

"Strange indeed." Gerald nodded.

Henry remained distant, gazing out the window across the dining room. Then suddenly he turned and addressed his aunt and uncle. "I agree, but how strange is it that my father had so much money?"

Apparently caught off guard, the pair didn't respond.

"He had to, right? First, there's the house and the way we lived in Philadelphia, not to mention how we got here. He paid for everything. Then, there's the log cabin...a castle in the mountains. And, everybody we talk to insinuates he must have struck gold, but I ask you, did you see a gold mine up there? I've found out he's never paid a bill in gold and never filed a claim."

"How do you know that?" Betty asked.

"Angus. He knew him best...except for maybe Aponi's father, Cholok. I just don't understand how he managed all...this."

Betty's face indicated she was adding his questions to her suspicions. "And now the lawyer and...that wife, organize this... what did he call it?"

Gerald answered, "An expedited reading of the will."

The three went silent again.

A small number of townspeople had been asked to attend the reading of Amos Cronin's will. The attorney, Bogart Simpson Clark, Esquire, serving in an official capacity as the administrator for Amos Cronin's Last Will and Testament, summoned all parties mentioned in the document.

Henry, and Elizabeth and Gerald, who were, naturally, first on the lawyer's list of names, left the dining room and joined the meeting when a waiter told them it was about to begin.

Howard and Martha Goodman were surprised to receive an invitation, as was Thomas Hardy, John *Doc* Brown, and Mary and June Thatcher, the sisters who were the owners of the livery stable. Angus MacGregor also received an invitation, although it did take Henry some time to persuade him to attend. Henry convinced Angus that the Scotsman had to be there because not showing up would be a great dishonor to his friend's memory. The redhaired man, whose honor had seldom been questioned, spit and sputtered, but reluctantly agreed to show up.

With all the pomp and circumstance physically possible to muster, Bogart Clark conducted the meeting as if he were being heard in front of the Supreme Court. The wife sat to his right in front of a window with curtains parted just enough to allow a narrow beam of sunlight to illuminate her finery. The meeting was being held in a private dining room at the hotel. The lawyer's office was too small, and the wife wasn't about to serve refreshments.

Gerald needed to grab Betty's arm to keep her seated and not go Philadelphia on the pretentious woman.

"This is a reading of the Last Will and Testament of Amos Cronin, as dictated and transcribed by me Bogart Simpson Clark, witnessed by Amelia Clark, and duly signed by Amos Cronin on August 15 in the year of our Lord, 1866, and notarized on that same day. This is an official document, and it has been registered in the State of California."

"Get on with it, you fop." Angus came in on the exact moment of the last period of Clark's dignified opening statement.

The unified chuckle that rose up reminded Henry that nothing was funnier than a suppressed church laugh.

Clark, however, continued without hesitation. The frozen-stiff wife also showed no reaction to the disrespectful display.

The opening paragraphs of official language were expected but what followed Henry assumed were his father's actual words.

Simpson began and the audience settled. "To my son Henry, I leave the entirety of my estate including all possessions, livestock, property, homes, and the lands I own in the Feather River Valley,

Carversville, and all the other properties I own in the state of California."

A couple of looks were exchanged and Betty murmured to Gerald, "Other properties?"

"I also leave him all the money I have in banks in Carversville and San Francisco."

The mention of big city banks received a couple of, "San Franciscos?" and one, "Why would there be two banks?"

Again, Clark pushed on. "With the following exceptions, Elizabeth Myers will receive the proceeds of the properties in Philadelphia, when or if, she chooses to sell. In addition, she will receive an allowance for all expenses she should incur during her life in an amount she and Henry agree."

Betty squeezed Gerald's hand.

"I also bequeath to Howard and Martha Goodman, twenty thousand dollars."

"Oh, my dear God," Martha yelled out loud then fell into her husband's arms.

"Also, I leave a thousand dollars to Tom Hardy for new scissors."

Tom Hardy looked at Doc and said, "What did he say?" Doc just smiled and schussed the barber.

"Doc is to receive fifteen thousand dollars, a portion of which he should use to hire and train another doctor to take his place when he retires."

Doc looked at Tom Hardy and said dryly. "Well, I'll be dipped."

"Mary and June Thatcher will get two thousand dollars per year for the care and feeding of every abused or abandoned animal that comes their way. Buy them, house them, care for them, and find them a new home as you see fit."

The two women, who had been completely surprised to receive an invitation, since their only contact with Amos was to occasionally treat and care for his livestock, sat speechless with mouths ajar.

The lawyer continued speaking but this time he addressed people he hadn't deemed necessary to invite to the reading. In a much lower and almost disrespectful tone he read the next section of the will. "I leave approximately thirty thousand acres of property I own along the Feather River Valley, described by deed, to Cholok of the Maidu Indian Tribe."

There was a gasp from the crowd, and a "that's a lot," was mumbled.

Clark went on, "The land is the tribe's ancestral home and is theirs by right. It was taken from them, and I'm giving it back."

The lawyer looked up and addressed the gathering, apparently off script. "Amos recently added this codicil to this document."

The lawyer lowered his voice and spoke much quicker than he had before, something Henry immediately recognized as suspicious.

"In case Cholok precedes me in death, the entirety of the property then transfers to his daughter Aponi."

Betty looked at Gerald, and Gerald looked at Henry, who happened at that moment, to be looking at the lawyer's wife. She was still basking in the sunlight but now had a slight but perceivable grin.

Clark raised his voice back to a courtroom tone and pronounced, "Finally, my partnership in the Hotel Ramona is hereby dissolved with my interests going to Angus MacGregor."

The red-hair man stood, then sat down, then stood up again. When he finally came to rest, Henry patted him on the back.

Clark sounded as if he was about to finish. He pulled a paper from a file and held it up. "I've been informed by this telegram, which I received earlier this morning, that for clarification of some minor terms, bank balances, statements, and the locations of the properties mentioned in the will, several representatives from the Wells Fargo Depository in San Francisco, and two representatives of the legal firm of Weiss, Roberts and Coleman will be arriving to meet with Mr. Henry Cronin." He shuffled the telegram back into the file on the table. "I was required by Amos Cronin to notify these firms immediately upon his demise and, apparently, they are arriving sometime today." He changed his tone, trying for friendly, "Naturally, being Amos's primary lawyer and executer of the will, I felt that expediency in the reading outweighed the necessity for their presence at these proceedings."

Henry stood up. "Meeting over."

The lawyer stammered. "I wasn't quite finished."

The folks started talking and milling about.

Angus shouted out. "I have some refreshments for you all in the dining room." Angus then leaned over to Henry's shoulder. "I'll get rooms ready for the visitors, and I wouldn't talk to Clark again until after you talk to them."

Henry nodded, started to leave, and everyone, save the lawyer and the wife, followed.

Before he could escape, Martha Goodman approached Henry tearfully. "Oh Mr. Cronin."

Henry smiled. "Now, did you call my father Mr. Cronin?"

She sheepishly said, "No. He insisted on just Amos."

"Then please...Henry."

She breathed easier. "Henry...is this for real? I mean we have been struggling for years and years and without your father's...I mean Amos's help to get started, I don't know where we, or for that matter, where this town would be. But, Henry, dear Henry, this is too much. Is it for real?"

"Mrs. Goodman—"

Now she too became insistent. "Martha, if you please."

"Martha," he grinned, "I don't know that much about my father, so I have to ask you, did you ever know him to say something that wasn't true?"

She shook her head. "No, never. He wasn't an easy man..." she looked up at the ceiling and apparently to God, "and the dog... well...but Amos, he helped us get started." She paused a second, took a breath, and said softly. "But he always kept his word."

"Then, that is your answer. Isn't it?"

Suddenly, she leaped forward, grabbed both his cheeks, and kissed him long and clean on the mouth. She then stepped back and put her hand over her mouth, embarrassed.

Her husband, Howard, stepped up. "I'd kiss you too, but I think that one spoke for both of us."

Betty and Gerald politely pulled Henry away and guided him to the nearest wall. Angus joined them.

"Henry, you should wait on these arrivals before going back to the cabin." Betty looked at him curiously. "You were planning on going back?"

"Yes, I was. Rufus is there and the stock needs to be fed."

Angus stepped in front, shaking his head and waving a finger. "I got that." He walked away, corralled one of his workers, gave some instructions, then returned. "I will take care of everything. You stay here and handle business. No worries."

Betty and Gerald took Henry by the arm and found a table where suddenly a pot of coffee appeared.

"Do you think that Zuni, Aponi, and the tribe know about the will?"

Henry didn't hesitate. "Absolutely. I'm certain they did. And somebody else did too. Cholok's and Amos's death are obviously related and Cudworth's connection is the key to their murder."

There was an awkward pause before Betty spoke again. "Did you read his letter yet?"

Henry patted his pocket and shook his head. "Not yet."

"Why?"

"I just didn't think it was related to any of this, so I was waiting till I was ready to read what he wrote."

Gerald gave him a stern look.

"Okay, I'm afraid of what he wrote."

Betty looked at him with love in her eyes. "I understand how you feel, but there is little doubt in my mind that letter will have answers to a multitude of questions. But you are right. Some things about the past probably could wait. However, I think there is more in that envelope than just why he did what he did back when you were born."

"Betty's right, Henry." Gerald spoke with certainty. "Go...find a quiet spot and read the letter."

Henry stood there for a minute, his hand tapping the letter's pocket. Finally, he stood and started to leave the hotel. He got to the porch, looked north, then south, then found himself thinking that the log near the river with Aponi next to him would have been the right place. His aunt was probably right, but he somehow knew there were answers that his father and his friend took to their graves.

CHAPTER 34
CARVERSVILLE, CALIFORNIA
DECEMBER 1869

Bogart and Amelia made a quick exit from the meeting, going through a side door unnoticed. A retreat from an audience which was a total reversal of their normal behavior. They always arrived and departed as if they were the most important people in the room—chins held high, nose tilted up, and their eyes never making full contact. It was the everyday social behavior of Amelia, and traits she demanded her husband adopt. The superior attitude wasn't a natural talent, as she came from humble stock— criminal to be accurate. She deemed her attitude a necessary worker-skill, a trade, a means of social and wealth advancement.

He offered his devotion and accepted her demands because he was a weak, broken man who, when they first met, became intoxicated by her beauty and sexuality. He was just a man who knew he possessed average looks, ability, and social position but would be immediately elevated to a position of admiration by his peers when she agreed to marry him.

She grew her abilities to dominate as their marriage aged but became more dissatisfied with her circumstance when his position in the legal community went from associate counsel in a San Francisco firm to sole practitioner in this outlying mountain town. The only reason she had stayed with Clark as long as she had was the inclination that Reginald Cudworth, one of the wealthiest men she had ever met, was as corrupt as she was.

"We need to hurry." Bogart pushed her out the door and down the stairs to the alley outside the hotel.

She was balking, not at the urgency, but at the effort that was necessary. "I will not be hurried. We will walk directly, but I will not let on that we are not in complete control."

They were now side-by-side and headed north to the white house. He was carrying a thick file and struggling to keep the papers within secure. She was having some difficulty fastening her winter shawl. The weather had become much more seasonable, allowing a sunny day to warm the mountain air for just a few hours in the afternoon. Their pace was set by urgency, but also an effort to minimize the chill.

"The representatives will be arriving this afternoon and I want to get all these papers signed by the boy before they get here." The file slipped again, and he grabbed it. "I want to tell Cudworth I accomplished what he needed and get instructions about how he wants me to handle the backlash it will cause."

The small smile she had on her face while sitting at the meeting returned. "I wouldn't worry about that. I believe he has anticipated the family's reaction and is prepared."

"I'm not thinking about him. I'm thinking about us. We must exist in this town after this is over and we need to be careful about our reputation."

She choked out a surprised response. "I don't think we will have to be concerned with what others think. We will never ever be successful taking chickens and apple pies as fees. Cudworth and the railroad is our ticket. His is the only opinion we need to worry about."

He started to speak, but her cold stare chilled him to the bone.

Wesley Strong was plotting his attack. He needed to anticipate the opponent and be prepared to parry while counter punching. He had a cigarette burning and had downed several double shots of whisky to bolster his courage. He'd fought in the Mexican-American war and had killed several men with a rifle and two in hand-to-hand combat. He was still fit and prided himself on being able to call upon a command presence when necessary. However, he was about to go up against the most formidable enemy he'd faced—a man with money and power. Cudworth never needed to raise a hand or pull a trigger; he only needed to pick up a pen.

The outcome of his assignment had been accomplished and the goals Cudworth had given him had been achieved, but Strong knew that the rich man would balk at giving him his due.

He saw the lawyer and the wife coming up the sidewalk. He tossed the cigarette down and ground it with his heel. They were a complication he didn't need right now.

"Hello Wesley." She grinned her pearly white teeth at him.

"Mrs. Clark," he responded unemotionally.

"Oh, we are way past Mrs. Clark, aren't we?"

Bogart tried to get past him but failed. "Is he inside? I...we... need to see him immediately."

Strong let the demand hang a second.

Amelia winked at him.

"I'll check." Strong turned on his heels and pushed the front door open.

They followed closely.

"Wait here," he said, now terse.

She pouted a, "Ummmp."

Strong walked down the walnut-stained floor to tall double doors with large brass doorknobs. He knocked once then went in, closing the door behind him.

"The lawyer and the wife are here."

Cudworth was behind his desk, dressed in a white suit which seemed a little tighter than it had before. He didn't look up from the papers he was reading. "Send them."

Strong stood silent and didn't move.

Cudworth looked up, then sort of shrugged. "What?"

"In or away?"

"Send them in," Cudworth barked.

Strong stood another second then pushed the doors open and found the two right there.

She came in first. "Reggie, so good to see you. Have you lost weight? Why, you look marvelous."

Cudworth grunted and didn't get up.

"I have what you need but I think we should talk about it," the lawyer said quickly.

Cudworth grunted again.

She ran a finger on the desk. "I told him not to worry about this. I said that Reggie Cudworth had covered all the angles. But... you know lawyers, he's just trying to watch out for you."

"Uh huh, what do you have?"

"The death certificate for Cholok of the Maidu Tribe." He opened the file while standing and again almost dropped everything.

276

She smiled, "Reggie, he worked hard to get this quickly, just like you requested."

The white suit said slowly, "Mr. Cudworth, if you please."

"Why certainly," she responded, but added with a soft coy voice, "Reggie."

Bogart stammered on. "I had to pull in a lot of favors to get this." His voice became high pitched. "After all, there was no body."

Cudworth rose.

Bogart gulped. "I had to get an affidavit from Sheriff Mitchell who said there was a written note and statements from Cholok's squaw."

Cudworth's face changed color and he slowly repeated, "The written note?"

Bogart stammered. "It wasn't part of the submission, and I left out what the note said so no damage done, right?"

"You had better hope not."

There was silence as the lawyer handed over the paper.

He read it quickly then handed it back. "Good."

"Do not show this to the lawyers from San Francisco or the family." He paced around his desk and pointed to a chair.

Clark took a step.

"It's not for you, you idiot."

She ballet stepped to the chair and sat with a little ankle exposed for effect.

Strong walked into the field of battle. "What's so important about this death certificate?"

Cudworth looked at the lawyer. "Tell him."

"Cronin added a codicil to his will." Clark stammered. "A codicil is—"

"I know what it means." Strong interrupted.

"In case the Indian, Cholok, died, his daughter gets the property."

Strong didn't understand why that was important.

The wife added the reason. "According to California law, a woman, especially an Indian woman, cannot own property."

"I still don't understand."

Cudworth looked at the others who were silent, who also looked as if they were without a full explanation.

"Confusion." He leaned back on the desk. "This started with a man who refused to sell me the ground I needed because of these...Indians." He almost spit the word. "But I found out through my friends here," he extended his open palm toward the wife, "that not only did Cronin leave the property I want to an Indian but added the daughter to the will...just in case." He winked at Amelia.

Strong resettled and waited.

"What you have to understand is that while this isn't Tombstone or Deadwood or some other lawless wild west town, it is ruled exactly the same way. The men in power used gunfighters and I use lawyers and judges. Same exact thing, just not as messy."

He walked to his side of the desk and sat down with a thump. "I need confusion, a wrinkle, a deviation from normal procedures, then I can step in, use my 'gunfighters,' and get what I want."

He put both hands on the desk and leaned over. "It doesn't matter if it's actually legal, it's about who is saying it is."

Everything came clear for Strong.

Cudworth then gave the next set of instructions. "Clark, you start the inheritance process immediately. Obviously, don't give them any details."

"What is this confusion you're talking about?" Strong wasn't ready to let it go.

Cudworth nodded to Clark again. "Go ahead."

The lawyer continued, "I am going to get Henry Cronin to file a quitclaim deed honoring his father's bequest. It is unlike a normal title transfer. It doesn't promise that the grantor, in this case Henry Cronin, has a clear title. It simply states that the grantor, the boy, is giving up any legal claim he has to the property. So, he transfers the property to the Indian girl, who, by law, can't own it...but now Cronin doesn't either."

Amelia removed a powder puff from her purse. "Once Bogart gets the Cronin boy to sign the deed, Reggie...I mean Mr. Cudworth files a claim with the government for the ground he wants. The Cronin boy has no more rights to the property and the girl doesn't own it. So...fait du complete." She examined herself in the little mirror and replaced the puff.

"Wait, what?" Strong got lost in the transaction. "You file a claim?"

Cudworth actually smiled. "We can thank Mr. Lincoln for this. The property is no longer owned by a Cronin so, by default, it is owned by the government. I file a claim under the Homestead Act of 1862 and buy it all for a dollar an acre." The last part he said as if he were eating ice cream.

He interlaced his fingers across the girth of his belly. "They can try to fight it in court, where they will find my lawyers and judges ready for them. This has been like a sport for the government...taking ground away from Indians. And know this for certain, there is not a possibility that some little Indian-girl, or boy-child from Philadelphia, is going to stop me from completing a multi-million-dollar connection between the east and west coast railroad."

The wife leaned forward a little, her facial expression almost demonic. "The moment Henry Cronin signs the paper...Reggie wins." She said his name, Reggie, slow and sexy.

Cudworth walked to the chair and extended his hand to the wife who smiled demurely and rose.

"I will submit a bill for my services." Clark coughed out.

"Indeed." Cudworth, paying him no attention, kissed Amelia's hand. "It will be my pleasure to pay this debt...once the paper is signed."

She rose, curtsied, and took her husband's hand as he led her across the room.

Strong held the door for the lawyer and the wife, then closed it behind them.

Cudworth spoke with disgust in his voice. "They want ten thousand dollars to get the boy to sign the title transfer to the Indian girl. She told me they plan to slip it into the stack of papers he has to sign to execute the other terms of the Cronin will. Ten thousand dollars—thieves."

Strong still stood with his hands on the doorknobs and his back to the power, summoning his courage.

"Is there something else?"

Strong spun around. "One thousand seven hundred and fifty dollars."

Cudworth slowly reached for a wooden cigar box. "Oh, now that's a lot of money."

"It is, and I would like to have it now, if you please."

Cudworth looked at Strong overtop of the cigar as he fired it up with a long wooden match. "I do like a good cigar, but I hate biting the tips off to get a good draw, don't you?"

Strong didn't answer.

"You want one?"

Strong remained silent, though he found it a little tougher than he expected.

"Wesley, I have to pay that lawyer and his whore wife about

two thousand dollars for a death certificate for that Indian because...there was no body to prove he was dead."

Strong repositioned his weight.

Cudworth continued, "And speaking of dead bodies, the other two, Stull's friends...and that fighting dog? Again...no bodies?" He drew a long breath and expelled grey smoke. "So...how do I know they're really dead? How do I know they won't show up at my door looking for money...just like you are? Tell me again, what do I owe you, exactly."

"Amos Cronin, Cholok, Sid Stull, Soapy Smith, Bite and...that dog are all dead. You owe me one thousand seven hundred and fifty dollars. It's what you agreed to, and what I'm entitled to."

More smoke rose from puffy lips. "Putting aside for the moment what you think I actually bargained for, I'm a little nervous about giving you that kind of money all at once. It might look bad for me if you suddenly started spending a lot of cash around town." He puffed and watched the smoke. "So, this is what I think is fair. I'll give you an extra fifty dollars a month, until let's say we reach five hundred dollars for any service you feel you rendered. How about that?"

Strong's jaw tightened and his face reddened.

Cudworth leaned back on the desk. "Anything else?"

Strong turned away.

"Oh, by the way, do you know where the bodies you allegedly...dealt with, actually are?"

"Their location wasn't included in your recent proposal." He spun to face Cudworth. "Are we renegotiating?"

Cudworth studied the glowing end of his cigar. "No, I am not. Close the door on your way out."

CHAPTER 35
CARVERSVILLE, CALIFORNIA
DECEMBER 1869

A quiet place to think in Carversville seemed impossible to find. Everyone was abuzz. The terms of the will were being shared like a spring downfall and Henry had no place to hide. He walked as quickly as possible past folks who were shouting out or were trying to step up to him. Eventually, he got past the people, the houses, and the stores, but he was running out of road. There were only two places left before the slope started up to the mountain. A big white house surrounded by a white fence and a perfectly cultured garden was on his left. A church which wasn't quite as well-cared for, but had character and grace was on his right. Naturally, he chose the church.

The red-painted double doors were unlocked, and he went in cautiously. A small man with a broom was sweeping up and paid him no attention. Pews were lined up in a typical row-by-row fashion and were similar to what he remembered in the cathedral in Philadelphia. The oak seats in this much smaller, much less grand edifice looked just as uncomfortable as the pews inside the towering domed roof frequented by a city full of rich churchgoers.

"I didn't know your father."

Henry swung around and saw that the preacher from the funeral service had come in from a side door.

"Oh, sorry. Is it alright if I sit awhile? I kinda have a lot going on right now, and I just wanted some peace."

"Right place for that, young man. And, yes of course. Take as much time as you need." He turned to leave.

"You really didn't know my father?"

"No, son."

"But you said good things about him."

The preacher nodded. "Sometimes it's enough to witness what other people think of someone to know the true heart of the man. I didn't know him, but I know folks who did and that was good enough for me."

"Thanks..." he then added, "and thank you again for your words today."

"Take as much time as you need."

The preacher walked away, and Henry was alone.

He patted his pocket again and took out the letter. He studied it for a minute. It had a spot of unbroken candle wax on the flap which had a fingerprint embedded in its purple surface. He broke the seal and carefully opened the flap.

He removed five pages. The three on top were all written with a steady hand with what looked like the same pen and ink. The fourth page was not margined the same and contained only a few paragraphs on only one side of the paper. It looked like the same handwriting, but it appeared hurried and sloppy. There were smudges and ink stains on the paper.

The last page was a complete surprise. It was a map, folded neatly and separated from the others. It had hand-drawn lines, strange symbols, and small drawings of figures, some men and some animals. No words were written on the front, but there was a poem on the back. He refolded it, then returned it to the envelope.

He looked at the first three pages and read the first lines.

Dear Son,

There have been so many times I have tried to write to you over the years but I was never able to find the words. Your Aunt Betty, my beloved wife's sister, wrote to me many times and told me of your growing up and about some of your adventures. I anxiously awaited each and every...

He stopped reading.

Aunt Betty was right, this could wait.

Henry put it, and the other two pages, back into the envelope then picked up the hastily written page.

Henry,

I am writing this in a hurry because I fear something bad is about to happen. If you're reading this, I'm dead, most likely murdered.

A man named Reginald Cudworth is an owner of a railroad company that wants some property I own so they can build a railroad. I own this land now but it really belongs to the Maidu Tribe.

On the other side of the mountains, there is a railroad being built connecting the east coast to the west coast. The east coast rail construction has reached Nevada and Cudworth's company is building the connection westward from San Francisco, but the property I own is stopping them.

He'll never get it from me, but he might do me some harm trying. What he doesn't know is, that if something happens to me, I left the property to Cholok who is the head of the tribe. The Maidu live there now as they have for hundreds of years. This evil man will do whatever he can to get his hands on that property, which will destroy the tribe and their village. He is powerful and has many friends in high government places who want this railroad to happen. I fear now doing what I did might have put Cholok in danger. I fear treachery is afoot.

From what your aunt wrote, you are very smart, like your mother, Rose. Son, if something happens to me, try to make sure the tribe gets the property, but be careful.

People are going to wonder how I managed to buy all the ground and build this cabin. The truth is, I found gold, and nobody knows how much or where it is. But that is not what this man is after. He wants Feather River and if I'm not here I'll need you to figure out how to make sure he doesn't get it.

I had planned on giving you the other pages I wrote in person because I still don't know how to say what I want to say out loud. The last page is a map, and I wrote a riddle on the back because someone who is smart enough to figure it out will be wise enough to know how to use what they find.

I wish I was there to say I love you,

Your father, Amos

He dropped the letter he held onto his lap and looked up.

Oh my God. What can I do? What should I do?

The door burst open. Gerald came in fast. "They're here, just arrived, the men from San Francisco. You need to come and meet them."

He rose slowly while putting the letter back in his pocket. "Let's go."

CHAPTER 36

CARVERSVILLE, CALIFORNIA

DECEMBER 1869

Henry arrived back at the hotel slightly out of breath and found the lawyer and the wife waiting for him in the lobby.

"This will take just a moment of your time." Bogart Clark approached him, holding out a few papers and a pen. "The meeting this morning ended suddenly, as you remember. These are the release documents enabling the people named in the will to get their inheritance as quickly as possible. They needed to be signed, but as you know, the meeting ended abruptly."

Henry looked side-to-side and saw no help coming.

"Only a moment of your time." The wife took Henry's arm and directed him to a table. "I'm certain these needy people will appreciate you taking the time."

Henry stood between them as the lawyer fanned out the papers. The lawyer then slid them to Henry one at a time. "Here is the paper for Angus." Henry signed. "Doc Brown." Henry signed. "Aponi." Henry signed. "Tom Anderson." The lawyer paused, shuffled his file and placed two more papers down on the table.

"This one is for the livery ladies, and the last one is for Howard and Martha Goodman."

Henry signed all of the documents quickly. "That it?"

The lawyer collected the documents and put them into a file without responding.

Henry pointed to the dining room door. "The lawyers and bankers from San Francisco are here, waiting. We should go in."

The lawyer shook his head. "Not necessary. Henry, they are here for you, not me."

Betty and Gerald came in, saw the lawyer, and beelined for Henry's side. "What's going on?" Betty demanded.

The lawyer with documents secured, responded. "Just getting Amos's money where it's supposed to go."

Now almost frantic, Betty looked at Henry. "You signed papers?"

The lawyer tempered the situation by handing a file of papers to Gerald. "Here's copies of everything, for your records." He nodded politely to Betty, put his arm out for the wife, and the two did an unhurried promenade walk for the front door.

There were five men, and four of them looked exactly like what they did for a living. Two were dressed in respectable blue suits and black ties, and the other two wore pinstriped tailored suits with wide lapels and matching vests. Blue suits were the bankers, and the striped ones were the lawyers. However, the thing that impressed Henry was, in spite of their outward appearance, he didn't immediately distrust them. Both pairs shook Henry's hand firmly with what appeared to be genuine smiles.

He regretted he hadn't had more caution with Clark's paper signing. Now, he thought he should be more prudent with these strangers, but somehow, he seemed to feel as if these men were trustworthy. Still, in the back of his mind, the words from his father's letter were now echoing—treachery is afoot.

There was one other man in the room. He was short, had thin hair combed over a growing bald spot, had horn-rimmed glasses, and wore a not-nearly-as-well-tailored grey suit. He sat alone and was almost hidden behind piles of files and papers on the table. Henry gave him several glances, curious to know to which group he belonged.

Henry went to the empty side of a table. Betty and Gerald sat in chairs near a window leaving him alone to deal with what was to come. They smiled encouragements, but it was clear to Henry he was on his own.

"Mr. Cron—"

"Henry, please." He interrupted the first pinstripe.

The man nodded politely and continued. "Henry, my name is John Anderson. I'm a partner at Weiss, Roberts and Coleman and I worked with your father for almost fifteen years."

Henry looked past the suit and saw grey hairs on the temples and lines in his face. He had bushy eyebrows and an accent he didn't recognize.

"He came to us," Anderson gestured to his partner, "Gabe Honeycutt and I, out of the blue one day and asked us to assist him with the purchase of large parcels of land."

Mr. Anderson waited a moment, but Henry was not capable of quick reactions.

"Yes, well then. Your father knew exactly what he wanted and gave us very explicit instructions to purchase specific properties that were owned by the United States Government. It was largely ground which the U.S. had recently claimed as a result of the war with Mexico...which of course you know we won."

Anderson seemed to wait again for a reaction that didn't come. "After the Mexican-American War, Mexico ceded roughly 55 percent of its territory to the United States, encompassing states like California, Nevada, Utah, most of Arizona and Colorado, and parts of New Mexico, Oklahoma, Kansas, and Wyoming."

"How much?"

The lawyer looked at Henry puzzled. "Excuse me?"

"How much land did you buy for my father?"

Anderson stumbled a bit. "Well, I don't know exactly."

The man at the end of the table had the answer. "One hundred and twenty-three thousand acres, or one hundred and ninety-one square miles," then he added, "more or less."

The fan circulating the ceiling air was the only sound in the room.

After a minute, Henry pointed to the new voice. "And who are you?"

Anderson volunteered the introduction. "This is Benjamin Height. He clerks for us and handles the details of your father's account. Actually...he's a lawyer as well, so you can rely on what he is saying."

Henry looked toward Betty and Gerald who were staring at him with blank expressions.

Mr. Honeycutt attempted to expand on the land purchase. "You see...at the time, the government was selling ground at a dollar and a quarter an acre. The price went up a bit over the years, so your father's total investment was more than that."

The end of table voice said, "One hundred and seventy-eight thousand seven hundred dollars," then added, "more or less."

Henry grumbled something, trying to regain some level of reality. "How was that possible? He lived in a cabin in the mountains. How could he have bought that much ground?"

Mr. Anderson now pointed to the bankers.

The first blue suit stood up, which sort of surprised everyone. "Mr. Cro—"

Henry put his hand in the air.

"My apologies. Henry, your father was a very, very wealthy man."

Henry said, "Cabin...mountains?"

"Maybe I can clarify." The second banker stood. He was much older than the first and appeared to be the authority figure of the entire delegation. He was portly, well-groomed, and sported a very important-looking gold watch chain. "My name is Gottlieb, and I'm the Vice President of San Francisco's Wells Fargo Depository. It will help, I think, if I explain our role here today. You see, around fifteen years ago your father arrived at our offices with two wooden boxes. After he spoke to a few of our people, I was called in to assist. The boxes contained about one hundred pounds of the finest, purest, gold ore I'd ever seen. Most of the gold discovered in California consists of river panned gold dust, or an occasional pile of nuggets. There are a few gold mines where larger deposits are mined but that ore comes from tons and tons of solid rock that requires heavy equipment and a large workforce. The gold your father had was in chunks, rocks as big as one's fist or bigger."

He poured a glass of water then continued. "The price of gold then was about twenty-one dollars an ounce. What your father brought in that day in wooden crates was worth thirty-three thousand dollars." He took a drink while looking like he was judging reaction. "We are not an assessor, or even a bank for that matter. We are a depository, a gold depository that buys and ships gold for our government. We are a private company, but we sell only to the federal gold depository in Washington D.C."

"There is obviously more to this story," Henry said.

"There is. When your father decided to buy additional pieces of ground, he would talk to his legal partners here at the table today about how much he would need, and then, over a couple of weeks, wooden boxes containing much more than was needed would be delivered to our depository via land transport from Hainesport, which I believe is the next town over from Carversville."

"So, he only bought property with the boxes of gold?"

"No, not exactly, he also had boxes delivered, converted the gold to cash then deposited into our accounts. Occasionally, we transferred money to the bank in Carversville, but in amounts, we assumed, were for living expenses. We all believe he shipped from another town and kept most of his transactions private to avoid notoriety. He never spoke to any of us about where the gold came from, but we suspect that it was to protect Carversville from being overrun by prospectors like so many of the towns where gold deposits were discovered."

Henry now coughed out a response. "How much?"

Gottlieb glanced at Betty and Gerald then back to Henry for permission.

"It's okay. How much?"

He cleared his throat. "Over the years he deposited...about six million dollars."

Betty actually slipped off the chair.

Henry stood up and walked to the window. "Tell me about the property he bought."

Mr. Anderson took back the reins. "Well, that would take some time."

The voice at the end of the table announced confidently, "I know."

Mr. Anderson gave him a stare but nodded to go on.

"Your father purchased property up and down the Feather River Valley. I did all the research, managed all the assets, compiled the deeds, transferred documents, paid whatever fees and taxes, and handled any legal disputes or issues and—"

Henry put his hand up and stopped him. "Cudworth. Tell me about Cudworth."

The voice became silent immediately.

The banker, Gottlieb, sat down and put his fingers together like he was contemplating his answer. "Reginald Cudworth is a very wealthy man who has made his money in a variety of different businesses. He started in shipping, got into some trouble with that, then moved to land speculation, and most recently, used his old connections in shipping to corner the market in Chinese labor. He has also managed to become involved with William Ralston, a banker and a gold speculator. They are partners in a deal to connect the eastern railroad to San Francisco. However," he looked at the lawyers, "there seems to be some conflict with the partnership and rumor has it Cudworth's position is extremely vulnerable."

"Is he dangerous?"

The four men all grumbled at the same time.

Gottlieb mumbled, "We are professional men and cannot engage in speculati—"

"Yes. He is extremely dangerous." The voice of Benjamin Height rose to answer Henry's question.

The men grumbled again, but didn't disagree.

Henry walked back to the table and sat down. "Sum it up, please."

Anderson tapped a pencil. "I believe it is safe to say that together with the properties you own in Philadelphia—"

Henry suddenly leaned across the table and said quickly, "Did Clark, the attorney handling my father's affairs ever give you a copy of my father's will?"

Anderson stammered a second and looked to his partner. He shook his head. "Why no, I thought we'd attend to that when we were here. Is it a problem?"

Betty stood up, arms down, fists clenched.

Henry stood up too and walked toward his aunt and comforted her while guiding her back to her seat.

Henry then looked to the end of the table. "Your name again is?"

"Benjamin Height."

"Mr. Anderson."

"Yes."

"Does your firm, Weiss, Roberts and Coleman have offices in cities other than San Francisco?"

"Why yes, we do. We are represented in the state capitol in Sacramento and the city of Los Angeles, more than two dozen attorneys—"

"How important am I as a client to your firm?"

He jumped at the answer. "Extremely important as is witnessed by our presence."

"Good. You have just opened a new branch office here in Carversville. Your clients will be me and the residents of this fine town, which I assure you will welcome you with open arms."

"I...I..."

"And your attorney here will be..." Henry stopped suddenly and leaned toward Height. "How much do you make?"

The voice at the end of the table for the first time seemed unsure of an answer. "I make $52.50 a month."

Henry turned and readdressed the head attorney. "And your attorney will be Mr. Benjamin Height who is promoted with a new salary of $150 per month."

The voice at the end of the table gasped.

Henry looked at him and smiled. "More or less."

Anderson sat down and said weakly, "Yes, of course."

Henry slid the file of papers that Bogart Clark, his former attorney, had given him, to Height. "I'll see to it you get a copy of my father's will. You'll also need to go through these papers I just signed. I think I made a big mistake, and I'll need your help to dig out of the mess I made."

Henry stood and walked to the men. "Thank you for coming here to help me. I appreciate what you've done in the past, and I'm sure this is but the beginning."

They all broke into broad smiles.

Henry put an arm on Gottlieb's shoulder. "Naturally, if you need anything you'll communicate though Mr. Height. Now, I am certain my friend Angus, the owner of this hotel, has made up rooms for your stay tonight and has prepared a fine dinner. Please enjoy your stay here in Carversville."

Betty and Gerald were standing proud, watching their boy dominate men of prominence and stature.

Henry beckoned to his aunt and uncle. "Should we eat, as well?"

She started to walk to him.

"Don't say it." Henry shook a finger.

"I won't." Betty put a hand over her mouth.

They walked together toward the door.

She couldn't hold it in and exploded. "I told you the wife was evil."

"I know, you were right. All better now?"

"No..." she chuckled, "but I'm getting there."

They were almost to the door when Henry turned around, "Hey, Benjamin, come have dinner with us...leave the papers. No one will touch them."

He smiled and stepped lively.

"Do you prefer Benjamin or Ben or what?"

"My mother calls me Benji."

"Then Benji it is. Tell me, how are you at all-out war?"

CHAPTER 37

FEATHER RIVER VALLEY, CALIFORNIA

JANUARY 1870

The temperature was well below freezing, but the sun had no resistance from the cloudless sky. It wasn't warm enough to melt anything, but it was bright enough to remind one of what being warm felt like. Several snowfalls had deposited about a foot of snow, more where it drifted against the fence, or the rock wall, or the windward side of the barn. A light morning breeze had come up with the sun. It fluffed tiny crystals of snow into the air like small ocean waves as it blew across the open space.

Betty wore a fur-lined leather coat pulled tight to her chin, and mittens that were twice the size of her hands. Normally, back in Philadelphia, a hat, cap, bonnet, or anything that covered her head and mussed her hair would have never happened, however, there wasn't anyone around to damage her vanity except for Gerald who had seen her at her worst and still looked at her as he did the first day they met. She stood on the front porch of the cabin, mittens wrapped over the rail, looking out over the pasture.

She and Gerald had spent the night in the cabin, and she couldn't help herself but to spend her time cleaning and straightening up. Henry wouldn't like it, but then again, he never did like her messing about in his room.

Gerald came out of the barn and hustled up to the porch, banging the snow off his boots when he arrived. "The livestock is all taken care of." He blew into his hands. "Damn, it's cold."

"Come, stand next to me. The sun will warm us up."

"I'd rather get next to the fire."

"Get over here." She chastised him.

They stood in silence for a bit, listening to what Amos must have heard every day of his life. Today, it was the mountain orchestra playing a song to the passing of the winter solstice.

She laid her head on his shoulder. "Are we doing the right thing?"

Gerald shrugged. "There are things that need attention that we've put off for too long. But I don't know, maybe it is the right time, maybe it isn't."

She didn't respond.

Puddle appeared, coming out of the forest like a mythical steed, his black coat gleaming against the blinding white snow. His chest was out, his head was up, and grey streams of air billowed from his nose. It was the end of the journey from the Maidu village, but it looked like he was just fresh from the barn. Henry, on the other hand, looked a bit weather-beaten.

Puddle cantered across the pasture effortlessly plowing through the snow. He grunted and whinnied and bobbed his head until the porch stopped his forward momentum.

Gerald hurried down and took hold of Puddle's bridle. "I got him, Henry. I'll get him brushed down and fed. You go warm up."

Henry stiffly dismounted, then gratefully handed the reins off to his uncle.

"Come on. I have hot soup ready for you." Betty gathered him up and almost pushed him through the door.

It took a little time to reacclimate, but sitting by the fire with the steam coming off the bowl of soup, the cup of coffee, and his socks helped get him warmed back to a livable comfort level.

"I don't know how my father did it. The cold penetrates everything and riding a horse...it's just torture. Meanwhile, it doesn't bother Puddle at all. He loves it, but me sitting up on a saddle, fifty feet in the air—"

"He's not that big."

"Might as well be." He blew on his fingers again.

Rufus was up in his loft on the woodpile. His wound was almost completely hidden by his coat which was growing back over the long scar. Somehow, he'd accepted his limited exposure to the elements and was seemingly content with a resting recovery.

"Tell me something," Betty said, bending over the soup pot. "How does Aponi handle the cold? Does it bother her as much as it does you?"

He looked as if didn't understand her joke. "She's used to it." His voice then softened. "At least...she doesn't complain about it."

"Uh-huh."

"Okay, okay. I get it."

Gerald came through the door. "It's getting late, and we have to go. The team is all hitched up."

Neither Betty or Henry looked at each other.

She put a lid on the pot and put the spoon in the sink. She took off her apron and walked to the hook where she had left her fur-lined leather coat. She reached up and started to take it down but stopped. She looked at Henry, then walked over, sitting down on the hearth next to him.

"This is the right thing, isn't it?"

Henry nodded. "Of course it is."

"There are things we need to do in Philadelphia that just won't wait any longer."

"We talked about this. I understand."

She sat quiet for a minute.

He did too.

"How's Aponi?" she said, suddenly.

He brightened immediately. "She's good." He turned to her and spoke quickly. "You should see how she handles things at the village. It's really amazing. There are a hundred people, maybe more, all relying on her leadership." He looked up at the ceiling and smiled. "Grown men, elders, hunters, wives…they don't come to her for decisions…they go to her to talk things out."

"How are you handling it?"

"I don't understand. What do you mean, handling it?"

Betty looked at him with a mother's love in her eyes. "Your feelings for her?"

"Uhh," his face reddened.

She patted his leg and stood abruptly. "Henry, dear, it's late, we have to get going, but I do have one more thing I need to ask you before I leave."

"What's that?"

"How is Benji working out?"

"He's good. He got his office set up and, as you know, we've had a couple of strategy sessions."

"Do you think you can handle this, alone?"

"I'm not worried."

"Why? You're up against a man with powerful friends who will stop at nothing to win."

Henry smiled and looked at her with confidence.

She chuckled and shook a finger at him. "I've seen that look before. The last time I saw it I spent an entire day with an Archbishop bailing you out of a lot of trouble."

"Yeah, that was fun, but this is as serious as it gets. I cannot forget the man killed my father."

"But how will you manage?"

He smiled, "I have a plan."

"I don't understand how anybody could come and go without Rufus barking his head off. I was out here at dusk and these things are new." There were many objects of various descriptions placed on Amos's grave. Most were partially covered with snow, but he pointed to a string of beads, a small clay pot, and a single arrow. "These were not here last night."

"That's a ceremonial arrow, Yurok, I think. They are a tribe, north of here, that has fought hard against settlers...very protective of their lands. The feather fletching is from an eagle—important and sacred."

"But...Rufus? He hears everything, how come he didn't react?"

"Probably recognized their scent."

"You just said their. You think there was more than one person here?"

She nodded and pointed "Look, there are a lot of different size tracks in the snow." She gestured to the tracks. "These are ours. Those are not. Other tribes...other friends of your father have visited."

He nodded.

She bent over and dusted snow from the clay pot. "This is from the matron of the Madai tribe. I recognize the bead work of the Hupa, and the arrow...that's from a hunter, a warrior. All these gifts are tributes to your father."

Henry shook his head slowly. "So many stories he could have told me."

She smiled and took his hand. "They will be revealed to you in time."

They walked together back to the cabin.

At the kitchen table, she poured a cup of tea for him.

"That's not the tribe tea, is it? Not my favorite."

Aponi mumbled, "Like father, like son," then pointed at him, "drink it, it's good for you."

She saw him glance over at the stack of papers Benji had prepared. "What's bothering you?"

"I've read those files over and over, and I'm nervous about my plan." He shook his head. "I need to spend more time reading."

"Okay, but are you still confident?"

He hesitated a split second before answering. "I'm trying."

She took a sip of her tea. "I know you will find the way."

"I'm glad you think so."

"I am confident."

"I don't know why. A year ago, I was pulling childish pranks and now I have the fate of your tribe in my hands." He dropped his gaze.

"Don't do that," she said tersely.

He looked up. "Do what?"

"Let doubt enter your thoughts. It will take up the energy you need to solve this."

He looked into her eyes. "I don't understand why you believe in me when there is no earthly reason why you should."

She burst into a grand smile and pointed a finger at his face. "That is exactly the reason."

He was mystified. "Huh? What reason?"

She beckoned to the cup. "Drink up."

He kept staring.

She took both his hands in hers. "When this is over, I'll tell you what I mean. Until then, just believe what I say. I have faith in you."

Somehow that calmed him.

"We need to get to the village. Go take care of your friends in the barn so we can get going."

He shot another look at the papers.

"There is no answer in them. You already know what you have to do, you just haven't realized it yet."

"I hope you're right."

"Go." She pointed, and he obeyed.

When the door closed, Rufus jumped down from his perch. He walked over to Aponi and put his head in her lap.

"He needs to believe, and we are going to have to help him."

The big dog grumbled.

"I know...like father like son."

CHAPTER 38
CARVERSVILLE, CALIFORNIA
JANUARY 1870

Henry asked to sit alone—an untouched cup of coffee in front of him was losing heat. He'd been staring out a small window in Benji's office for thirty minutes. The street scene was a normal winter's day, nothing to deserve his attention. the hustling and bustling of the people of Carversville were of little importance to Henry this day.

Aponi sat out of his eyesight a few feet away, while Odina was doing his impression of the statue of an Indian in front of a cigar store. Benji was at his desk quietly going through legal documents one at a time.

The clock on a shelf chimed.

Benji looked up and, without a lot of emotion, broke the silence. "It's time to go."

Aponi rose, approached Henry quietly, and put her hand on his shoulder. "Ready?"

Henry looked up and saw her sparkling eyes. He touched her warm hand and closed his fingers on hers. "No matter what happens—"

"Don't you say another word." She lightly smacked the back of his head.

Henry laughed and rubbed his head. "My Aunt Betty does that to me."

"I know. She told me it works."

He laughed. "Alright. Let's do this."

The three smaller people went first, the mountain trailing two steps behind. Out the door, down the steps, then turning north, they picked their way along a shoveled path of snow, avoiding the muddy patches as they went.

Henry, in the lead, looked back over his shoulder, "Careful where you walk. We don't want to ruin Cudworth's carpet."

Bogart Simpson Clark had laboriously prepared all the papers for the settlement that had taken weeks to organize and was about to take place. He was being extremely careful as he wanted to avoid a future confrontation with the law offices of Weiss, Roberts and Coleman although secretly he thought it was unavoidable. Malpractice was certainly on the table, but the amount of money Cudworth promised him outweighed the fear of losing his license to practice law.

The wife did not share his concerns. She'd not given much thought to anything but what she was going to wear. After much consideration, she ordered a special outfit. It was a taffeta dress with equal vertical stripes in different shades of blue. She was told by the San Francisco designer it was inspired by New York's latest fashion, and she quoted its features to anyone who would listen. "It has bishop sleeves emphasizing the fullness at the elbow which tapers to my wrist where it features gold and blue fringe.

It's definitely a day dress, because evening gowns had off-the-shoulder necklines and short sleeves." It took weeks to get and days to alter but now here she was, perched in her finery, in a settlement conference that, at its end, would change their lives forever.

Clark saw that Cudworth, unlike his fashion-crazy wife, was all business as usual. However, he did detect an ever so slight lightness in Cudworth's step, like a weight had been removed from his shoulders. "Sir, I have everything they will need to sign right here. Its only four signatures, two from him and two from the Indian girl."

Cudworth pointed a pudgy finger at his desktop. "Put them there," he paused as he plopped down into his chair, "but let's not rush them into it. They know what they have to do, but I don't want to spook them. So, we will take it slow."

"Very well, sir." The lawyer nodded his head, almost bowing. "One more thing, though."

"What's that?"

"I think we should put the check for purchase with the papers in the file, so they can see it. I think it will help motivate them to sign."

"Hmmm." Cudworth reached for the cigar box, then stopped. "No. I'm going to wait on that, but good idea."

The lawyer beamed.

The wife, not paying any attention, was looking for her powder puff and mirror.

There was a knock on the door.

"Enter." Cudworth barked.

A wide, bald Chinese man came in. "They are coming up the walk."

Cudworth nodded. "Keep them waiting for five minutes, then knock on the door."

The wide man turned and left without a word.

"He's a big one." the wife remarked.

"Mr. Strong is no longer in my employ."

She found her puff. "Pity."

Henry surveyed the entry hall where they waited. It was large, almost cavernous. On one long side, doors to several rooms, whose purpose was unknown, were closed. On the other side, an open archway led to a living space with tall windows that opened to the gardens, and couches and chairs that appeared unused. There were shelves on a long inside wall that held a few pots, and vases, but no books.

At the far end of the hall, an oversized double door was shut tight. A large Chinese man, almost as wide as one of the doors, was planted in front, securing the entry.

Henry looked at Benji. "Are we all set?"

Benji nodded confidently. "I spoke to the staff yesterday. We're ready."

Henry nodded and went back to pacing.

Suddenly, without provocation, the Chinese man turned, opened the door, and beckoned them forward.

Cudworth was behind his desk, Clark was to his right, and the wife sat to his left smiling demurely.

"Come in." Cudworth's voice bellowed.

Henry looked left and right—the wife was occupying the only chair.

The Chinese man came into the room after Odina, who took a position against the wall, about three steps from Aponi. The Chinese man stood at attention on the opposite wall.

"Well, well. It looks like this whole thing will finally come to rest today. I have to tell you I'm very pleased you have decided to settle this." Cudworth's movements were beaming confidence. "Henry, I hope you've not been too inconvenienced with this delay of your return to Philadelphia."

"What makes you think I'm going anywhere?"

Cudworth seemed caught off guard. "Why, I just assumed... being isolated up in the mountains, the cold..." He coughed, then grumbled. "Never mind about that." His voice turned from cordial to business. "Here are the papers that convey the property to me." He slid four documents forward. "There are marks where you need to sign."

Clark stepped forward. "I have put—"

He stopped talking because Henry's look would have stopped a charging bull.

Henry addressed Cudworth and pointed to Aponi. "Explain it to her."

Cudworth leaned back in his chair, resting his head and casting his eyes to the ceiling. "Okay...Mr. Cronin signed a quitclaim deed giving up all rights to the property his father, Amos Cronin, willed to your father, Cholok. The deed named you, Aponi, as the new property owner." He took a little breath. "However, in California, a woman, especially a woman who is...not a citizen, cannot own property. Therefore, since Mr. Cronin gave up all his rights to the property, the state will regain jurisdiction over the land."

Benji had picked up one of the papers and with his head down added, "That has not been adjudicated as yet."

Cudworth looked at Henry's diminutive counsel like he'd just noticed he was in the room. "Who's this?"

Henry didn't answer him but asked a different question. "A court hasn't decided on who owns the property yet, correct?"

"Technically, yes," Cudworth turned his attention back to Henry. "But...I have it on information from very well-placed people that the court will rule in my favor."

Benji again offered some important information missing from Cudworth's dissertation. "Judge Marcus Donahue, the judge in this case whose son, Peter, is your partner in the railroad company?"

Cudworth chuckled. "Quite a coincidence, isn't it?"

Henry chuckled back, which put Cudworth off. "Yes, it is... quite the coincidence."

Cudworth pushed on. "Well, as you can see, your position is untenable. The court is about to rule in my favor because it's the law." He leaned across the desk. "Do you really think that the court that marched 100,000 Indians across three states in the dead of winter is going to give this property to an Indian girl and stop the railroad from connecting the Atlantic to the Pacific Ocean?"

Benji corrected Cudworth's history. "Actually, the court didn't do that. The court ruled it wasn't legal, but President Andrew Jackson said, 'Let the Supreme Court try to stop me,'"

Cudworth almost came out of his chair. "I don't know who you are, but you're right." He looked at Henry and pointed his finger into his face. "Try to stop me."

There was silence, and Henry knew he would have to thank Odina later for not tearing the fat man's head off right there and then.

Cudworth plopped back into his chair. "I think you should sign these papers, and accept my offer, before I change my mind, and the court gives you nothing."

Henry stepped forward and looked down. "I don't see a check." He turned to Benji. "What's the amount?"

"Thirty-three thousand acres at $1.25 per acre equals $41,250," Benji replied.

"Uh huh...yes. Well two things to consider before we discuss the amount. If the court rules for me, which I believe they will you'll get nothing. This settlement meeting today is intended to 'do the right thing.'" He made little quote marks with his fingers. "But...as to the amount... Well, that is the amount your father paid, but there have been some changes to value, and I, as do my partners, have some concerns about the tribe's welfare...when it comes to that much money received all at once."

"Do tell." Henry appeared disinterested, again off-putting Cudworth.

"We believe a payout over time is a better solution, so that is what's offered...a thousand dollars a month for three years."

"So, $36,000 instead of $41,000."

"Like I said...there have been some value changes."

Henry looked at Aponi and smiled. He walked to the edge of the desk and pushed the papers to the side. "There are several reasons why this is never, ever going to happen."

A fearful look pushed up onto Cudworth's face.

Clark stepped back and clutched a paper to his chest, and the wife slumped just a little.

Henry looked at Aponi. "You or me?"

She patted his arm. "This is you."

He sucked in a breath. "Correct me if I'm wrong, but your position in court is: since I gave up the property rights, Aponi cannot inherit because she's a woman, correct?"

Cudworth just nodded.

"Well...she's not just a woman anymore."

Cudworth, the lawyer, and the wife stared at him.

"She's a married woman. Meet Mrs. Henry Cronin, my wife."

Benji withdrew a marriage certificate and placed it on the desk. Clark grabbed it and read.

"The property is now, legally, back in the hands of the Cronin family."

Cudworth stammered, "I don't understand?"

"I gave up the rights when I signed the quitclaim deed that," he pointed to the lawyer, "Mr. Clark snuck it in with other papers I signed without telling me what it was. He was obviously working for your interests, not mine."

The lawyer stepped back, face white.

"The property then went to Aponi but you are challenging that in court claiming she can't own property because she is a woman...an Indian woman. Correct?"

Cudworth didn't answer.

Benji did. "Correct."

"So, Aponi is married, no longer single, she married me, a Cronin, and is now also an American citizen, so—"

"No case." Bogart Simpson Clark exclaimed quietly, "Oh my God."

Cudworth slammed the desk. "I'll fight this to the end."

"You're already at the end...you just don't know it yet, but you're about to find out." He pointed to the papers on the desk. "The real reason you don't have a check on the table is because you don't have any money."

The wife slumped a little more.

"Of course, you remember your partner, Mr. William Ralston?"

Cudworth sucked air.

"I've met with him several times...didn't like him...nasty man. But we did have one thing in common, we both despise you."

Cudworth blinked.

"The fact is your shipping company is bankrupt, your

311

construction labor company is out of work and also broke, and you spent all your cash on the other pieces of property you needed for the rail line. In short, you've borrowed every cent you could, on everything you own, including this house."

Cudworth tried to speak but couldn't, apparently wordless.

Henry stood up, turned his back to Cudworth, and walked to Aponi. "How am I doing?"

"Not bad."

Henry spun around. "You have no idea how rich my father was, do you?"

"Well, he had enough to buy..." he stammered, "but I..."

Henry nodded to Odina.

The mountain opened the door, and the house staff came in one-by-one. Two Chinese women, a black man wearing coveralls, an older woman wearing an apron and a kerchief on her head, and Reverend O'Neil. They found a spot to stand between the wide man and the mountain.

"Get these people out," screamed Cudworth at his bodyguard.

"Ah...sorry, he's no longer your employee. You brought him from your labor company after Mr. Strong left, didn't you?"

Cudworth nodded.

"He is the cousin of Mai and Xing Yung." He pointed to the two women who bowed slightly. He continued slowly, "Cudworth, there have been some...value changes... that are going to affect you, personally."

Cudworth looked up at Henry who'd come around the desk to face him. "I want you to hear this loud and clear. Everything you own, I now own. Ralston had your notes and mortgages, but now I do. I bought them and I'm calling in every debt you owe, effective today."

Benji waved a small stack of papers. "Every single one."

Cudworth gulped. "My house?"

The wife started for the door.

Aponi cut her off. "Sit back down."

She did.

Clark did nothing.

"Let me make the introductions. This is Ingrid Johansson your former cook. She is now an employee at the Hotel Ramona apprenticing under Angus MacGregor. This is your former assistant, Xing Yung who is now the new President of the construction company whose business was built on importing and abusing Chinese labor. Her sister, Mai Yung, who speaks Mandarin, English, French, and Spanish, is now a language teacher. Mr. Samuel Johnson, your gardener, had his name given to him on the plantation where he was a slave before emancipation. He will be a teacher of agriculture. Sam Johnson and Mai Yung will be teaching in a new school that our own, Reverend O'Neil, will help oversee. It is a school that will be public, non-denominational, and will include students from the Maidu tribe."

Cudworth appeared numb.

"Guess where the school is?"

Henry laughed at Cudworth's silence. "You're right. Right here. You're sitting in a classroom in the brand new Carversville Center for Learning."

Clark now started inching for the door, leaving the wife behind.

Henry noticed. "Oh...you two can go if you like, but I don't know where. You will be disbarred by the end of the month. Right, Benji?"

"Guaranteed."

Amelia ran out, screaming. "No."

He followed. "Wait for me."

Cudworth started to get up.

Henry pushed him back into the chair. "I'm not done yet."

Cudworth was grabbing his chest.

"Stop it, you're not dying." Henry pushed the chair around with his foot.

Aponi was standing on the other side. "You murdered Cholok, and Amos Cronin."

Cudworth was now even more pale than he was just a moment before.

She moved in front of Cudworth and continued. "Didn't you wonder where Mr. Strong disappeared to? Well, I'll tell you, he's in jail. There was never enough evidence to connect you to our fathers' deaths, even though there was a note written by Amos Cronin with his blood on it saying you killed him. But now... things are different. Henry, how did he put it?"

Henry answered. "Values changed."

"It was just rumor at first, that you had our fathers killed. No hard proof, but you didn't anticipate that the assassins you hired, or should I say Wesley Strong hired for you, would talk when they drank. Sid Stull and his two buddies had plenty to say when they got drunk. The bartender heard them bragging. People in the saloon heard them say you hired them. But...still, it wasn't enough for the local sheriff to arrest you. And then suddenly they are gone, disappeared."

"Presumed dead." Henry added.

"Thank you." Aponi continued. "It all just stopped because there was no evidence. But then you did something really, really, stupid. You didn't pay Wesley Strong. He didn't go away. He got drunk and talked. So...now he's in jail waiting for the federal marshal, because why, you ask?"

Cudworth just stared.

"Because...killing an Indian is a federal crime and not under local jurisdiction. A federal marshal, who you don't know and can't control, is coming to investigate. With Strong's testimony you will be convicted."

Cudworth sank into a much smaller version of himself.

Aponi was seething with anger but spoke in a slow, cold voice. "You murdered our fathers for money, and now you're going to hang."

There was complete silence.

"Well," Henry said cheerfully, "that about wraps it up. Anybody hungry?"

The group left one by one and closed the double doors behind them, leaving Cudworth still sitting in his chair.

Everyone was out onto the walkway, but Henry hadn't closed the front door completely.

The gunshot echoed down the hall and out to the entire town.

Henry then closed the door and put his arm around his wife. "I'm thinking steak."

They started walking, falling in sync with each other's steps.

"Oh," Henry whispered, "Good story about Strong and the whole federal marshal thing. Is what you said true?"

"I have no idea, made up the whole thing." Aponi winked at her husband.

"I wonder where Strong really is?" He looked back at Odina, who was still, as always, two steps behind.

The mountain remained stoic, but Henry perceived a slight smile.

They walked a little further down the street. She suddenly stopped and looked up at him with a serious expression. "Hey, you owe me $41,000."

He looked at her then broke out laughing. "Ah...I'm good for it.

CHAPTER 39

FEATHER RIVER VALLEY, CALIFORNIA
JANUARY 1870

Icicles had formed on the trees. Long prisms containing kaleidoscopes of color hung down from limbs that bowed under their weight. A freak storm rolled through the mountain pass and caused this unusual event. Storm clouds, that for some atmospheric reason were much lower in the sky than normal, were trapped against the outlying mountain. All night the wind howled like a wild animal trapped in a cage. In the morning, when the temperature rose to somewhere above freezing, the clouds boiling in the eastern sky broke free of their containment and rushed into the valley, shadowing over the tribe's village. Within minutes the sky began to spit hail, forcing the tribe to run for cover. A downpour of rain followed, which lasted only a few minutes before winter found its way into the valley and resumed its role as king of the mountain. Cold returned with a vengeance, forcing out the rare storm which left its ice sculptures behind.

"Beautiful, but very dangerous." Aponi was standing with Henry just outside their hut. She yelled at children in Maidu playing near the trees, which Henry imagined was a warning to be careful.

"Does this happen often, the ice?"

"No, I've seen it only once before."

Henry hid a smirk.

Aponi spun around and looked up at him with confrontation on her face. "What?"

"It's not a sign, is it? An omen?"

Her expression turned from confrontation to hurt, and she walked back into the warmth of the hut.

Henry came in behind her knowing he should apologize, although he wasn't quite sure why. "I'm sorry."

She was sitting on a platform covered with thick furs and colorful blankets. "I shouldn't have expected you to understand our ways so quickly. You have done well with most of our traditions, but I think you feel some things in our culture are beneath you."

He didn't know what to say, so he said nothing.

She patted a spot next to her.

Henry sat, put his hands in his lap, and waited.

Rufus, whose nap was apparently disrupted by their presence, jumped off his very comfortable loft and ran out the door. The sound of children suddenly laughing cheered up the occupants he'd left behind.

"Our culture is centuries old. Yours is about as long as one or two generations of a family. My family and this tribe, according to our stories, has existed for twenty-one generations—one tribe, one village, over six hundred years. We had to move many times, only the last time because of white men. But...we have maintained our identity, our heritage, our village, our tribe. Some things are strange, even to me, but they are traditions. Don't you have traditions, or stories, or figures from the past that influence your lives? A warrior, or a medicine man or a leader of great ability? Do you not have traditions that maybe you don't fully understand but honor just the same?"

"Yes, of course we do. I think—"

"Don't think." She put a finger over his lips. "This is our way. A way that may soon disappear from our life. A way that the children laughing outside may never know about. We don't have the same kind of history that white people have. You have records and books. We have only stories carried by elders who tell them over fires at night...which will continue until our people stop listening." There were tears rolling down her face.

Henry took her hand.

"What the tribe has now is the end of what we were, not the beginning." She squeezed his hand. "What you and I have is the beginning of our new generation, but we cannot forget our past... yours and mine. We will not be able to preserve what was, but we can honor and respect the history of our ancestors."

Henry leaned forward and kissed her tenderly. "I'm trying."

"I know you are." She kissed him back.

Rufus came back after the children had been recalled to their huts. He jumped back up on his pile of logs, something that kind of resembled his perch at the cabin.

They were splitting the time between the village and the cabin. He had duties with the livestock and had business with Benji. It took only an hour now to traverse the mountain path. Puddle was making the trip without any guidance from a rein.

Henry found being the recipient of a great deal of money was also a great deal of work. It really wasn't what he wanted to do but he knew not a person on the earth including his bride would have an ounce of sympathy for him. On one journey from the village to the cabin to see Benji he handed him a telegram from Aunt Betty. He knew she would never forgive him for getting married without her, but he hoped she would understand.

WESTERN UNION
TELEGRAM

BAO 535 CTD073 3:15 PM JAN 16,1870
CT WWY014 WW13 PHILADELPHIA, PENNSYLVANIA

HENRY CRONIN CARVERSVILLE CALIFORNIA

ALL DETAILS OF THE SALE OF PROPERTY AND UNNEEDED
BELONGINGS DONE STOP TAKING THE SAME ROUTE TO
CALIFORNIA STOP SHOULD ARRIVE BY END MARCH STOP WILL
UPDATE PROGRESS STOP KISS APONI FOR ME STOP

LOVE, AUNT BETTY

"I had a thought."

Aponi looked at him suspiciously. "What?"

"Aunt Betty and Gerald will be arriving soon." He paused.

"And?"

He spoke his next thoughts quickly. "Maybe we should let them have the cabin and move up to the village full time. Then maybe build another cabin for us over the summer. Gerald loves working with the animals and I think Aunt Betty would get used to mountain life, eventually."

Aponi didn't say anything. She was in the kitchen making a

soup or a stew. Henry didn't know which one until it was time to eat.

"What's wrong?" He saw that she was just stirring the pot, not concentrating.

"Nothing, but I was thinking."

"Uh oh." He now looked at her suspiciously.

"I think it might be better if we stayed here and just thought of adding another room instead of another building." She added quickly, "For the moment, I mean."

Henry looked at her the same way Rufus tilted his head when he didn't get the scent right away.

She came over to him and pulled him up out of his chair, then laughed. "You are really terrible at reading sign."

"Huh."

"I'm pregnant. We are going to have a baby."

The only thing that came out of his mouth was pure joy.

She put her arms around his neck. "It's a boy."

"What? How?"

"How am I pregnant or how do I know it's a boy?"

He used hand signals because his mouth wasn't working well.

She laughed again. "Mothers know."

He uttered, "A boy."

"Amos, we should name him Amos."

He shook his head, "Cholok."

She laughed again. Then kissed him. A kiss that would last a lifetime.

They had not been back to the Maidu village for a couple of days because Henry was still trying to remember what day, month, or year it was.

I'm going to be a father.

However, he did eventually recover, and they were sitting outside near the community fire. A dance had just finished, and people were milling about.

"There was something I keep forgetting to talk to you about." Henry had a stick in his hand and was probing the fire's glowing embers.

"What do you want to know?" Aponi replied.

"A while back when I was having doubts about how to handle things, I said to you that I didn't understand why you believed in me when there was no earthly reason why you should." He paused and looked at her intently. "And then you said—"

"That was exactly the reason."

"Right. You remember. So...what did that mean?"

"No earthly reason." She took the stick from him and probed the fire much harder than he had. Flames shot up and embers danced, glowing into the night. "My father often told us about the legend of the Coyote. It is a mythical tale passed down generation to generation about how when the tribe was challenged by something that held certain defeat, the gods would send the Coyote to help. It has magical powers, and he is the hero who is called on to fight against monsters. One of the stories is about how he was summoned by a warrior chief to fight and kill the Thunderbird, the killer of people." She hit the fire again. "Toward the end, my father told my mother and me that he had called on the gods to send the Coyote to stop the Thunderbird from taking our land."

"So, he thought my father was the Coyote?" Henry nodded, "I can see that, they were fighting against what was an almost unbeatable foe."

Aponi looked into his eyes and shook her head. "No, your father was not the Coyote. The gods sent you. You defeated the Thunderbird. You are the Coyote."

He looked at her for what seemed like a long time. "Nahh, I'm just a kid from Philadelphia. Besides, I don't even know how to howl."

She laughed. "Do it."

"What?"

"Howl."

"No way."

"Do it." She laughed and then jumped up and started to run away.

He jumped up and started running behind her.

Somewhere in the distance a coyote called out to its mate.

They both stopped running, looked at each other and then laughed.

He put his hand on her belly. "Now, this is a story that is worthy of passing down."

THE END

EXCERPT - THE CRONIN CHRONICLES BOOK 2

TREASURE

FEATHER RIVER, CALIFORNIA

MAY 1952

"Come on... come with me. I have a surprise for you." Marcus Cronin walked ahead of his granddaughter toward the log cabin. "Close the car door. We don't want any critters climbing in."

Olivia walked behind her grandfather and was trying hard to keep up. It wasn't that she was undersized for her twelve years; it was because he was oversized. "Wait up."

He didn't stop, and he made her a little mad when he increased his gait.

"Please wait for me, Grandpa."

Marcus turned and stopped. "Okay little girl, but I like beating you. One day very soon I won't be able to anymore."

She ran up and took his hand and pointed to the building. "It's old and kinda yucky. Why are we rebuilding it?"

Marcus laughed. "It is yucky, isn't it? Well...I'll tell you why. Everything we are as a family started right here with your great-great-great-grandfather and grandmother. I decided to rebuild it after the winter snow crushed part of the roof. In fact, I am going to make it a thing of beauty."

"That will be a challenge." She tilted her head at the old log cabin then added, "And a lot of work."

"You're right about that, but we've already started. In fact... that is the reason I brought you here today."

They reached the porch of the cabin and Marcus helped her up. The door was open. They went inside and found the interior was in much better condition than the exterior.

"No one has lived here for many years, but there are still family picnics, and sometimes one of the family spends the summer. But..." Marcus got real excited, "when we pulled the damaged roof off, we discovered a trunk in the attic space that has been there for...well, I can't imagine how long. Anyway, I opened it, and I found something I want to give you." He walked her over to a steamer trunk that was covered with cobwebs and dirt. The clasps were hard to open but the old man got them open. The lid creaked.

Olivia peeked inside. What looked like an old saddle blanket was folded neatly on one side and a beaded leather vest lay next to it.

"This is what I wanted you to have." He withdrew a small wooden box and handed it to her.

She looked up kind of like a child about to open a strange Christmas present. Inside was a brown leather journal.

"Your great-great-great-grandmother, Rose Cronin, kept a diary of her journey in a wagon train that crossed the country in the 1800s."

Olivia carefully opened the book. The hand that wrote on the page made graceful strokes. She started to read but some loose pages fell out. She opened them and read.

Dear Henry,

There have been so many times I have tried to write to you

over the years, but I was never able to find the words. Your Aunt Betty, my beloved wife's sister, wrote...

She stopped. "Grandpa, who is Henry?"

"He was your great-great-grandfather. His mother was Rose and his father Amos."

"Amos? He was the one who—"

"Yes dear, he was the one."

A single paper fell to the floor. She bent over and picked it up. It had curved lines, trees, little drawings of men and animals, and there was a poem on the back.

"What's this?"

"Looks like a map to me."

"Of what?"

"I don't know. I think you'll have to figure that out on your own."

OTHER BOOKS BY THIS AUTHOR

SMOKE: A White Collar Crime

SMOKE (Book 1)

Reckoning (Book 2)

Henry (Book 3)

WHY

(Standalone)

ABOUT THE AUTHOR

This is the fifth book published by Paul Eberz. THE CRONIN
CHRONICLES - Legacy is preceded by WHY, published in 2023,
which deals events surrounding the assassination of JFK. Eberz
also published a mystery trilogy: Smoke – White Collar Crimes,
(2020), Henry (2022) and Reckoning (2021).

Legacy is the first in a series of CRONIN CHRONICLES. Amos
Cronin leaves a legacy for his offspring which was much more
than just a fortune. Journey is the prequel to Legacy and is the
adventures of young Amos and his wife Rose's journey across the
country in a covered wagon. Treasure takes place almost a
hundred years later when great-great-great-granddaughter, Oliva
finds the Amos map in an old trunk. The stories of two more
Cronin generations are in the cue.

Eberz retired from the construction industry where he held
executive positions in Fortune 500 companies and traveled the

country working with Native American Tribes. Born in Philadelphia, he now resides in Virginia.

Contact the Author:
Email: Paul_Eberz@yahoo.com

www.ingramcontent.com/pod-product-compliance
Lightning Source LLC
Chambersburg PA
CBHW071050250626
47159CB00002B/432